CLEMENTINE CRANE PREFERS NOT TO

Also available by Kristin Bair

Agatha Arch is Afraid of Everything

Writing as Kristin Bair O'Keeffe

The Art of Floating

Thirsty

CLEMENTINE CRANE PREFERS NOT TO

A Novel

KRISTIN BAIR

alcove press

Books should be disposed of and recycled according to local requirements.
All paper materials used are FSC compliant.

Published in the United States by Alcove Press, an imprint of The Quick Brown Fox & Company LLC.

Alcove Press and its logo are trademarks of The Quick Brown Fox & Company LLC.

Library of Congress Catalog-in-Publication data available upon request.

ISBN (hardcover): 979-8-89242-325-0
ISBN (paperback): 978-1-63910-110-8
ISBN (ebook): 978-1-63910-111-5

Cover design by Sandra Chiu

Printed in the United States.

www.alcovepress.com

Alcove Press
34 West 27th St., 10th Floor
New York, NY 10001

First Edition: October 2025

The authorized representative in the EU for product safety and compliance is eucomply OÜPärnu mnt 139b-14, 11317 Tallinn, Estonia, hello@eucompliancepartner.com, +33757690241

10 9 8 7 6 5 4 3 2 1

In honor of all the hot-flashing humans
brave enough to say, "I prefer not to"

It is a thing hundreds of thousands of women have done.

—Nora Helmer, *A Doll's House* by Henrik Ibsen

CHAPTER ONE
Linchpin

At 6:47 AM on January 14, 2023, Clementine Crane realized she might burst into flames.

This was not a metaphor. Clem's soul was not about to ignite. The sparks of her emotions were not being fanned. Passion had not been fueled in her heart. This was fire. Combustion during which substances combine chemically with oxygen to produce light, heat, and flame.

Think inferno.

Conflagration.

Full-on motherfucking blaze.

Clem sucked in a breath. Good god, she was hot. Hotter than she'd ever been in her life. As she stood alone in her kitchen, prepping the family calendar, sweat seeped from her forehead like water from a squeezed sponge. Seeped from the bottoms of her feet, her belly, thighs, and neck, even her elbows.

Who knew elbows could do anything but bend?

Her face, now a maraschino cherry, felt dense and gummy, like an underproofed loaf of sourdough, and a prickly, unfamiliar sensation was spreading through her lower abdomen. It wasn't nerves or a UTI.

Definitely not desire. No, this was something new, something unrecognizable, something else entirely.

She dropped her forehead to the countertop. Moaned. It was cold. So sweetly cold. When she rolled one cheek against it, then the other, Hagrid, the family dog, moved to her side. He was a Newfie, an enormous black-and-white quadruped who took Clem's well-being quite seriously. With his tongue lolling from his mouth, Hagrid had a penchant for looking both mournful and ecstatic in the same moment. And although Clem was fairly tall, Hagrid's head bumped her hip. When she reached down and tugged at his ear—his favorite touch—a snaggle of drool dripped onto her bare foot.

Quite sure detonation was imminent, she quickened the pace of her weekly catch-up, jamming the date and time of her annual physical into her already overstuffed chest cavity as neatly as possible between Anna's next orthodontist appointment, Evan's upcoming college prep meeting, Brewster's check-in at the otolaryngologist, and all other commitments for her family of five.

Years before, when the intensity and frequency of then-baby Brewster's ear infections were ramping up, when he and Clem were both rendered sleepless by his excruciating pain, she used to flub the word *otolaryngologist* every time she called the doctor's office to make yet another appointment. To master it, she'd practiced as she paced with sobbing Brewster tucked into the space between her neck and shoulder.

gogolist

gogolisto

otogogolisto

Why such a complicated word? she'd often wondered as she'd worn a gully in the hardwood floor between the coffeepot and the window. *What's wrong with* ear doctor?

otogogolist

otogoglist

otolargyngoglist

otolaryngist

But after managing Brewster's 2.4 million ear infections, endless rounds of antibiotics, and so many ear tube surgeries she could probably insert the damn things herself, the word for one of the most common childhood doctors rolled off her tongue as easily as *firefly*.

otolaryngologist

Bookending these carefully considered appointments were, for all five members of the Crane family, biannual visits to the dentist and annual visits to the optometrist. Myopic messes, every one of them.

In addition, there were dates and times for Brewster's upcoming musical, Anna's ice hockey games, and Evan's swim meets. Holy hummingbirds, how was it all supposed to fit? Why did *she* have to make it fit? Why did *she* have to play so many roles in the family production of life?

mother
rememberer
caregiver
cook
coach
referee
nurse
laundress
kin-keeper
architect of experience
coordinator of chaos
emotional barometer
admin
alarm clock
alchemist
therapist
head cheerleader
defender
taxi driver
linchpin

That last one? Linchpin? That was it. The truest. The most comprehensive. The role into which every person with a uterus who played mother, wife, and gainfully employed human was thrust.

"Alexa," Clem asked, "what is a linchpin?" She needed an official definition.

The soft, robotic voice replied, "A linchpin is a pin inserted crosswise which holds together elements that function as a unit."

Linchpin.

Clementine lifted her steaming head and yelled, for the third time that morning, in what the kids called her *serious voice*, "Anna! Brewster! Evan! Get up and get moving! Now!"

Silence.

Thirty seconds later, she yelled a fourth time. This time with an edge that implied she knew a little something about animals that eat their young.

As expected, she heard a stomp and Anna's angry "Fine, Mother! We're up!" Thanks to TikTok, fourteen-year-old Anna was a "gentle parenting" convert, a believer in the approach to child-parent relations that favored partnership, calm communication, and mutual respect over threatening a life of misery when one's offspring refused to get out of bed.

Clem looked out the window. More snow was falling as meteorologist Heather of the Weather had promised. More snow on top of the nearly three feet they already had.

"I hate you," Clem said, glaring first at the windswept bank of it against the back fence, then at the branches of the sycamore from which spiky balls hung like glistening morning stars.

Firmly anti-winter, anti-cold, anti-snow, anti-ice, anti-nor'easter, and anti-blizzard, Clementine begged every year for her and husband, Torvald Crane, to pack up the kids for a move from frigid New England to tropical Costa Rica like one of those spunky families on *House Hunters International*.

"We'll open a bed-and-breakfast," she always said. "Or a hemp farm." She knew nothing about either industry, but it wouldn't have mattered if she had. Tor was a card-carrying member of the *I wear shorts in January* club, a cold-weather connoisseur who'd likely leave his wife before his beloved Massachusetts.

"Winter is the season of renewal," he responded each time.

"It's not," Clem always growled. "Spring is the season of renewal. Winter is the season of being frozen, cold, and dead."

"You can't have spring without winter," he said. "And besides, nothing's dead, just dormant."

"Nothing except me," she always muttered.

But Tor never responded to that. By then he was lost in his private hibernal veneration. Thanking the gods for icy windowpanes and cross-country skis.

Clem lifted her hair into a bun. The roots were sopping wet, and her long curls were frizzing up. *Fever,* she thought. *I must have a fever.* Jittery, breathy, anxious in her belly, she padded to the bathroom and pulled the thermometer from a drawer. Back in the kitchen, she uncapped it and aimed it at her forehead.

Ninety-eight point six degrees. No fever.

The *green zone,* Brewster used to call it.

She crammed the kids' upcoming appointments with the oral surgeon onto her calendar and into her chest cavity. It had been at least five years since she'd run out of room in her head for such things.

When her watch beeped seven, she peeled out of her cardigan—armpits, back, and neck damp with sweat—then lurched to the bottom of the stairs, her clammy feet sticking to the tile. *Thwck, thwck, thwck.* "Brewster! Anna! Evan! Get moving! Twenty minutes until the bus!" Clem hadn't known how loudly she could yell until her kids became teenagers.

A door slammed on the second floor. Evan yelled at Anna. Anna yelled at Brewster. Brewster yelled at no one in particular. Not an ideal start to the day, but at least they were out of bed.

When Clem leaned over to scoop food into Hagrid's bowl, sweat dripped from the tip of her nose onto the dry nuggets. He lifted his massive head from the floor, nudged her ankle, and sighed.

Her watch beeped again. She had ninety minutes until her first meeting of the day. "Hurry!" she hollered up the stairs, then sucked in another breath. There was so much more she had to squeeze into the calendar—fundraisers, birthday parties, parent-teacher conferences, school pictures, holiday gift shopping, music lessons, haircuts, mani-pedis, vacation plans, her work events, Tor's work events, and book club gatherings. The cleaners came every other Thursday at eight AM. Beanpod delivered groceries every Monday evening at seven.

And, good god, don't forget the trainer. That unnaturally muscled beast arrived twice a week in her Tango Red Audi S5 to put Clementine and Tor through the paces. Lift this, stretch that, sprint faster, kick higher. Mondays and Fridays, religiously. Clem despised her.

When another wave of heat rolled through her body, Clementine tore off her turtleneck. The back of it was as drenched as if she'd stepped out of the shower moments ago. *What is going on?* She tossed it onto a stool, then placed both hands on her chest cavity. Against her palms, it throbbed with urgent things and the terrible consequences that could befall the Crane family if any were neglected—crooked canines, a lapse in reading skills, uncorrected myopia, chicken pox, tetanus, a busted eardrum, a failed class, stomach chub, rotting molars, ragged cuticles, the bubonic plague, and, God forbid, the loss of a competitive edge.

Clad now in nothing more than wool trousers and a bra, Clementine speed-transferred the dates and times of each meeting, appointment, and event from her internal calendar to the wall calendar in the kitchen. She was practiced. And fast. Anna in purple; Evan in red; Brewster in green; her and Tor in orange and blue, respectively. Hagrid in basic black. All this and a shared Google calendar because she clung desperately to the distant hope that one gloriously spectacular day, Tor might look—actually *look*—at this calendar or that calendar or maybe his wife's exhausted face and act independently instead of waiting to be told what to do.

Drop Anna at the rink at 5:00 and Evan at the pool at 5:15.

Pick up Brewster at the theater at 6:00.

Practice Evan's *they/them* pronouns.

Pay sports fees before January 30.

Hug Evan.

Hug Anna.

Do not hug Brewster. He was in the *I'm too old for hugs* stage.

Order a goose for the annual Crane family Valentine's Day celebration.

Venmo the trainer.

Slip a water bottle into Evan's backpack. Dehydration was their worst enemy.

Put money into Brewster's lunch account at school. Hunger was his worst enemy.

Order a Pride flag for the front yard.

Take Anna to get a birthday gift for her friend Laila.

Make a grooming appointment for Hagrid.

Order a new sleeping bag for Anna. She lost hers.

Order a new hockey helmet for Anna. She lost that too.

And so on.

But Torvald Crane taking charge of something beyond the mortgage and health insurance was as likely as the woolly mammoth being de-extincted. A few weeks before, Clem had heard a story on the radio about the well-funded scientists determined to achieve this genetic feat. The host had pointed out that attempting to "jump-start nature's ancestral heartbeat" by resurrecting the *Mammuthus primigenius* could be viewed as a rather selfish goal considering the number of dire problems facing the world, but Clem disagreed. She understood the need to believe that the impossible was, in fact, just the opposite.

The kids filed into the kitchen in varying states of preparedness.

"Uh, Mom," Evan said, shoving their laptop into their backpack, "what's happening here?" They gestured at her nearly naked torso.

She waved them off. "Coats and boots," she said, handing each a muffin. "It's snowing again."

Anna rolled her eyes, and although she didn't say it, Clementine heard it loud and clear: *My family is so weird.*

Thirteen-year-old Brewster averted his eyes and raced out the door.

Once the house was kidless and quiet, Tor strode into the room. What a lovely thing, Clem thought, to be able to stride into a room *after* she'd strained her voice wrestling the kids out of bed, *after* she'd thawed half a dozen muffins for them, *after* she'd shuffled them out the door, *after* she'd fed Hagrid, *after* she'd crammed one thousand appointments and to-dos onto the family calendar and into her chest cavity—*after* everything.

When was the last time *she'd* been able to stride anywhere? She huffed and looked from the yellow school bus pulling up outside to her husband. He was freshly washed, shiny with a good scrubbing, well scented, firmly muscled, rested. "Good morning, my little squirrel," he said, smiling as he poured granola into a bowl.

The nickname, pulled from Henrik Ibsen's play *A Doll's House*, used to make Clementine feel cared for and loved. Ibsen was her and Tor's favorite playwright, and they'd seen *A Doll's House* on one of their first dates twenty years before. These pet names had always been a thread of affection between them—a touchstone in even the busiest of times—but over the past few months, being called *little squirrel* or *little lark* or *little pet* or *little* anything made Clem seethe. She lifted her hand from her bulging, throbbing, sweating chest cavity, clenched it into a fist, and imagined popping her husband square in the schnoz, flattening his well-plucked proboscis.

"Um, hon," he said, nodding at her nearly naked torso, "you look beautiful, but I think you forgot something."

Clementine glared at him, then looked out the window as the bus was turning off its blinkers. He didn't ask *Why aren't you wearing a shirt?* or *Why is your face as red as a boiled lobster?* or *Is there anything I can do to move things along here?* or *How are the kids this morning?* All she got was *I think you forgot something*, as if strolling around their kitchen without a shirt in the middle of a New England snowmageddon was an everyday occurrence undeserving of inquiry.

She listened to the snowflakes hit the window and thought about the rocket debris from a recent Chinese space launch that supposedly landed in the Indian Ocean. When pressed by the international community, China had insisted most of the debris had burned up on reentry, but no one had proof of such an outcome. No one had yet determined if an engine or window frame or throttle or trim wheel had landed on any of the Maldives' 1,192 islands. No one had investigated if anyone on the 187 inhabited islands had been bruised, maimed, or even killed as a result of the incident. Understandably, NASA was pissed, so much so that the administrator had issued a rebuke—an unusual step—accusing China of "failing to meet responsible standards regarding their space debris."

If only there were such a rebuke for husbands, she thought. A "failing to meet responsible standards regarding their goddamn life debris."

She watched Tor take a quart of almond milk from the fridge, pour it over his granola, chuck a handful of walnuts into the mix, then sprinkle a bit of cinnamon on top. He opened the silverware drawer to get a spoon but, like Clem hours earlier, discovered that there were none. No teaspoons. No tablespoons. No serving spoons. Not even any of those tiny, useless sorbet spoons they'd gotten as a wedding gift. Clem waited for her husband to realize he must either choose a fork with which to eat his granola or go to the fancy dish cabinet in the dining room to retrieve one of her grandmother's silver spoons. With his milk already poured and his granola in danger of becoming mushy, she knew he would not choose the latter. When he slowly pulled a fork from the drawer and sat down at the table to scroll on his phone, avoiding her eyes, she smoldered and turned away.

"Not a single spoon," she whispered through gritted teeth. "Not one."

He ignored her.

On any other day she would have taken this further, asked him the whereabouts of the twenty or thirty spoons usually found in the drawer, but distracted by the rivulets of sweat dripping into her cleavage, creating a pool so deep a dozen guppies could take up residence, Clem instead picked up her phone and texted Georgia.

G, help! I may be dying.

What?

Dying.

Dying how?

I'm on fire.

What? Where's Tor? I'll call 911!

Before her husband's death a few months before, Georgia had been unflappable, but ever since, she'd become much more reactive. Quick to panic. Quick to worry.

No, no. Not really on fire, G. Not dying that bad,
I hope. But so fucking hot.

Fever?

No, but dizzy, can't breathe right,
sweat oozing from every pore.

The phone was quiet for a good ten seconds, then, You, my dear, are having a hot flash.

A what?

A hot flash.

Clem had some distant recollection of her mother sweating in the kitchen, hurling a roast chicken into the sink, and sticking her head into the refrigerator.

Welcome to the next stage of womanhood.
Perimenopause.

Clem had heard this term before but had never related it to herself.

Impossible. I'm only 44.

I had my first at 43.

Holy crap.

A hot flash.

At forty-four.

Clem started to type a response, but another heat wave rolled up through her middle. She was dizzy, foggy in the head, and nauseated. Not nauseated, really; that wasn't quite right. It was more like she needed to swallow but couldn't. Holy crap, she had to cool down. She stood, set her phone on the island, unlocked the sliding door to the backyard, and stepped onto the patio. Hagrid followed. The frosty stones felt delicious on the bottoms of her bare feet. She sighed and moved down the walkway toward the sycamore. The kids had cleared the path after the weekend's big snow, but she was now wading through five or six fresh inches that had fallen overnight.

"Clem," Tor called, "you're letting in the cold air."

She didn't pause. Hagrid padded along behind her, then veered off in the direction of the deepest drift.

"Clem!" Tor yelled. "Close the door. Our heating bill is going to go through the roof."

As she moved through the crisp air, steam lifted from Clem's head like a cloud.

"Clem, what are you doing out there? Get back in here."

Clem pondered the great divide between Tor's *here* and her *there.* And when a snowflake landed on her nose, she realized that nothing—nothing—had ever felt as good as that single frozen drop on her bare skin.

"Clementine Crane!" Tor called. "Come back in. Get a shirt on. You're going to freeze."

Now he was concerned about her well-being.

Just past the sycamore, Clementine turned to face the towering mountain of snow. When the kids were little, they'd spent hours patting down the steep drift from the top of the fence to the ground, then sliding the entire length of it on the slick bottoms of their snow pants.

She unbuttoned, then unzipped her trousers. She wiggled them down to her ankles, stepped free, then kicked them a few feet along the path. Her black underwear didn't match her faded purple bra. Her legs were prickly with stubble. Her nails protruded like broken swords from the ends of her toes.

Clem glanced at the Marks' house next door and saw Georgia smiling at her through a snow-crusted window. When she waved, Georgia raised the pane. She leaned her gray head over the sill and called, "Morning, Clementine!"

Clem smiled. Even in an inferno like this, Georgia Mark could make her feel loved.

"That must feel so good!" Georgia said, then shivered and shut the window.

Clem heard Tor calling her name and looked back. He was leaning on the doorframe in his seersucker shorts, bowl in one hand, fork in the other. His sky-blue shirt beautifully contrasted with the white snow.

Bastard.

From the other side of the fence and down the way a bit, Clem heard a loud crunch. She leaned in that direction, listening. *Crunch, crunch, crunch.* Through a crack between two boards, she saw a shadow. A big one. Probably Bill Weston, a neighbor who had the wingspan of an Andean condor.

"Clem!" Tor hollered. "What is going on?" His mouth was full of granola and walnuts. "Talk to me."

Clem shook her head. Wagged it furiously like Hagrid when the fur around his ears froze. She was done talking, and, for the moment, she was done steaming. She stepped off the path into the thigh-high snow, then hurled herself facedown into the deep drift, arms and legs spread like the branches of a stellar dendrite snowflake. She groaned as her temperature plummeted. The snow was cold. Magnificently cold.

CHAPTER TWO
Big Feelings

An hour later, Clem walked into Byrock's public library, refreshed and ready for work. She was feeling much more like herself, as if that hot flash might have been the first and last of its kind. She felt hopeful when she paused at the fish tank in the children's room to greet Frankie, the beloved celestial goldfish whose bulbous eyes stared permanently at the stained ceiling tiles above.

Unlike every other being in Clem's life, Frankie demanded nothing. She didn't need a new helmet or a ride to school. She didn't beg for pancakes on Saturday mornings. She didn't need money for snacks or the trendiest water bottle. She had no doctor or dentist appointments to manage. She was a fish swimming quiet laps in her tank, resting now and then in the doorway of her turquoise castle. Oblivious to the constant chatter of young visitors and their gummy fingerprints clouding her worldview, Frankie was one of the few things of late that inspired and balanced Clem. To express her gratitude, Clem had made a habit of slipping a few extra flakes of food into Frankie's tank when no one was looking.

After doing just that, Clem hung her coat on a hook and scurried down the hall to join the team in the conference room. She dropped into her usual spot next to Meghan, children's librarian extraordinaire, and surveyed the materials for the week's craft—the shape of a human cut from stiff poster board, a bowl of googly eyes, a glue stick, construction paper, crayons, and a pair of child-safe scissors. Crafts were one way the team coped with Bathsheba Wheaton, library director from hell, who insisted on weekly staff meetings even though 90 percent of what they discussed could easily be handled via email or quick chats at the circulation desk.

A few weeks before, their craft assignment had been to create a tree in autumn. Most everyone's had featured typical New England fall foliage. Tried-and-true leaf-peeper stuff—orange, yellow, and red leaves against a spicy blue sky. But Clem's had been different. Bare, black limbs starkly contrasted with a scurry of pale-gray clouds. When her colleagues had looked quizzically at her distinctive piece of art, she'd said, "It's post late-November squall," referencing the annual doozy of a storm that inevitably knocked every last leaf off every deciduous tree in New England. The storm that signaled once and for all that autumn was over and winter was about to unleash its arctic torture.

"I loathe that squall," she'd told them, politely adhering to Meghan's *don't say "hate"* rule. "I loathe winter even more," she added, as if there were a soul in the room who didn't already know that.

Her colleagues had tried to be empathetic, but like so many New Englanders, they lived for that day each year when they could zip up their parkas, strap on their snowshoes, and head out into the wintry wild. Clementine was alone in her loathing.

As usual, Meghan had written craft directions in colorful, loopy letters and displayed them in the center of the table. Today? *Make a person having a big feeling.*

"Oh, I've got this one," Clem whispered to Meghan, grabbing her cutout.

"What's it going to be?" Meghan said.

"Not telling."

Meghan nudged her. "Come on."

Clem shook her head.

"Excited?"

"Nope."

"Mad? Frustrated? Lonely?"

"Nope."

"Joyful?"

"Meghan, we have three feet of snow on the ground and more on the way," Clem whispered. "What are the chances I'm going to make a joyful human?"

Meghan tsk-tsked. Big feelings were a big topic in the children's room, and the day's craft seemed especially apropos as Bathsheba began to discuss—for the hundredth time—titles. Not of books, which would make good sense, but of employees. "As you know," she said, "the board has agreed to consider our list of updated titles."

Clem cleared her throat, intentionally loud.

Bathsheba whipped her eyes in Clem's direction. "Yes, Clem?" She had this way of scowling that made Clem want to either hide under her desk or morph into a Komodo dragon.

"You're going to lobby for my proposed title, right?" Clem's voice wobbled near the end of the sentence. She'd been pushing for this change since September, and battling Bath's resistance was exhausting. As the only daughter of a dominant father and submissive mother, Clem had been programmed to accept what was offered and ask for no more. She was good at it.

Bathsheba sighed.

"In case you've forgotten," Clem said, rummaging through her cup of crayons, because while she'd gotten better at saying what she wanted out loud, she still couldn't look at Bath when she did, "that title is Connector of People to Magical Things." She glanced around the table. "Does anyone have red?"

Bath plucked a red crayon from her own cup, passed it dramatically to Clem, and said, "You have a perfectly functional title, Clementine. Director of Media. This is a common title for people with your set of responsibilities, and as far as I know, there are zero Connectors of People to Magical Things."

Clem closed her eyes, trying not to let the f-word suck her into a pit of emotional quicksand. "I don't aspire to functional," she said. Good god, she'd never aspired to that. *Functional* was for multi-tools and washing machines, not humans. When she'd interviewed for the job ten years before, she'd talked passionately about Homer and Hurston, Kahlo and Basquiat, Maria Callas and so much more. Magical things she knew a lot about and could contribute to a community centered on people and stories.

Frustrated, Clem drew a large, red circle for the mouth of her human, then plucked two googly eyes from the bowl and placed them on the face. One wiggled up, the other wiggled down. Feeling like that was about right, Clem popped the top from her glue stick. "Director of Media stuffs me into a box I don't fit into," she said. "My job is much more than media."

"But media is a significant part of it."

"There are many significant parts."

The catch in Clem's voice made everyone in the room look up from their cutouts. Meghan, Samantha, Jing, Victor, Walter, and Jade. Even Keisha, who usually looked up only for discussions about technology issues or chocolate chip cookies. Clem was well known for her dependable, even-keeled, people-pleasing nature. She rarely complained, always took on extra work without being asked, and consistently said yes when everyone else said no. Until recently, challenging her boss hadn't been in her repertoire.

Clementine pressed her googly eyes into place, then insisted, one more time, on the new title: Connector of People to Magical Things.

Her phone buzzed. Anna.

mom

mom

mom

i forgot my beaker tongs for science

Unless you duct-taped all required items to Anna's body, something was always left behind.

Why did you bring beaker tongs home?

2 pluck my eyebrows

With beaker tongs?

yah TikTok challenge

The pocked red marks along Anna's eyebrows suddenly made sense.

mom

mom

mom

I'm here. Processing the plucking.

failed the challenge

I noticed.

can u bring tongs

Anna, I'm at work.

mom

I'll drop them off at lunch.

i need them by 11:30

my book 2

mom

Which book, Anna?

collection of short stories by the moby duck guy

Moby Duck?

sry autocorrect

dick

Anna.

name of book mom

moby dick

by whats his name

What's his name?

that guy who wrote it

Herman Melville

i guess

Clementine grunted. She *guessed*? Anna Crane, beloved daughter of book-obsessed library passionista Clementine Crane, had the audacity to say "I guess" when asked the name of an author she should know almost as well as her own? How many times had Clem told her and the boys the story of Ahab's self-destructive obsession with the white whale?

YOU GUESS?

yah

Clem knew Anna didn't feel or care about the fury in her all-caps response. The outrage. The indignation. The overwhelming sense of failure and disappointment in her own parenting. How could the daughter of Clementine Crane—Connector of People to Magical Things—not be able to answer the question "Who wrote *Moby-Dick*?"

Talk about big feelings.

FINE.

Clem knew Anna didn't read her final text—just trusted that her mother would appear by 11:30 with her beaker tongs and book.

And as usual, Clem would. It was a wretched pattern, and Tor blamed her for it. "How is Anna ever going to learn to fend for herself if you step in every time to make sure she doesn't fail?" he asked whenever she complained. "You've created a monster." Clem had always nodded when he'd insisted the pattern was her fault because she never said no, but she was starting to realize that was bullshit. The truth was much deeper than that. Much more complex. Like so many women, both she and Anna were strange little automatons in a traditional family structure that had been firmly in place for generations. The structure in which the dad "provides" and the mom meets all needs.

Bathsheba burst into Clem's thoughts. "Clementine? Are you still with us?"

Clem set her phone on the table. "I am."

"I was saying that the other problem with your proposed title is that it has too many words."

Clem's eyes shot up to the brown stain on the ceiling tile over the table, the one shaped like a snowman. She felt like she'd been punched in the stomach. "Too many words?" she said. "Are you kidding?"

"I am not."

Clem grimaced and pointed at the cart of books waiting to be shelved at the end of the table and the floor-to-ceiling bookshelves on the other side of the window. "Look around, Bathsheba!" she said. "We work in a library. A place full of words. A place reliant on words.

A place that would not—could not—exist without words. The very foundation of this edifice is constructed with words. How can anything in our library have too many words?" She snatched a pair of child-safe scissors from the table and began to cut a fiery flame from a sheet of red construction paper.

Her phone buzzed.

> Please call The Nail Finery to reschedule yesterday's missed pedicure. Your toes are our business.

Another missed appointment. Clem wiggled her daggerlike toenails in her boots.

She ignored the text and continued snipping paper. "All day, every day," she said, "I connect people to stories, books, audiobooks, puzzles, and spaces to read. I connect old people to young people, unusual people to unusual books, artists to writers, musicians to sculptors, anxious folks to Zen masters, naysayers to yea-sayers, and so on. Bathsheba Wheaton, I *am* the Connector of People to Magical Things, and this is the title I choose."

With the entire team staring at her, Clem realized this was the most detailed, heartfelt monologue she'd ever given about why she deserved her proposed title. And now that she had, she felt a divine glow radiating from every pore. It was glorious.

Bathsheba sighed and nodded in the same way she'd sighed and nodded at least five or six times in recent months during less dramatic standoffs about the same topic. "Wouldn't it be nice, Clementine," she said, "if titles were something we were actually allowed to choose?"

Clem snipped another flame from red paper, this time pretending it was Bath's neck. She felt oddly pleased they were finally arriving at the heart of things. Didn't everything in the world come down to control? Down to who got to make decisions and who had to abide by them? In the past, Clem had always accepted her status in this hierarchy—every hierarchy. School, friend groups, work, volunteer organizations, marriage. She'd found comfort in them and appreciated the ease with which she could identify herself in the world: "I am a B student. I am a faithful friend. I am a responsible wife. I am a devoted mother. I am an obedient patient." But that first hot flash had ignited something in her, and although she didn't quite know how it was going to play out, Clem knew that going forward, things were going to be different.

"And why aren't we allowed to choose titles?" she said to Bath. "The ones we have in this library are boring and trivial, but the people who hold these jobs are not." She waved a red flame at Samantha. "For example, Head Librarian Samantha is interesting and clever. Right?" Clem waited until all parties around the table, even Keisha, were nodding. "Yes, she is Head Librarian, but if we really think about who she is and what she does, her title could be . . ." Clem paused.

Crap.

Her belly rolled in the same way it had earlier that morning in her kitchen. An ember in her middle began to smolder. Suddenly she couldn't swallow in any kind of satisfactory way. The backs of her hands were beginning to burn. Her cheeks too.

Shit. Not another hot flash.

"The Alchemist," she finally said. Her voice was breathy.

"Or," Keisha burst in, "the Mad Scientist."

Clem looked at Keisha. Bathsheba looked at Keisha. Everybody looked at Keisha. Had she ever spoken outside of conversations about library technology? She was an amazing techie, a brilliant problem solver, but most often a silent one.

Samantha, with her signature cloud of white Einstein hair, chuckled. "I like those, Bathsheba. Especially Mad Scientist."

"Oh, don't you start," Bathsheba said. "We're moving on. There are other things to cover this morning."

When she sighed and nodded yet again, Clem could no longer hold her tongue. "Well, all right then, Director of Dramatic Sighing and Nodding."

Oh my god. Had she really said that?

A second later, Keisha and Samantha burst out laughing, Meghan coughed, and Victor snorted so hard coffee shot out of his nose. In the past, Clem had always been able to stop herself from blurting out the sharp responses that popped into her head, but clearly that was changing too. She ignored Bath's admonishing gaze by reading an incoming text from Etsy: You left a Valentine's Day item in your cart. Hurry! Only 7 left!

Fuck Valentine's Day. She hit the order button for the light-up heart, then stuffed the receipt into her burgeoning chest cavity, right next to the receipt for the chocolate-covered strawberries she'd ordered the day before. Valentine's Day was an annual tradition in the Crane family. A big one thanks to a pernicious mix of Tor's steady pressure for her to make every holiday as special as possible and Clem's insatiable need to please.

She groaned when her phone buzzed once more.

Hello, little lark.

Clem chomped down on the inside of her cheek. Why had she ever agreed to these infantile nicknames? All these nods to Ibsen had begun as playful and cute, and when she and Tor were first dating, she'd loved them. "We both adore Ibsen," she'd crooned to her roommates.

Fuck Ibsen.

Back then, she'd never considered that Torvald—or any man in a contemporary marriage—would expect his wife to be exclusively in charge of all things hearth and home. But now that she'd begun recognizing herself as a contemporary Nora Helmer, being called *lark* or *squirrel* made her want to grab one of the giant icicles hanging from the roof outside the window and drive it straight through her husband's heart.

Did you drop my green sweater at the cleaners?

She played dumb. *What green sweater?*

You know, my favorite.

The stinky one with a hole in the right elbow?

I wouldn't put it that way, but yes.

I haven't seen it.

Even though the text exchange ended there, Clem's brain continued to boil. Her husband, a smart man who'd gone to a top architectural school and received numerous awards for designing beautiful, energy-efficient homes, would know where his damn sweater was if he ever cared for the thing himself. If he ever took the initiative to drop it off or pick it up at Fresh & Fold, which was less than three miles from the Cranes' house. But no, whenever that sweater started to stink, he simply plopped it onto the pile of Clem's clothes he knew were headed for the dry cleaner. The rest was up to her.

As Bathsheba turned the conversation to the week's new releases, sweat began to pool in the hollow between Clem's bottom lip and chin. Her phone buzzed once more. Brewster. Clem's youngest was not a texter, so this could mean only one thing. He was hungry.

MOM IM STARVING

This bottomless pit of a boy had drained all the money from his lunch account. It was a weekly occurrence.

MOM IM STARVING

I CANT MAKE IT THRU THE MORNING

I CANT MAKE IT ANOTHER HOUR

NOT ANOTHER MINUTE

It was obvious why this Crane child was a theater kid.

I WILL PERISH

PERISHING NOW

AAAHHHHHHHHHHHHHHH

PLEASE ADD MONEY

NOW

$$$$$$$$$$$$$$$$$

Clem shook her head. Knowing this would not stop until Brewster had gotten something in his stomach, she opened the "add money to school" site on her phone. But as she began to transfer money from the bank, her glasses slipped down her nose on a rivulet of sweat.

Brewster buzzed again.

mom

MOM

MOM MOM MOM MOM MOM

u there mom

I SAID IM STARVING

DOES THAT MATTER 2U

DO I MATTER 2U

Clem held her glasses to the bridge of her nose with one finger and tried to breathe through the heat. The stomach thing was now also a lung thing.

"Earth to Clem, Earth to Clem."

Clem heard Bathsheba's voice through the ghostly fog that was settling into her brain.

Text your father.

whaaaat

Brewster, text your father.
I'm in the middle of something.
A couple of somethings. Too many somethings!

MOM dad cant put $$ in my lunch
account hes clueless about this stuff

Clem tried to imagine Tor successfully adding money to Brewster's lunch account. Tracking down the website, figuring out the login info, and deciphering the not-so-intuitive steps, all in time to keep Brewster from turning to cannibalism.

He's a smart man. He'll manage.

But she knew the second part of that statement wasn't true. Tor *was* a smart man, but this was not, as he would say, in his wheelhouse.

Fuck his wheelhouse.

In all the years the kids had been in school, he'd never once engaged in the minutiae. Sure, he did the visible stuff—clapped at concerts, did drop-off and pickup, coached hockey and basketball until the kids surpassed his know-how, and so on—but the man didn't know teachers' names or test dates. He never quizzed the kids on spelling words or state capitals. He didn't know who was bullying whom or who the kids were crushing on. And he certainly didn't add money to lunch accounts. Tears welled in Clem's eyes because she knew, even though it was 2023, that her husband considered these kinds of tasks to be her work—women's work. It was infuriating to admit that although from the outside the two of them looked like a "modern" couple with an equal balance of responsibilities inside the home, there was nothing balanced about them.

MOM now is not the time to joke i am starving

Didn't you buy an extra breakfast
when you got to school this morning?

YES but that was A WHOLE HOUR ago

I AM STARVING MOM

MOM

I WILL EAT MY OWN ARM

Text your father.

MOM

Sweetheart, I realize no one is noticing,
but I, your mother, am on the verge of imploding.

whaaaaat

mom i need food $$ food $$ food $$ fooooooood

FOOD

FOOD

Good god, how much more could she take?

Fine, Brew, fine.

Under the table, Clem slid one boot off, then the other. She pressed her toes into the puddle of wet slush on the linoleum. The moment of relief from the heat as her socks absorbed the chill was transcendent enough for her to complete Brewster's lunch money transaction.

You're all set, Brew. Go eat.

omg thx mom

You're welcome. Please don't eat your arm.

hahahahahaha

Unlike Anna, she could still count on him to read her final text.

"Clementine, do you have anything else you need to discuss today?" Bathsheba said.

Clem sighed. The relief from the heat was fading fast, and warmth was already beginning to build inside her thick wool socks. On a day that had begun with her very first hot flash, why in the world had she chosen to wear thick wool socks?

She pushed her right foot against the floor until the jagged nail of her big toe popped through the end of the sock. Cool air gushed in. When she sighed out loud, Bathsheba shot her an annoyed glance.

"Clementine?" Bath said. "Is there anything else?"

As Clem struggled to remove the sock without anyone noticing, she glanced at her colleagues' craft humans. Jing's was happy. Walter's looked confused. Jade's was pissed off. Victor's looked constipated. And Keisha's? Hers looked smart and shy, much like Keisha herself.

In so many ways, Clem loved the attention this library gave to emotions. She remembered her own big feelings when she was a kid. Sad, mad, lonely, scared, guilty, embarrassed, happy, excited, confused, ashamed, enchanted. The list went on and on. Back then, no one talked about feelings—big or small—at least not in her family, school, or town library. No one asked her to draw a picture or make a craft human that expressed those feelings.

At five years old when she'd lost her stuffed tiger at an amusement park, she'd been so distraught that she'd hidden in the backyard for an hour. Her parents hadn't noticed.

And when Rusty Blackburn broke her tender twelve-year-old heart, she'd had no idea what to do with the giant bubble of loneliness she carried around for months after.

What a gift Meghan was to the library community. Teaching kids—and their families—about big feelings so early in life.

"Actually, Bathsheba," Clem said, as she pasted red-and-orange flames all around her craft self, "I do have one more thing to say about titles."

Bathsheba grunted. "What is it?"

"Meghan's title should be Feelings Teacher."

Meghan clapped her hands. "Clementine, that's perfect!" she said.

Clem smiled and, right then, a flurry of texts blew up her phone—a reminder about the boots she needed to return, a receipt for a book she'd preordered, a last-minute location change for Brewster's cast party, a motivational message from a yoga studio. Her cheeks were blazing now. Did anyone notice?

Her phone buzzed. Tor.

Maybe you're in a meeting?

Sweetheart, I called the dry cleaner.
They don't have my sweater.

Clem knew from years of experience that her husband wanted her to be impressed that he'd taken the initiative to call the dry cleaners all by himself. He wanted a pat on the head and a *Good job, hon*. Normally she would have offered up the laudatory ode he so desperately needed, but today she couldn't do it. She also couldn't bear the heat a moment more. She pressed her right toe into the top of the sock on her left foot and pushed it off.

When both socks were off, Clem realized that her long, curly hair was beginning to expand. Soon she'd look like a Chia Pet, the norm whenever the temperature rose above seventy-five degrees. With her body in complete rebellion, she leaned and pressed her cheek to the cool table, then moaned audibly. When she sat up, three googly eyes were stuck to her face and the sweaty outline of her head lingered on the table. Everyone was staring.

"Clem, are you all right?" Bathsheba said.

Clem swallowed and pressed her feet, now bare, on the linoleum. "Not quite, but I'll be okay."

Bathsheba was too young to understand. Though a day ago Clem would have said the same about herself. Way too young for a hot flash.

Bathsheba nodded.

Clem plucked two googly eyes from her cheek and tried to ignore the sweat now soaking the waistband of her pants. She reread the craft directions: *Make a person having a big feeling.*

This may be the biggest feeling I've ever had, she thought as a gaggle of three-year-olds waddled past the window behind Janine, the assistant children's librarian. A precocious girl in a bright-blue fuzzy hat turned, caught Clementine's eye, and stuck out her tongue. Clem couldn't remember her name, but she'd seen her plenty of times, usually challenging a grown-up about this or that.

Bathsheba redirected the group. "Clem, I will take title changes to the board for consideration, but for now, you"—she looked at Samantha—"are Head Librarian, and you"—she looked at Clem—"are Director of Media. Can we please get on with the list of this week's new releases?"

"Excuse me," Clem said, then stood.

"Clementine?" Bathsheba looked irritated. "I said—"

"No, no, Bath. It's not the title thing," Clem said. "I'm upset about that, but I'm also not well today. I have to go." She could tell by the weight of her hair that she'd graduated from Chia Pet to unkempt bonsai bush. Sweat was streaming down her shockingly hot forehead, carrying the last googly eye in its current. Bits of construction paper were stuck to her forearms.

She leaned her craft self on the sandwich board in the center of the table. The likeness was uncanny. A poster board Clem with an unruly mane of dark hair and a name tag glued to her chest: CONNECTOR OF PEOPLE TO MAGICAL THINGS. Craft Clem was surrounded by so many flames she looked like she was being catapulted from a volcano.

"Clementine, you know we won't be able to hang this," Bath said. Each week, the team hung their crafts on a bulletin board in the children's room for the kids to admire. Meghan believed in letting kids see that adults were creative too. It was a rule that every craft had to be shared, but occasionally there was an exception. Once, when the assignment was to illustrate a favorite hobby, Victor made a beer can. Another time, when the assignment was to create a beloved relative, Samantha had drawn a picture of her son who had passed away. For different reasons, neither made the cut.

"I don't care, Bath," Clem said. "Put it at my desk. Burn it. Whatever." She stood, picked up her bag, and said, "Rage. My big feeling today is red-hot rage." Then she stepped away from the table.

"Clem?" Samantha said.

Clem ignored her and pushed out the door. She was still barefoot, boots and socks abandoned in the puddle of slush under the table. She shuffled down the hallway, heading as fast as she could to the snowy nirvana outside.

"Clem, wait!" Samantha called, running along behind her. "Are you having a hot flash? It's okay! Let me help! I have a cooling pack in my desk."

Clem waved her off. "Not now, Sam," she said. While she knew Samantha was the only one old enough to understand what she was going through, she wasn't ready to talk about it.

Clem padded into the children's room. In the adjacent garden, the gaggle of three-year-olds, now bundled in snow pants and mittens, was building something that looked like a monster with three heads. When the girl in the blue hat spotted Clem through the window, she pointed and called out to her minions. The minions followed her finger with their eyes, then giggled.

Thankfully, the children's room was empty. Quiet and still. Frankie was doing laps in her tank, though Clem could barely see her through the fresh smear of greasy fingerprints on the glass. She stared at the fish, channeling her tranquil state of being. And like always, it worked its magic. Who needed the Dalai Lama or Yoda when you had Frankie the fish? Clem felt herself calming enough to let an idea—an unexpected idea—take shape.

She looked out the window and waited. When she was sure the kids were deep in their snow tasks, she dug a Ziploc from the bottom of her purse. She shook potato chip crumbs from it and, using the empty coffee mug on Meghan's desk, scooped water from Frankie's tank into it. Once the bag was half full, she scooped up Frankie, plopped her in, sealed the bag, and tucked it into her purse, hoping it didn't leak. "All right, Frankadoodle," she said, slipping the small jar of fish food in as well. "You and your peaceful sensibility are coming with me."

Before sneaking out the door, Clem grabbed a crayon and jotted a note on the back of a library card application. Careful to disguise her handwriting, she wrote in bubbly, slanting letters: *I've borrowed Frankie. Don't worry! I'll keep her safe and well.* She taped the note to Frankie's tank, then tiptoed out of the library and into the snow, barefoot.

CHAPTER THREE

The Perfect Storm

Clementine Crane wasn't a thief. The only thing she'd ever taken illegally was a piece of gum from her fourth-grade teacher's desk, a crime about which she still felt shame whenever someone handed her a stick of Juicy Fruit. But with Frankie the fish tucked into her purse like a stolen Matisse, all that changed. Clem knew she needed to get away from the library . . . fast.

Once safely in her car, she revved the cold engine and whipped out of the parking lot. She skidded across Main Street on a patch of ice, veered around a snowplow, and glanced in the rearview mirror to make sure no one was following her. She even altered her normal route in case Little Miss Blue Hat had taken note and summoned the authorities. Usually a cautious driver, Clem knew she couldn't dilly-dally. She was now a fugitive. A larcenist. A barefoot, rage-filled, overheated fish-napper with revelations about marriage zipping through her head and evidence of her misdeed sloshing around in a Ziploc on the passenger seat beside her.

When she reached the Cranes' deep-blue Cape on Baker Street, she slid into the driveway and slammed on the brakes. Though she'd planned to pull directly into the garage, minimizing the chance of being spotted, Tor had left his beloved snowblower blocking her bay. She inched forward until the bumper of her car kissed the massive machine, then unzipped her purse and peered in.

"I've got you, Frankadoodle," she whispered. "We're almost there."

When Frankie swished her tail, a bolt of joy shot through Clem. *This fish adores me,* she thought, smiling bigger than she had in months. For a moment, it was like a slow-motion scene from a movie in which the protagonist is hoisted onto the shoulders of her admirers and toted through a crowd of cheering fans. Clem felt cherished and revered. But when a plow passed behind her, grating its blade on the pavement, she was startled back into reality. Frankie was a fish. A celestial goldfish with bulgy eyeballs. Fish didn't adore people. They probably hated people. Who would think warmly of someone who was responsible for your eternal confinement in a tank?

Clem climbed out of the car, incredulous that she was turning to a fish for adoration. How had she gotten to this point? If she'd been able to stomp dramatically into the house, she would have, but with her bare frozen feet feeling like blocks of cement stuck to the ends of her legs, she duckwalked instead. Once inside, she hobbled up the stairs to her and Tor's bedroom. And there she locked herself in her walk-in closet, pulled the Ziploc from her purse, and set poor Frankie on a shelf.

When her phone pinged, she jumped, half expecting it to be Meghan or Little Miss Blue Hat, demanding she return Frankie to the library immediately. But it was Anna.

MOM

All caps. Clem sighed.

MOM

Clem ignored the text. She stood, stepped into her slippers, then went downstairs to the dining room, where she grabbed her grandmother's crystal punch bowl from the fancy dish cabinet. It was the perfect size for a temporary fish tank. Not too deep, not too wide. Clem checked her watch. Brewster was due home from school at 3:15. She had ten minutes.

MOM

MOM

MOM

Busy, Anna.

MOM

wht hapnd 2 moby duck

u nvr brought the bk

MOM

Sorry, Anna. Something came up.

Back upstairs, she filled the punch bowl with water, then lowered the Ziploc into it. She didn't know much about caring for a fish, but she knew enough to let the temperatures equalize before setting Frankie free in her new digs.

Moments later, she heard the front door open. "Mom!" Brewster's voice blasted through the house. "Mom? You here? Mom? I'm hungry!"

Clem remembered the first time Brewster cried from hunger as a baby. The unrelenting bleating of the lamb.

It hadn't stopped since.

Later that evening, after Heather of the Weather did her snow dance, Clem and Georgia—along with nearly every other adult in Byrock, Massachusetts—made a last-minute trip to the grocery store to stock up on necessities—eggs, milk, bread, coffee, and snacks. Most could have muddled through with whatever they had on hand, but nor'easter prep in New England was hard to resist.

As they were pushing past a woman loading pancake supplies into her cart, Clem told Georgia about the crunching sound she'd heard in their yards that morning. "Something was moving around in the ice and snow. Did you hear it?"

Georgia shook her head. "You know very well that I can't even hear the teakettle unless I'm standing right beside it. How would I hear a crunching sound coming from outside the house?"

"I heard it right before I dove into that snowbank, right after you pushed up the window and called to me."

"I heard nothing, Clem. I'm sorry."

"Did you see anything?"

"Only you in all your glory."

Clem grinned and added two bags of popcorn to the cart. One for Brewster and one for everyone else.

"But you're sure *you* heard something?" Georgia said.

"I am."

"And it wasn't Tor?"

Clem shook her head.

"And it wasn't your brain in its first hot flash?"

"Nope."

"Unusual things can happen during hot flashes. I used to get so foggy and confused."

"I wasn't imagining it."

Georgia nodded. "So, what do you think it was?"

"Something big," Clem said. "Something really big." When she lifted her arms over her head to demonstrate, she bumped a display and knocked a few bags of pet-friendly snow melt to the floor.

"That big?" Georgia said.

"Bigger," Clem said. She tossed two bags into the cart and restacked the rest. "I know it sounds impossible, but whatever it was, it was massive."

"Bill, maybe?"

"No," Clem said. Bill Weston was big but not *that* big. "This was definitely an animal."

"What kind?" Georgia said, placing three bananas in the cart.

"I don't know," Clem said, "but I'm going to find out."

Georgia cocked her head but didn't laugh, and this very reaction was yet another reason Clem loved her so much.

From the beginning of their friendship, Georgia had never chuckled, mocked, or turned away from Clem. They'd met on Halloween shortly after the Cranes moved to Byrock years before. Clem had gone for a stroll in their new neighborhood wearing an inflatable giraffe costume, and Georgia, the first person she met, had skipped the handshake, gone in for a hug, and howled with laughter when Clem's giraffe head, at the tiptop of her very long neck, bopped Georgia's husband, Henry, on the buttocks. That was the day Clem began to live out her lifelong dream of having a best friend.

She'd always had lots of friends—coffee friends, roommate friends, meet-at-the-gym friends—but a bestie had eluded her. Her last near miss was Penny Bexler, way back in eighth grade. For the first three weeks of school, the two girls had eaten lunch together, a sure sign of best friend status. They'd walked to class, spied on their crushes, and ditched the raisins both their mothers insisted they bring as a snack. That kind of willingness to rebel was hard to find. But when Chen Li moved her things into the locker next to Penny's, Clem's brief foray into best-friend-ness ended as quickly as it had begun. Penny and Li bonded over a mutual love for Tchaikovsky's *1812 Overture* and red Converse high-tops. Penny never looked at Clem in that best friend way again. Li was in, Clem was out.

While she'd scrambled to find a gaggle of friends to eat lunch with, Clem decided that was the last time she'd ever risk her heart. Having a bestie didn't seem worth the pain. And she'd continued that way right up until the moment she'd met Georgia. Thankfully, their friendship had never disappointed her. Instead, it had done all the things a best friendship should do: buoyed her, supported her, and made her feel like she could do anything. The two even had matching mugs with their likenesses etched under the words: *Clem and Georgia. Besties Forever.*

"What kind of animal do you think it is?" Georgia said. "Coyote? Deer?" She put a pint of cottage cheese into the cart. Shelves were emptying fast. The ice cream freezers were already bare except for a few lonely gallons of vanilla.

"Too small."

"A moose?"

"Maybe," Clem said.

"Moose like deep woods and mountains, Clem. Maine and Vermont. They're not much into the northern suburbs of Boston." Georgia grabbed the last quart of 2 percent milk.

"Maybe it's an adventurous moose."

"Clementine, it's got to be at least twenty-five years since a moose was spotted in this town."

"But it's happened, right?"

"Sure. We're in New England. A wayward moose is possible, but not likely."

"That's what they say about aliens," Clem said, "but more and more people are jumping onto that spaceship." Her phone buzzed. Anna.

MOM

MOM

i need a ride

at library

come get me

I'm at the store with Georgia.
I'll pick you up in 30 minutes.

"What else do you need today, Georgia? Cookies? Shrimp? A loaf of bread?"

"I'm all set."

MOM

MOM

not 30 minutes

library is closing early

ill be cold

frozen

This from the kid who played ice hockey.

Sit tight.

As Clem and Georgia moved toward the checkout lines, Clem said, "There is one other possibility."

"What's that?"

"It could be a woolly mammoth."

Georgia stopped the cart and looked at Clem. "A what?"

"A woolly mammoth. There's a group of scientists trying to de-extinct it. Maybe they were successful."

"Why would anyone want to de-extinct the woolly mammoth?" Georgia pushed into the shortest line.

"To heal our planet."

"I don't get it."

"They're trying to bring back species that have gone extinct and whose absence is missed in the ecosystem." Clem lifted Georgia's items onto the conveyor belt.

"The woolly mammoth is missed?" Georgia said.

"It is. Grazing mammoths used to clear layers of snow so cold air could reach the dirt. That helped the grasslands to thrive, and grasslands are a vital part of our ecosystem."

"Hm." Georgia looked dubious.

"I'm telling you, they were important."

"And you think one of these resurrected hairy elephants could be tromping around our neighborhood?"

"Maybe."

"Like the dinosaurs in *Jurassic Park*?"

"Not really. Dinosaurs lived millions of years ago. Mammoths only died out four thousand years ago. They're not an ancient species. Humans lived among them."

Clem's phone buzzed. Tor.

Sweetheart?

Clem braced herself.

Yes?

Honey, I'm still looking for my green sweater.

Oh, for fuck's sake. That green sweater was the ugliest piece of knitted nonsense ever to be sold in a clothing store. "Tor can't find that hideous sweater of his," she mouthed.

Georgia rolled her eyes.

Little lark?

Yes?

I really need this sweater.

For what?

Does it matter?

Tor, I'm at the store with Georgia.
I'll look for it when I get home.

Thank you.

Clem dropped her phone into her purse, then set the bag of groceries in the cart.

"Clementine," Georgia said.

"What?"

"Where is Torvald's sweater?"

"I don't know."

"You didn't hide it or give it away?"

"I didn't."

"Honestly?"

"Honestly."

Georgia raised her eyebrows.

Clem's phone pinged with a reminder to make snickerdoodles for Anna's upcoming bake sale.

Respond YES to confirm.

YES

Clem added the bake sale to the calendar and stuffed it into her chest cavity. Tor got none of these school-related texts. E-invites to parties, calls for cookie donations, activity forms, medical forms, field trip approval forms, Venmo for this and that, teacher conferences, and so on. These never crossed his phone or his mind. He got to pass each day singularly focused on whatever it was he chose to focus on. What a privilege. Anyone who said marriage was proportional had never been listed as the primary parent.

"Hats on," Clem said, and she pushed the cart through the exit. Snow was cascading down from the clouds.

As they moved through the parking lot, Georgia leaned on Clem. "Have these scientists said they've managed to resurrect a woolly mammoth?"

"No, but I think they may have secretly succeeded."

"Come on, Clem."

"What? Why not?"

"How would they hide it? It's a woolly mammoth! It would be impossible."

Clem opened the hatch of the car and loaded the bags. "Didn't Henry always say anything is possible?"

"Yes, but he hadn't been privy to your woolly mammoth story."

Clem's phone pinged. She pulled it from her purse. Georgia's appointment with the vascular surgeon. Please confirm.

Clem typed *YES* as fast as she could. A month before, after several bouts with numbness, an unnerving hour of aphasia, and one unexpected tumble, the doctor had discussed the possibility of an arterial blockage. That had led to a neurology referral, which had led to the discovery of a 70 percent narrowing in Georgia's carotid artery. They'd scheduled an endarterectomy for February 2.

Clem guided Georgia into the car, checked that the appointment was in her calendar, then tucked it gently into her chest cavity.

At the library, Anna hurled herself into the back seat with her coat, backpack, and hockey bag. "Mom, I lost my microscope. Mr. Cauley is going to kill me. Have you seen it?" She rooted through the pile of sports gear, books, and fast-food wrappers on the floor.

"Anna, say hi to Georgia, please," Clem said.

"Hi, Georgia! I'm so sorry! I'm panicked." Anna leaned over the front seat and kissed Georgia on the cheek.

"Don't worry about me," Georgia said. "Look for your microscope."

"Anna, did anyone say why they're closing the library early?" Clem said.

"I don't know, Mom. Ms. Meghan was whispering with Ms. Samantha on the stairs, and then Ms. Samantha was whispering with the other librarians. The next thing I knew, they were shuffling everyone out the door."

"Whispering about what?" Clem knew they must have discovered that Frankie was missing. She squeezed the steering wheel and let the car idle as she peered up the granite steps.

"You work here, Mom. Don't you know?"

Clem's phone pinged. Meghan's name popped up on the car's display screen.

"I think we're about to find out," Georgia said.

The car's audio system read the text out loud. *"Clem, Clem! Call me. Frankie is missing!"*

Anna and Georgia both sucked in a breath. They knew how much Clem loved that fish.

"I'm so sorry, Clem," the audio system read in its monotone voice. *"It appears she's been kidnapped. Well, fish-napped."*

Anna leaned into the front seat. She looked from Clem to Georgia and back. "Fish-napped? Oh my god. Mom, I am so sorry."

This was the kindest thing Anna had said to Clem in weeks. The long stretches of being distant and unkind broke Clem's heart, even though she knew they were a natural part of the teenage years.

Clem gripped the steering wheel even harder. Out loud she said, "Frankie? My Frankie? Someone has kidnapped my Frankie?" but inside her head, she was yelling, *What the hell? Why did it take them so many hours to figure this out? Didn't they see the note earlier today? And the empty tank?*

Georgia reached over and set a hand on Clem's arm. "Do you want to go in, Clem? Anna and I can wait here."

Clem rubbed her eyes. "No, I can't go in there if Frankie is missing."

"Are you sure? Maybe you can offer some information," Georgia said. "Did you see anything out of the ordinary today?"

"No, I was in for a meeting this morning, but then I worked from home. I didn't see a thing." Clem's mouth throbbed as she spoke. Deception was horribly uncomfortable. She had lied throughout her life about as often as she'd stolen things. Thankfully, her phone pinged, and the audio system read out loud, *"Clem, we told the children we removed Frankie to clean the tank. We promised them she's safe in the secondary tank in the back offices. We'll stick with this story until we know more."*

Clem swallowed.

"Secondary tank?" Anna said. "I didn't know there was one."

"There isn't," Clem said.

"Oh."

Georgia put her hand over Clem's.

"Mom, it's okay if you want to go in," Anna said. "I can live without the microscope another day."

"No, Anna. We have to find it." Deflecting attention from an undesirable topic by refocusing energy onto something else was a parenting strategy Clem had perfected over the years. "Please, look for the microscope. I can't even think about Frankie right now. Who would do such a thing?"

Anna leaned back. "Okay, Mom. Whatever you want."

"Now," Clem said, "did you leave the microscope in the car?" Her voice was shaky. She considered lecturing Anna on how she should put everything in her backpack the night before school so she was properly prepared, but she knew—because of the previous 3.2 million conversations about this very thing—it wouldn't make a damn bit of difference. Like all humans, Anna was who she was, and, likely, she would be losing and finding things for the rest of her life. Tor, the consummate organizer, always said, "Talk to her, Clem. She can't keep going like this." But throughout the years, their daughter had proven she could and would. Besides, if Tor was so concerned, why didn't he talk to her?

"I don't know," Anna said. "Maybe."

"Look in the black hole."

Anna did a flip into the third row of seats in Clem's Highlander, aka the black hole. The space into which all things disappeared—water bottles, library books, money, laptops, winter hats, knee pads, hockey pucks, wigs for school plays, Hagrid's favorite stuffed bear, and so much more. Once, they'd even found a friend of Evan's who'd fallen asleep and been forgotten.

A moment later, Anna popped up. "Hey, look," she yelled.

"You found the microscope?" Georgia said.

"No, but I found a snack." She held up a Tupperware of rotten apples.

"Yuck!" Georgia said. "Any chance you see your dad's green sweater back there?" She nudged Clem.

Anna rummaged around for another minute. "Nope. No sweater here."

Clem slunk deep into the driver's seat when she saw Bathsheba pulling into the lot. She knew she should go in too, but she couldn't.

When the flashing lights of a passing snowplow lit the interior of the car, Anna hollered, "Ta-da! My microscope! Got it!"

Clem sighed. "Great. Now what are you supposed to use it for?"

Anna somersaulted back into the second row of seats, buckled her seat belt, flicked on the overhead light, pulled a binder from her backpack, and flipped through it. "No idea. Now I have to find my assignment sheet."

Once home, Clem tugged on Georgia's arm. "Come on. I have to show you something," she whispered.

"Your hiding spot for Tor's sweater?" Georgia said as they made their way up the stairs.

"Oh, stop it," Clem said. "I told you already. I don't have Tor's sweater."

"Then what?"

"You'll see."

She led Georgia into her and Tor's bedroom, then unlocked the door to her walk-in closet—Clem's refuge from the world. Before letting her in, Clem stared into Georgia's eyes and said seriously, "This is a secret. You must promise you won't tell."

"Without even knowing what it is you're going to show me?"

"Yes."

"What do you have in here? A woolly mammoth?"

Clem grinned. "Honestly, that would probably be better."

Georgia cocked her head. "Whatever it is, I'm sure it's fine. Open the door. My legs are tired."

"Promise you won't tell anyone?" Clem said.

Georgia sighed. "Promise."

"Thank you," Clem said, then turned the knob and guided Georgia into the dark space. She shut the door behind them, locked it, and flicked the switch. For a moment, they were blinded by the sudden burst of light.

When their eyes adjusted, Georgia said, "Clementine, what is that?" She was pointing at the punch bowl where Frankie was doing slow laps, her fins flipping lightly back and forth.

Clem didn't answer.

Georgia moved closer, then leaned down until she was nose to nose with Frankie. "Oh, sweetie," Georgia said. "Please tell me this is not Frankie the fish."

Clem grimaced. "This is not Frankie the fish."

"Clementine?"

"What?"

"Is this Frankie the fish?"

"Maybe."

"Maybe?"

"Yes."

"Yes?"

"Of course it's Frankie, Georgia. Who else would it be? Do you know any other celestial goldfish swimming around town?"

Georgia dipped her fingers into Frankie's punch bowl. "Clementine, what is Frankie doing here? Did you rescue her from the kidnappers?"

Leave it to Georgia to come up with a scenario in which Clem was the hero, not the villain. That made it even harder to tell the truth. "No," Clem said.

Georgia was the only other person she'd ever invited into this sanctuary, and after all these years, it had become as much her space as it was Clem's. She even had her own chair by the window. How many times had they sat there in the early years watching Henry and Tor push the kids on the swings? Watching Anna, Evan, and Brewster bump down the slide and climb the sycamore? How many times had they sat right there talking about marriage and life and dreams after Clem had put the children to bed?

Georgia sat down. "If you didn't rescue her, how did she get here?"

Clem sat down and waited quietly.

"Oh, Clem," Georgia finally said. "You're the kidnapper, aren't you?"

"Technically, I'm the fish-napper."

"Oh, sweetie, I should have known." Georgia reached out and took Clem's hand. "What a day you've had."

Tears welled up in Clem's eyes for what felt like the hundredth time. "It happened so quickly, Georgia. One minute I was having a hot flash in a meeting at work, arguing with Bath about my title and trying to keep up with Tor and his damn sweater texts, and the next I was sneaking out of the library with Frankie in my purse, barefoot."

"Barefoot?"

"Long story."

Georgia squeezed Clem's hand. "It's okay," Georgia said. "It's going to be okay. We'll work this out."

Clem squeezed back. She wanted to believe her. She really did. But how could she with everything that was going on? The hot flashes, the fish-napping, the lack of support at work for a title that fit her person and position, Tor's sweater, managing every damn need and emotion of every person in the family, the woolly mammoth. And now, on top of everything else, a growing roar of anger somewhere deep inside.

Later that night Clem did a search for symptoms of perimenopause. The list was much longer than she had expected:

Mood changes
Heart palpitations
Hot flashes
Heavy periods
Changes in sexual function
Changes in sexual desire
Sleep disruption
Itchy ears
Brain fog
Bone loss
Changes in cholesterol levels
Headaches
Night sweats
Vaginal dryness
Joint and muscle aches
Frequent urination

She called Georgia. "Why didn't you tell me?" she said when she heard her friend's voice.

"Tell you what?"

"Tell me how much more is coming in perimenopause!" Clem realized she was wailing. Actually wailing. Had she ever wailed before? She was pretty sure the answer was no. "Hot flashes are only the beginning. Why didn't you say anything? Brain fog? Itchy ears? Night sweats? High cholesterol?"

"You really need to stay off the internet, Clem."

"If you'd talked to me about all this, I wouldn't need to be on the internet."

"That first hot flash was a lot," Georgia said. "I figured we'd talk more once you got used to those."

"I will never get used them," Clem said.

Georgia chuckled. "It seems like that now, but you will, dear Clem. You'll never like them, but you will get used to them."

After they said goodbye, Clem checked off the perimenopause symptoms she'd already experienced: heavy bleeding, hot flashes, no sex drive, and brain fog. Why hadn't she known any of this would be coming? Why hadn't her gynecologist or PCP ever discussed it? Why wasn't she armed with solutions? Or at least some coping tools? Why was she completely clueless about how her own body would change as she aged?

While one part of her simmered with anger, another part was comforted. There'd been moments in recent months when she'd thought for sure she was dying or losing her mind. The fact that she wasn't was a relief.

As always, before falling asleep, Clem sent her final text of the night to Georgia.

Night, G.

She waited for the usual response.

Night, C.

CHAPTER FOUR
Hypocritical Chickenshit

But that night, at 1:38 AM, Clem woke with a river of thoughts and worries flooding her brain.

My right boob hurts.

What is the etymology of sycamore*?*

Did Anna figure out her science assignment?

How much snow will we get this week?

Did that Ziploc damage Frankie's fins?

What time is my Pap smear in the morning?

Could a potato chip crumb kill a fish?

How do you grow a woolly mammoth?

Heather is an unfortunate name for someone working in weather.

Heather. Weather. Heather. Weather.

Did I pay Evan's tutor?

Did Evan meet with their tutor this week?

How will the children react when they learn Frankie has been fish-napped?

Where is Tor's green sweater?

I hate Pap smears.

I forgot to take Evan to meet their tutor.

I hate winter.

What new hell was this? Clem had always been a decent sleeper. Decent enough anyway. Able to wake with the kids, fall back asleep. Wake to Tor's meteoric snores, kick him in the leg, fall back asleep. Able to cope with any and all nocturnal obstacles tossed in her path. She'd suffered but slept just enough to survive. But on this night, after her first hot flash? She felt she might never sleep again.

What time is my first meeting tomorrow?

I have to pee.

How often does Georgia think of Henry in a day?

Did anyone find debris in the Maldives from China's wonky space launch?

How much is a plane fare to Costa Rica?

Did I put out the recycling?

I am the Connector of People to Magical Things.

An hour later, finally drowsy enough to move past her brainly wanderings, Clem's eyes drifted closed. But as she was about to fall asleep, a snore burbled out of Tor's nose.

Shit.

Knowing there was never a one-off, Clem braced herself. As expected, another snore surged. Then another. At first, they came quietly and far apart, like thunder from a distant storm, but as Tor relaxed deeper and deeper into sleep, the burbles got louder, more raucous, and more frequent. Clem leaned close to her husband's face and glared at the culpable schnoz.

"I hate you," she whispered. She wasn't sure if she meant the entire man or his nose. "Turn over," she said, prodding his ribs, and when he finally shifted onto his side, she heard the telltale clink of metal under his pillow.

"Holy fucking hummingbirds," she whispered.

Years before, when Heather of the Weather first joined the local news, she'd immediately started telling everyone about her annoying obsession with all the wacky ways people around the world tried to manifest snow. Each time she introduced a new ritual, she asked viewers to test it out with her. Tor and the kids were all in.

White crayons in the freezer?

They'd done it.

Ice cubes flushed down the toilet?

They'd done it.

A stack of pennies on the windowsill?

They'd done it.

But their favorite was putting spoons under their pillows. There was no proof that this, or any of the rituals, produced the desired result, but, for whatever reason, they believed this to be the most successful method of encouraging snow.

Clem slid her hand under Tor's pillow and pulled out three teaspoons and a tablespoon. "Oh my god." No wonder there hadn't been any spoons at breakfast.

Wide awake, she set the spoons on her bedside table, grabbed her phone, and stuck her head under the covers. She searched for *animals that have hot flashes.*

The results?

Zero.

There were a handful of animals, she discovered, that went through perimenopause and menopause, but thus far, none had been found to have hot flashes.

Only humans with uteruses had to suffer this way.

And even worse, she discovered that for most animals, menopause not only signaled the end of menstruation, ovulation, and fertility but also the end of life.

The. End. Of. Life.

Buh-bye, Lady Jane.

Rather than suffering hot flashes, desert-dry vaginas, debilitating bouts of depression, hair loss, wide-awakeness in the wee hours, widening hips, burgeoning bellies, saggy boobs, thinning hair, stiff joints, itchy ears, and all other delights of perimenopause and menopause, most animals with uteruses died.

Passed away.

Expired.

Gave up the ghost.

Kicked the motherfucking bucket.

Sayonara, sister.

Why?

Because, Clem read, females were no good to their communities unless they were able to push out babies.

She seethed. That's all animals with uteruses were worth?

With a little more digging, she discovered that there were a few exceptions to the death-at-menopause rule, including beluga whales, narwhals, orcas, and short-finned pilot whales. Through research on these animals and their dried-up, dormant ovaries, scientists had discovered that for menopause to make sense, a species needed two things: reasons to stop reproducing and reasons to live on afterward.

Ugh.

It worked for orcas, she learned, because all offspring stayed with their mother for life. If the mother didn't go through menopause, she'd have way too many kiddos in her pod and she'd be competing for food with her own children and grandchildren. Dying off immediately didn't make sense because, as the elder, she had institutional knowledge.

"How depressing," Clem said out loud.

Torvald interrupted his own snore. "What?" he said, patting the top of the comforter to locate her. "Honey, what are you doing? Turn off your phone and go to sleep." Within seconds, an audacious snore rumbled across the bed and ripped into Clem's heart.

To stop herself from lobbing a spoon at her husband's head, Clem texted Georgia. *Why do women live past menopause? From what I've read, we're more dead than alive at that point.*

Georgia responded almost immediately. She was awake too. Grandmother syndrome. As grandmothers (and best friends), we're still good at loving the young ones while moms pick peapods and slaughter enemies.

Gotta love evolution.

Go to sleep. Do that word meditation you saw on TikTok.

Clem chuckled. Wouldn't Anna love to see a text from eighty-seven-year-old Georgia encouraging her to do a TikTok thing? Anna had been begging Clem to join for months. "Come on, Mom," she'd said over and over, "I'll even dance with you." Clem kept telling her that she didn't have time to dance, but, in truth, she was tragically uncoordinated and petrified of embarrassing herself. Despite her near-daily lecture to her kids about being themselves and not worrying what others thought of them, Clem spent a hell of a lot of time worrying what others thought of her. *I'm a hypocritical chickenshit.*

Georgia texted one last time. Stop thinking. Word meditation.

Otolaryngologist popped into Clem's brain.

She mouthed it silently over and over.

Otolaryngologist.

Otolaryngologist.

She pictured Brewster's ear. The softness of his little-boy lobe.

She slowed down the word.

Oto-laryn-golo-gist.

Her eyes began to close. She was getting sleepy.

Otolaryngologist.

Otolaryngologist.

Otolaryngologist.

But then, out of nowhere, her stomach did that strange roll, and for a few seconds she couldn't catch a breath.

Oh, for god's sake. Another one?

Otolaryngologist.

Otolaryngologist.

As heat built on her forearms and forehead, Tor's snore ratcheted up like a cyclone-force wind. *Will this torture never end?*

Clem whipped off the covers and pulled her nightgown over her head. She scrunched it into a ball, used it to sop up the pool of sweat between her breasts, then threw it to the floor.

Motherfucking otolaryngologist.

Then, as she was about to detonate, Clementine heard it.

Crunch, crunch, crunch.

It was the same sound she'd heard when she'd plunged face-first into the snow. She sat up.

Crunch, crunch, crunch.

What would make such a tremendous noise?

She rolled out of bed, ran to the window, and yanked up the blind. The spoons had definitely worked their magic. Fat, dense flakes were drifting down from even fatter clouds. When she tried to raise the sash, the old frame stuck until she knocked it a few times with her elbow. Then she jiggered it up.

A single sniff told her it was sledding snow, and she said a quick thanks that the kids weren't interested anymore—even Brewster. They were too busy. Too old. Too mature. Too cool.

Back when they were little, even the lightest dusting had them dragging her and their inner tubes to the golf course in town, then over and over whipping down the steepest hill at top speed. She'd done it, of course. Good New England moms sled when their kids yell, "Snow!" But she'd loathed it as much as they'd loved it.

Crunch, crunch, crunch.

The crisp air felt so good on Clem's skin that she pushed the sash higher and pressed on the screen with her palms. When it gave, she popped it sharply with her fist, then stuck her head out and watched it tumble down until it landed silently in a deep drift below. Hagrid nudged her with his nose.

"Yeah, I know, I know," she whispered, rubbing his head. "You love the stuff."

"Clem?" she heard Tor call. "Clem, get back here. What are you doing over there?"

Clem felt the familiar chasm between Tor's *here* and her *there.*

"Clem, it's freezing," he said.

She heard him pull the extra blanket from the bottom of the bed and watched a frozen cloud form from her breath. Then she leaned farther out, raking her breasts through the snow on the sill. It was glorious. The heat in her body was beginning to subside. She could breathe.

Crunch, crunch, crunch.

She was surprised that the motion light on the corner of Bill Weston's house hadn't clicked on. Normally, the thing was so sensitive the slightest breeze could trigger it. Clem sucked in a breath. It came again—*crunch, crunch, crunch.* There *was* something out there. A shadow moving through the dark yards. She wasn't imagining it. She stretched as far as she could out the window, but the jumble of fences, trees, and backyard sheds prevented a clean line of sight.

Inspired, Clem pushed the window shut, pulled on her robe, and sprinted out of the bedroom and down the stairs. Hagrid followed. In the kitchen, she opened the sliding door and stepped into the yard, barefoot once more. Then she marched through the snow, knees high, to the intersection of fences and peered through the hole the kids had sawed out years before when they were determined to spot aliens landing in Bill's yard.

The crunch was fainter now, but through the hole, Clementine saw what looked like a rump—a large, dark rump moving through the shadows. A rump higher than her head.

What was it? Had aliens finally landed? Was it a wayward moose, as Georgia proposed? Or had those scientists, as Clem secretly wished, succeeded at de-extincting the woolly mammoth?

She set her hand on her dog's happy head, listening as the *crunch, crunch, crunch* faded in the distance. "Heather is promising another eight inches today," she said. "Soon, dear Hagrid, even you will get buried by it." He grunted hopefully. Like Tor and Heather, Hagrid was a psychrophile. King of the psychrophiles, perhaps. Romping gleefully on the coldest, snowiest days of the year. Sprawling on the stone patio and refusing to go inside.

"I'm a thermophile," Clem had told Tor shortly after they'd met. He'd shrugged. The difference hadn't seemed important to either at the time, but back then they didn't have a house with a thermostat to fuss over or vacation spots to decide upon.

The kids had turned out to be exactly like him. "I'm outnumbered," Clem always said.

"Dominant gene," Tor always responded.

Clementine didn't hate people who enjoyed cold weather. Not all of them anyway. But they were strangers to her. They enjoyed wool hats and knitted scarves. She preferred linen shorts and flip-flops. They took great pleasure in chili and thick stews. She'd rather dine on gazpacho with a squeeze of lime. They reveled in the generations-old debate, down versus feathers. She was happiest with a hot breeze and a cool sheet.

As long as psychrophiles didn't proselytize, she could put up with them. In most cases, the good outweighed the bad.

But Heather of the Weather? Clem abhorred her. The grand proselytizer who'd made it her mission to convince every human to love winter. Clem despised her make-it-snow rituals—putting spoons under pillows, wearing pajamas backward and inside out, running around the dining table five times before bed, brushing your teeth with your nondominant hand, singing every time you walked by an open freezer. It was a load of nonsense.

Though Clem had grown up in Massachusetts, she'd always longed for warmth. Her mother told stories about how, as a baby, she'd only stop crying in winter if every part of her body was layered up. Her grandmother had even crocheted a nose mitten for her, and although Clem had laughed about this with her family, she'd secretly believed it was a brilliant idea. Quite marketable too.

How she'd been born into a family of psychrophiles was a mystery. Both of her parents were skiers and cold-weather hikers. Until Clem was old enough to make a big stink, family vacations in January were spent in Vermont and in June, northern New Hampshire. Once, they'd even traveled to Switzerland. For ten days and nights, they'd slept in a hotel with the balcony door open. "Ah, the crisp air," her mother gasped daily. "Breathe it in, my family. Breathe it in."

Because Clem had always believed that once grown, she'd settle in Arizona or southern Florida or some other steamy place on Earth, she was shocked when she'd fallen in love with Tor and agreed to move back to Massachusetts.

As soon as they bought the house on Baker Street, Clem began to create hot spots for herself. A massive fireplace with two cords of wood delivered each fall. Cozy nooks with heavy quilts. A heated mattress pad on the bed. Slippers she could warm in the microwave. A remote starter for her car. And for Anna's hockey games, a heated stadium seat.

Although they did go on at least one ski vacation each year, Clem insisted on a warm one during the kids' spring break.

Bermuda.

Costa Rica.

Bahamas.

Thailand.

She didn't care how far they had to fly to be toasty. She only knew that when she stepped out of a car, plane, bus, or train, she needed to be warm in order to be happy. It didn't matter if she and Tor were in a fight, if the kids were fluish or cranky, or if toothy lizards were crawling on the window screens. Once engulfed by balmy air, Clementine Crane was at peace.

CHAPTER FIVE
The Gathering Begins

The next morning, a quick search taught Clem that the sycamore tree took its name from two Greek roots—the first meaning *fig*, the second, *mulberry*. But when she found herself wanting to know more, she called the Moses Arboretum.

"The information is correct," the man on the phone confirmed, "but if you go deeper, you'll find that the sycamore is actually a type of maple." His tone implied that this arboreal muddle should confound Clem, but instead, it made perfect sense.

"Sycamores are hardy trees," he continued, "with incredibly strong root systems that anchor them in the ground. Nothing knocks them over. That's why they thrive in this part of the country."

Clem looked out the window and nodded. The sun was shining down from a glacial blue sky, and snow was glistening on the sycamore's limbs. It was the rare kind of day that gave hope to New Englanders like Clem who couldn't wait for spring to arrive. The ultimate bait and switch.

"What's your role at the arboretum?" Clem asked.

"My title is Keeper of Living Collections."

"Not just trees?"

"No, trees are living things that are full of living things that are surrounded by living things—bugs, birds, squirrels, caterpillars, worms, vines, flowers, and even bacteria. It's a whole universe."

"And it's all under your purview?"

"It is."

Clem smiled. "Is Keeper of Living Collections on your business card?"

"Yes."

"In your email signature?"

"Yes."

Hearing this made Clem want to be the Connector of People to Magical Things more than ever. "Did your boss give you this title, or did you choose it?" she said.

The man's laugh sounded like rustling leaves. "I chose it," he said. "The person who held the position before me was called Lead Arborist, but who wants that title? You might as well call me Tree Manager."

"Blah," Clem said.

"Exactly. I was an odd kid who spent a lot of time in the woods, and when I seven, I started introducing myself to people as the Keeper of Living Collections."

"How'd you dream that up?"

"No idea, but I used to walk up to complete strangers in grocery stores and malls and say, 'Hello, I'm the Keeper of Living Collections.' It embarrassed the hell out of my parents, but they couldn't curb my passion."

Clem tried to remember when she'd decided she wanted to be the Connector of People to Magical Things. She hadn't dreamed it up as a kid, but the idea had been bubbling for a long time. Throughout her whole life, she'd been known for connecting friends and strangers with cool stuff. Musical groups. Books. Historical places. Objects with stories behind them.

"And your boss agreed to this title?" she said.

"It took her a while, but she came around. Change is hard for a lot of people."

"Sure is," Clem said, then explained her role at the library.

"What's *your* current title?" the Keeper asked.

"Director of Media, but I'm lobbying for Connector of People to Magical Things." Saying it out loud made Clem shine brighter.

"That's perfect," the Keeper said. "I'd much rather walk into a library and talk with the Connector of People to Magical Things than the Director of Media. Has your manager agreed to it yet?"

Clem laughed. "No, and it's not looking good."

"Stand firm like your sycamore," the Keeper said. "She'll come around."

A few hours later in the ob-gyn's office, the Jupiter-like belly of a near-to-bursting preggo commanded the attention of nearly every woman in the waiting room. It was an impressive sight. That shiny, bulbous belly protruding from between a pink cropped sweater and a low-slung pair of jeans. Prior to this visit, Clem would have stared too, but instead she was focused on the red-faced woman sitting directly across from the pregnant wonder, the one with her eyes closed, her hair drenched with sweat, and her neck slick with perspiration.

"Hot flash," Clem whispered. She recognized it immediately.

A nurse opened a door and poked her head into the waiting room. "Charlene," she said.

Clem's phone buzzed. Anna.

i forgot my new skates can u bring them to skool

"Charlene?" the nurse repeated.

Yes, Anna. I'll leave them in the office.

When the nurse called out a third time, the sweating woman raised a single finger and opened her eyes. "Right here," she said. With a grunt, she stood, then plucked at the shoulders of her soaked blouse. "This is ridiculous," she said, then shook her head and walked toward the nurse.

As the door closed behind them, Clem leaned forward and whispered, "Charlene! Charlene! Come back! You are my people!"

Half the women in the waiting room glared at Clem, clearly annoyed that she'd spoken out loud, breaking one of the sacred rules of waiting rooms.

"You wait," she hissed at them as another hot flash hit. "Someday you'll understand." With her cheeks beginning to gleam like perfectly ripe strawberries and steam radiating from her head, Clem's brain popped with questions. Why hadn't she ever noticed the sweat-soaked women before? Why, when *she* had been the hugely pregnant wonder sitting in this very same office, hadn't she taken note of them? Surely they'd been present. Why hadn't Dr. Sheffield ever pointed them out? Explained to her that someday, in the not-too-far-away future, she, too, would be drowning in sweat? Heating from the inside out like a volcano? Why hadn't one of the nurses told her that this was the fate toward which every human with a uterus was hurtling like a meteor rocketing toward Earth?

The door opened, and this time the nurse called, "Clementine?"

Clem stood, waggled her legs back and forth to unstick her drenched thighs, followed the nurse through the door, and dropped into a chair in the back hallway next to the scale. She knew the routine. She also knew that somewhere in the maze of offices and examining rooms, Charlene was boiling over.

The nurse took her temperature. "How are you today?"

"Hot," Clem said.

"Your temperature is normal."

A bead of sweat ran down the side of Clem's nose.

The nurse wrapped the blood pressure cuff around her arm. "Your blood pressure is normal too." She rested her fingers on Clem's wrist. "Your pulse, though," she said, "is a bit rapid."

"No kidding," Clem said.

"Please step on the scale."

Clem leaned over to remove her shoes.

"No need to take those off," the nurse said. "I'll adjust for them."

"Ha," Clem chortled. She knew this was an empty promise.

A first-timer to the ob-gyn's office might have missed the ever-so-slight rise in the young nurse's eyebrows right then—a clear response to the chortle—but Clem was seasoned. She knew that in addition to training these young nurses in medical techniques, they also trained them not to react to gross or unsavory behaviors.

Chortled at by a grumpy patient?

Don't raise your eyebrows.

Weight gain?

Don't raise your eyebrows.

Two heartbeats during a first ultrasound?

Don't raise your eyebrows.

No heartbeat during a second ultrasound?

Don't raise your eyebrows.

A seeped fart when the speculum is inserted?

Don't raise your eyebrows.

When her shoes were off, Clem stood and sighed. Better, but why in the world had she worn tights? The most confining, heat-trapping piece of clothing in a woman's wardrobe. She might as well have been wearing a suit of armor.

"Ma'am, the scale," the young nurse said, clearly getting nervous about how long this was taking. There was a schedule and a doctor and a waiting room full of patients.

Clem heard the desperation in her voice, and as recently as a week ago, she would have been quick to hop on the scale and ignore her own needs. Quick to prove herself as the people-pleasing, embarrassment-avoiding woman she'd always been.

But she couldn't stand the heat a moment longer, and the thought of trying to satisfy this nurse instead of reducing her own discomfort was suddenly impossible. For the first time in her life, instead of acquiescing to the nurse's request, Clem prioritized her own need. She stood, reached under her skirt right there in the hallway, grabbed the waistband of her tights, and tugged.

"Ma'am?" the nurse said. Her eyebrows shot up—way up—indicating that removing clothing in a public space was an unprecedented event for which she had not been properly trained.

Clem didn't care. This hot-flash heat was so peculiar. Unlike any other she'd ever experienced. More suffocating than summer humidity. More stifling than an overstuffed subway car in August. One minute she was sitting in her gynecologist's hallway, and the next she was trapped in a fur coat on Venus.

She tried to remove the tights without also pulling off her underwear, but when that proved impossible, she simply lifted her skirt a bit higher, pulled the tights and underwear to her knees, plopped back onto the chair, and yanked both to her ankles and off her feet. Then she lifted the edge of her skirt and fluttered it to create a breeze.

Her phone pinged. Georgia.

News of Frankie is out. Check FB.

Clem clicked through to Facebook, then Instagram. The fishnapping news was everywhere. Her heart cleaved. The posts included a *before* photo of Frankie, her tank surrounded by a shoal of smiling kids, with Little Miss Blue Hat front and center, and an *after* photo of Frankie's sad, empty tank.

Rather melodramatic, don't you think?

Seriously, Clem?

Frankie is fine after all.

You and I know that. But Bathsheba,
Meghan, and all those kiddos? For all they know,
Frankie has been flushed.

Georgia!

What?

I would never flush Frankie!

Of course you wouldn't, but they don't know Frankie's with you.

As Clem scrolled through Facebook, she saw the post had already gotten more comments than the wildly popular announcement of a grown-ups–only Dungeons & Dragons group. Clementine read them with one eye squeezed shut.

Shocking!
Frankie the fish has been what?
Library fish gone missing? What kind of a world are we living in?
Kidnapped? Like Charles Lindbergh?
Celestial goldfish zapped to the heavens!
It's got to be an inside job.
What kind of kookadoodle would do such a thing?

What kind indeed.

Clem looked up from her phone when she felt the nurse's eyes on her.

"Ma'am," the nurse said, "are you ready to go to an exam room? Dr. Sheffield will see you now."

"What about the scale?"

"We'll get your weight next time."

Right then, a nurse came marching down the hall with the near-to-bursting preggo close behind. When they got to Clem's black tights and hot-pink underwear, which were stretched across the hallway like a ribbon, the nurse paused.

"For god's sake, it's not the Mississippi River," Clem said. "Step over it."

The pregnant woman's eyes widened with fear. Clem waved a hand at her. "Sorry about this," she said, but she didn't mean it. She didn't want to scare her, but she did want to be seen, and she wanted this young wonder to know what would one day befall her ripe, gushy, slushy body.

As the woman stepped over Clem's underthings and scurried after the nurse, Clem vowed this would be the last time she ever wore tights. She would be bare legged the rest of that winter season and every season thereafter.

Then, feeling that bubble of anger expanding in her middle once more, she also vowed never to apologize again—to anyone—unless there was a truly meaningful reason for doing so. Screw all the empty, insincere apologies she'd gotten used to flinging about: "I'm sorry this is late." "I'm sorry for taking your seat." "I'm sorry. I didn't hear you." Blech. "I'm sorry, but I disagree" was the worst. Why should she ever apologize for disagreeing?

Despite the thick hot-flash fog she was swimming through, Clem also recognized that she was waking up from a very long sleep. It was an unsettling combination of feelings. Big feelings. Meghan would be proud.

"Ma'am?" the nurse whispered.

"Yeah, yeah, yeah," Clem said. She gathered her underthings and followed the nurse into an exam room.

"Good morning, Clementine," Dr. Sheffield said. He was sitting on the stool he used to wheel himself between the small desk and his strategic position between a woman's legs.

"Good morning, Dr. Sheffield." Clem was immediately suspicious. It was unusual for a doctor to arrive before a patient. Unprecedented, really.

"I heard the ruckus, so I thought I'd get here first." He stood and washed his hands in the sink. "What's going on? You've never been a ruckus raiser."

Clem opened her mouth to apologize but then remembered that the sorry she'd given to the young preggo moments before was the final superficial one she'd ever give. "I've never lived through hot flashes," she said.

Dr. Sheffield dried his hands and turned. "Aha."

"Why didn't you tell me this was coming?" Clem said. She felt hoodwinked. How could she be so confused about her own body at forty-four years old?

"Let me step out while you undress. Leave your bra on. Robe open in the back. Then we'll talk."

"No need, Dr. Sheffield." Clem dropped her things on the floor, stripped off the rest of her clothes, and looked him straight in the eye. "You're my doctor. You've seen me through three births and one miscarriage," she said, gesturing at her body, indicating the this and that of things. "There's nothing here you haven't seen before."

This routine of undressing in the exam room before the doctor came in, then donning the paper robe and lap cover, was as ridiculous as expecting the nurse to adjust a patient's weight for shoes. It was a ruse. A failed attempt at creating an invisible wall between patient and doctor, easing the tension caused by sitting stark naked in front of a person you barely knew, then letting them prod you with cold metal instruments. But really, it made things worse.

Unlike the nurse in the hallway, Dr. Sheffield was indifferent. "Fair enough," he said. "Get on the table and tell me what's happening."

Clem climbed up, lay back on the pillow, and set her heels in the stirrups. Dr. Sheffield wheeled across the room on his stool and settled himself between Clem's legs. "Scoot down, please."

Clem lifted her bum and scooted, then launched into a description of the hot flashes—the heat and the sweat, the erratic pulses, the breathy disappearance from herself, the inability to swallow properly, and the fledgling rage. "You've got to give me something for this," she said. "A pill, a shot, a cream."

"Down a little more, please."

Clem scooted.

"A little more."

Clem scooted.

"And a wee bit more, Clementine."

"Oh, for fuck's sake," Clem said, and she scooted one last time so hard that she almost rammed her nether region directly into his face.

"There we go."

Dr. Sheffield began the exam. Never an eyebrow raised. "I wish I had a magic pill for you," he said. "Antidepressants help some women with hot flashes, but not all."

"I'm not depressed."

"Are you sure?"

Clem pinched her thigh to stop herself from lifting her foot out of the stirrup and kicking Dr. Sheffield's shiny bald head. "Yes, I'm sure." Doctors loved to yell *depression* every time a woman complained. It was much easier, Clem was learning, than doing the work that would actually help them.

"Clementine, I'm going to insert the speculum. You'll feel a bit of pressure."

Clem winced as the branches of the speculum stretched wide within her.

"How's your sleep?" he asked.

"Awful. I wake up every night at one thirty-eight AM."

"I'm going to collect a few cells, Clementine."

Clem winced.

"Is your period still regular?"

"Yes, but it's a lot heavier lately."

"Uh-huh."

"Can you elaborate?"

"Well, Clementine, you're likely in perimenopause, the stage before menopause. For the hot flashes, we could put you on venlafaxine and see if it has any effect."

"That's an antidepressant?"

"It is."

"But I'm not depressed."

"I'm sorry, but there's little else we can do."

There it was again. That word. *Sorry.*

"I'm going to remove the speculum," Dr. Sheffield said.

"Really?" Clem asked.

Dr. Sheffield lifted his head. "Yes, really. I am going to remove the speculum now."

"Not that," she said. "The *sorry.* You said you were sorry that you can't do anything more to help my hot flashes."

Dr. Sheffield removed the speculum and set it on the desk with a clunk. "Well . . ." He paused.

"See?" Clem said. "You are not truly sorry. Saying so is a knee-jerk reaction, not an authentic response." She was being quarrelsome but couldn't help herself.

Dr. Sheffield sighed.

"I'm never saying *sorry* again," Clem said, "unless I truly mean it. I decided this today. In your hallway."

"Fair enough." Dr. Sheffield smiled as he rolled over to the sink. "All set."

Clementine scooched back and sat up.

"I'll leave you to get dressed now, Clem. Everything looks good, but you'll get a call if anything comes up in the test results. You know the drill."

Clem nodded. "And the perimenopause?"

"What about it?"

"Can we talk about it now?"

Dr. Sheffield checked his watch. "I have another patient to get to. If you really want to talk, please make an appointment with the receptionist."

Clem stared at him in disbelief. "Of course I really want to talk. Don't all women?"

Dr. Sheffield shook his head. "Actually, no."

If only Clem carried a couple of cymbals in her purse. She'd pull them out and clang them together every time a man said something about women so far from the truth it was absurd. She knew in her heart that every woman who hit this stage of life wanted to come in to her doctor's office, discuss perimenopause, and get some help, but few felt welcome or comfortable enough to do so.

"What about Charlene?" she said.

"Charlene?"

"The woman who had an appointment right before me. She was in mid hot flash in the waiting room when the nurse summoned her. Soaked to the skin. Red as a raspberry."

Dr. Sheffield glanced at the door as if Charlene might be standing there. "You know I can't discuss other patients with you."

Clem studied the three posters hanging on the walls: One outlined the prenatal development of a human, another detailed the female reproductive system, and a third featured the stages of pregnancy and birth. There was not one poster that depicted a woman melting into a puddle with flames shooting out of her head. Not one that showed a woman lying in bed at 1:38 AM with a litany of panicked thoughts running through her brain. Not one that featured the words *perimenopause* or *menopause*. No wonder Clem knew nothing about this stage of life.

"Clementine," Dr. Sheffield said, "make an appointment. We'll talk."

"One question, Dr. Sheffield. How long will these hot flashes last?" She expected him to say a few weeks or, at the most, a couple of months.

"It's different for every woman, but the average is between two and ten years."

"Ten years?"

"Ten years."

Holy fucking hummingbirds.

As she stormed back through the waiting room, tights and underwear stuffed into her purse, Clem studied the women. She ignored the pregnant ones as well as those who looked hopeful. Instead, she focused on the handful who were quite obviously in the middle of or beginning to recover from a hot flash. With no forethought, Clem took the floor.

"Hello," she said, fluttering her hands at the soggy, flushed women. "I am Clementine Crane, Connector of People to Magical Things. And from what I see, you are probably in perimenopause, like me. Now I don't know much about this stage of life yet, but I do know that that doctor in there"—she pointed at the door to the examining rooms—"isn't interested in us. He doesn't even *see* us. And neither does the rest of the world." Clem pulled a bundle of tissues from her purse. She patted her forehead with one and handed the others to the dripping women. "But *I* see us, and *I've* got a plan to make everyone else see us too." She realized that was a slight exaggeration. She didn't have a plan, but in that moment, she was making one. "I'm going to build a—" She paused. What was she going to build? An initiative? A coffee klatsch? A union? "An empire," she finally said.

"An empire?" said a slick-skinned brunette.

"Yes, an empire."

"That's a bit insidious, isn't it?"

A little evil in exchange for hot flashes didn't seem like such a bad thing to Clem, but, still, insidious wasn't the goal.

"I'm a history teacher," explained a blotchy redhead. "And every year I teach my students that empires are driven by at least one of three things: power, control, and expansion."

Clem pulled her hair into a high ponytail. "Well, women at our stage of life are definitely driven by those," she said, "but we've also got two things traditional male empires don't have: rage and humor. And we're going to use those to conquer the world."

The brunette grinned.

"Have there ever been any funny empires?" Clem asked the history teacher.

"They're all pretty comical if you ask me," the woman said. "A bunch of moody men elbowing each other out of the way for the shiniest crown."

Clem paced back and forth. "Here's the plan. We're going to be the first pissed-off, sleep-deprived, lava-shooting empire of the galaxy," Clem said. "Watch out, world."

The sodden woman who hadn't yet spoken nodded and raised her fist. "I'm in," she said.

"Me too," said the brunette.

"What do we need to do?" the history teacher asked.

"Give me your email addresses. I'll be in touch about next steps."

Truth proved to be a magical thing. All but one woman gave her their contact information. Even the preggos.

Clem wasn't yet sure what she was going to do with the email addresses she'd gathered or even what she meant by building an empire, but she knew she'd figure it out. When she got to the parking lot, she spotted Charlene resting her head on the steering wheel of her car. All the windows were down. Snowflakes were blowing in and settling on her hair.

"Charlene!" she yelled, running to the Mazda.

Charlene raised her head slowly and looked at Clem. "Yes?"

"I'm Clementine Crane, Connector of People to Magical Things. I, too, am having hot flashes. You are my people." Clem knew it was an unusual way of introducing herself, but when she did, it was as if a flock of nightingales began to sing.

It took a moment for Charlene to catch up. Clem could see she was in that muddy hot-flash fog that Clem was quickly becoming familiar with. "You're suffering these too?" Charlene finally said.

Clem fluffed her Chia Pet hair and nodded. "Can't you tell?"

"Do your ears itch?" Charlene said.

"Not so far," Clem said. "But I read that's coming."

"It's awful." Charlene buried her index finger in her right ear and wiggled it wildly. "If I thought it would help, I'd pull a Van Gogh and cut off both ears. Old Sheffield up there pooh-hooed every complaint I made. He doesn't care."

"I know," Clem said, "but I do."

Charlene smiled. "Thanks."

And with that, a new friendship was born.

That night, unable to sleep, Clem opened TikTok and watched a video about Greenland, a place she'd never thought much about, mostly because nearly 80 percent of it was covered in ice. She had no interest in such places. "In recent weeks," the voice-over explained, "Greenland's highest point has seen its first-ever recorded rain."

Holy shit. Greenland is having a hot flash.

Clem considered the history of the world.

Rain. On one of the world's most reliably frozen lands. What would Heather of the Weather say?

And after the rain?

The disembodied voice explained that 337,000 square miles of Greenland's ice sheet had begun to melt.

Like me, it's heating up.

This news both comforted and crushed her. Paired with the lack of sleep, hot flashes, the state of her marriage, Georgia's health concerns, Bath's resistance to a job title that mattered, Dr. Sheffield's dismissal of her perimenopausal symptoms, the suggestion that she was depressed, the burden of managing the needs of every damn human in her life—it was all too much.

As Clem tried to imagine standing alone in the center of 337,000 square miles, Tor's nose burbled. She reached over and pushed his pillow.

Those miles of ice didn't melt completely, the voice explained. Don't be silly. The record-breaking rain caused only a surface melt, enough to make seven billion tons of water flood the summit.

Seven *billion* tons.

Tor's nose burbled again, and Clem dropped her head in defeat. From years of experience, she knew that that was the lead-up to what she called a Krakatoa, a snore equal in decibels to the 1883 volcanic eruption that killed nearly thirty thousand people.

In isolation, Greenland's ice melt might seem inconsequential. Hell, it rained on a frozen spot of land every day somewhere in the world, didn't it? Rain fell, ice melted. It was the rhythm of the seasons. But, as Clem learned, this warm-up in Greenland was anything but inconsequential.

She thought about this and more as she clicked through to Anna's TikToks. There she watched her daughter dry the blades of her skates, tie her laces, cuddle Hagrid. She watched Anna fly down the ice, tell a story about the day's win, and dance to a song Clem had never heard before. Anna had 21,536 followers.

Clem was so astonished that this many humans would watch her daughter pack up her hockey gear that she did something she'd never thought she'd do. She created an account for herself.

Moments later, when the next hot flash began, Clem ran to her closet. She closed the door, locked it, flicked on the light, and followed the TikTok instructions Anna had given her a hundred times before.

Click on the plus sign.

Swipe to a 60-second video.

Hit the red button.

Once she was recording, Clem didn't talk. She let the camera document her heaving breath, the brilliant scarlet that crept up her neck and across her cheeks and forehead, and the sweat that began as small beads but within seconds became white water rivers streaming down her temples.

The advice she'd heard Anna give to friends echoed in her head.

Stop and start the video.

Change angles to keep it interesting.

Clem wasn't sure that witnessing a hot flash would be interesting to anyone, no matter how many angles she included, but she needed to document this.

Don't post long videos. People get bored.

After twenty-five seconds, Clem stopped filming. She added trending music, text, and a few hashtags: #hotflash #womenshealth #perimenopause #menopause #obgyn.

Finally, she captioned it: "If you know, you know."

At 2:42 AM, she posted it.

At 2:44 AM, she leaned close to the punch bowl and whispered, "Good night, Frankie."

At 2:45 AM, she padded back to bed in the snow-bright dark.

At 2:46 AM, her ears began to itch. She thought about Charlene as she searched the internet for ways to stop it. A mix of white vinegar and rubbing alcohol was popular, as was baby oil. Antihistamines helped some women but not all. Whatever you do, professionals warned, do not itch your ears with Q-tips.

Fuck that. Clem opened her bedside drawer, reached in, and felt around in the dark. After patting down her vibrator, a tube of lip gloss, and an old purse, she finally found a handful of Q-tips. She grabbed one, jabbed it into her right ear, and wiggled it around until relief hit like an orgasm. She couldn't wait to tell Charlene.

At 2:52 AM, she sent her usual text to Georgia.

Night, G.

She waited until she got a response.

Night, C.

Then she closed her eyes, placed a hand over her chest cavity to hold everything in place, and finally drifted off to sleep.

CHAPTER SIX

Women Are Superheroes

The next day when Clem arrived for work, a police officer was blocking the entrance to the library's parking lot. He blew his whistle and waved her toward the street.

She rolled down her window. "Moving snow today, Officer?" she said. Trucking snow from parking lots and roads to snow fields on the outskirts of town was an annual event, an effort to ensure citizens had safe places to park and walk. The snow-moving people had been working around the clock for weeks.

"Not today," the officer said.

"What's happening, then?"

"A protest," he said.

"Where?"

"Right here at the library, believe it or not."

"About what?" Clem said.

"That missing fish," the officer said. He stepped away to direct another car toward the street.

Clem's chest seized. "A protest about Frankie?" she said when he returned.

"That's the one. You know her?"

"Doesn't everybody?"

"Not me."

The officer was older. Gray haired and tubby. "My kids are grown," he said. "The library didn't have a pet fish when they were little."

"That's too bad," Clem said. "That fish is the most popular thing in the library." In her head, she was shouting at herself, *So why the hell did you fish-nap her?*

"You must work here."

"Many years now." Clem's heart was thumping.

"What do you do?"

Clem paused. "I'm the Connector of People to Magical Things." Every time she said it out loud, it felt more and more like the right fit.

The officer smiled. "That's the nicest job title I've ever heard."

"Tell that to my boss. She prefers my current one—Director of Media."

The officer grimaced. "I like yours much better."

Clem craned her neck to look behind her. "I don't see any protesters," she said.

The officer pointed up the hill. "They're in front of the library. Listen."

A moment later, Clem heard a cacophony of drums and voices. "Find Frankie! Protect our kids! Find Frankie! Protect our kids!" It sounded like there might be hundreds.

"Whoa," Clem said.

"It's a crowd," he said.

"I assume it's been a peaceful protest," she said.

"So far, but these parents are ticked off. They're afraid the fish is only the beginning."

"Of what?"

"A dangerous trend."

"Huh?"

"They're afraid their children might be next."

"Next to what?"

"To be kidnapped."

Clem coughed. "Why would they think such a thing?"

The officer shrugged. "If it can happen to a fish, it can happen to a child."

"That doesn't make sense. A fish isn't a child. There's no comparison."

"Parents don't see it that way. When something breaks a circle of safety, it feels like anything can. They're vulnerable right now."

Clem nodded. It was a little farfetched, but since she was the fish-napper, she wasn't in a good position to argue the point any further.

"Park beyond the church today," the officer said, pointing to the street. "We need to keep a path clear for emergency vehicles."

A few blocks down Main Street, Clem wedged her car between two snowbanks, each higher than her head. She grabbed a latte and a scone at Brenda's Bakery, then baby-stepped her way down the icy sidewalk, gripping lampposts every few yards to steady herself.

As she neared the library, the cacophony crescendoed: "Find Frankie! Protect our kids! Find Frankie! Protect our kids!" Once she rounded the corner, she had to push through the dozens of parents marching up and down in front of the library's main entrance. Some carried signs emblazoned with messages like *Find the Fish* and *Keep Our Kids Safe*. Others wore outrageously bright goldfish cutouts pinned to their earmuffs and wool caps.

Halfway through the crowd, parents began to recognize her. "Clementine! Clementine Crane! Join us! Help us find Frankie!"

Clem protected her coffee while offering murmurs of sympathy. "Don't worry. We'll find her. We'll get her back. I know she's out there," she said, silently berating herself for being a disingenuous boob.

By the time she reached the steps, they'd shifted their chant to "What do we want? Frankie! When do we want her? Now!" Each *now* was punctuated with raised fists, drumbeats, stomping feet, and vigorous shakes of tambourines. That police officer hadn't been kidding. These people were scared. And mad.

The front door of the library opened a crack, and Samantha stuck out her head. "Clementine," she called. "Clem! Come on in!"

Clem tiptoed up the steps, trying not to draw any more attention to herself. She was sure someone would be able to smell her guilt. "You're honest to a fault," her father used to tell her. And it was true for so many years. But now she'd accidentally-on-purpose taken something that hundreds—maybe thousands—of people cared about.

Once inside, Samantha wrapped an arm around her. "I'm so sorry you had to make your way through that crowd," she said. "I know how important Frankie is to you."

Clem looked at the ground and shook her head. "It's hardest on the kids. I'm a grown-up. I should be able to manage my feelings."

"Even grown-ups struggle," Sam said. "Isn't that what Meghan tells us?"

Clem nodded. What would Meghan say once she found out that Clem was responsible for the sorrow and fear of the children and their families? Would she wrestle her to the ground? Disown her? Have a breakdown? Call for her arrest?

"I texted you earlier to come in the back door," Sam said, "but I must have been too late."

"It's okay," Clem said. "It's probably better I witness it." She turned and started walking to her desk.

"Hey," Sam called, "how are the hot flashes?"

Clem paused. "Awful. How long have you been having them?"

"Four years."

Clem's eyes got big. "Four years?" Dr. Sheffield's words echoed in her head: *The average is between two and ten years.*

Sam nodded.

"Every day?"

"Every day. Haven't you seen me race out of here like I'm being chased?"

"Yeah, but I figured you were taking a break from Bath's nonsense."

"That's a fringe benefit," Sam said. "Mostly I'm trying to cool off."

"Superheroes," Clem said. "Women are fucking superheroes."

Later that morning, after the protesters had gone home to thaw, Bathsheba cornered Clem in the L–N fiction stack on the second floor. "Clementine, we need to talk."

Talking was the last thing Clem wanted to do. "What is it?"

Bath pressed her lips together in a way that made Clem want to staple them shut. "It's this title business," she said. "You need to stop pushing for this change. You're getting everyone riled up."

"Director of Media is a flat, boring title that says nothing about who I am or what I do," Clem said. As she spoke, a shimmer of something shot through her. The glee of rebellion, perhaps? Even though she disliked Bathsheba, she'd always been respectful and deferential. Blind allegiance was in her bloodline. This baby step into sedition was something new.

"Clem, *Director of Media* is used by ninety-nine percent of libraries for employees with your responsibilities. As I've told you numerous times, it's a perfectly functional title."

"And as I've told you numerous times, Bathsheba, I don't aspire to functional." Clem tried to imagine Tor being told at work that his only goal should be functionality. It wouldn't happen. How could Bath not want to move the needle on how women were represented in the workplace? How could she not want to bring a touch of originality and creativity to the playing field?

"There's nothing wrong with functionality," Bath said.

Clem squeezed past her boss and marched out of the stacks with her arms pumping. She knew she might look like a two-year-old who'd been told no more cookies, but since she'd never said no to people before, figuring out how to do it was a process.

"Connector of People to Magical Things," she called over her shoulder. "That's me!" Then she headed to her cubicle, picked up Craft Clem that Meghan had set on a stack of file folders, and danced her across the desk.

To distract herself, she shifted her thinking to Valentine's Day. There were still details to tend to in order to create the extravaganza the Crane family expected. She'd ordered the chocolate-covered strawberries and the new light-up heart to replace the one that fizzled out last year, but as she tried to remember the best temperature at which to roast the goose, another hot flash rolled in. Embarrassed to heave and sweat in front of the three library patrons standing near her desk, she ran to bathroom to weather it as privately as possible.

There, her phone pinged.

mom

mom

mom

mom

mom

Clem leaned into the sink and wiped sweat from her forehead with the back of her hand.

Yes, Anna?

did u order pjs

PJs?

valentines day pjs duh

Clem groaned. *Oh, shit.* That's what she'd forgotten. The pj's. *The* pj's. How could she have forgotten?

Nearly two months before, she'd put a darling set of matching family Valentine's Day pajamas into her online cart. She'd chosen a soft, stretchy set with small white hearts dancing on a red background, and the set had sizes to fit all, even Hagrid. But she'd never hit "Place order."

How could this have escaped her? Matching Valentine's Day pj's were *the* annual tradition in the Crane house. Yes, the chocolate-covered strawberries and the light-up heart were much-anticipated elements of the day. Yes, everyone needed the right card in order to feel perfectly loved. Yes, the roast goose had to be tenderly prepared. But the pj's? Those were the crème de la crème. Each year, Clem handed them out the night before so everyone could sleep in them and wake up full of love.

mom

mom

mom

u there

what do this yrs pjs look like

Clem dragged her sleeve across her forehead to clear another liter of sweat, then pulled up the store account on her phone. She was afraid to look. She knew damn well, after many years of placing these orders, that if she didn't do it before the second week of January, the best collections were gone. Snapped up by the overattentive moms whose chest cavities had not yet reached their bursting points.

"Shit," Clem said. "Shit, shit, shit." She hovered her thumb over "Place order" and finally pressed down.

Sold out.

Desperate, she clicked on the "Still available" tab and scrolled. Every remaining set was awful. Hideous. There was one with aliens that had hearts for heads and another with fields of heart-shaped flowers set on a lime-green background. The designers must have been drunk.

"Shit," Clem said. No matter what she did now, Valentine's morning was going to feature three grumbling teenagers in scratchy, no-stretch pajamas decorated with hearts that looked more like heads of broccoli than the shape of love.

Her phone pinged.

mom

She couldn't tell Anna the truth.

mom

Clem stepped into a stall, locked the door, and dropped onto the toilet, sweat seeping from every pore.

mom

pjs

pjs

pjs

Clem searched until she found one set that had sizes to fit everyone, even Hagrid. They were horrible things. Brown and blue, not red. Creepy smiley faces, not hearts. Cheap polyester, no stretch. But they'd arrive on time, and that was most important.

Clem hit "Place order."

Anna, get back to thinking about school.
I've ordered the pjs, but I want them to be a surprise.

They sure would be that.

That night, at 2:45 AM, when Clem finally flopped into bed, yet another hot flash began. She ran to her closet, held her phone at arm's length, clicked on TikTok, and began to film.

This time, she didn't even try to look presentable. Within seconds, sweat was streaming down her neck, drenching her breasts, and soaking the waistband of her pajamas. Her face was swollen and bumpy as if she had poison ivy, and her heart was hammering. She fluffed her wet, frizzy hair, then closed her eyes and swallowed, trying to manage the uncomfortable moment of panic that accompanied the first minute of every flash.

During the second minute, she talked to the camera. "It's like I want to take a deep breath but can't," she explained. "It's similar to the feeling you get when you're at the dentist and your mouth is propped open by that horrid plastic thing. And suddenly you need to swallow, so you raise your hand, and the hygienist says, 'Go ahead. Swallow. Nothing's stopping you,' but you can't because that horrid plastic thing is in the way. Then panic hits and you want to rip that plastic thing out of your mouth and hurl it across the room. You know that feeling? Well, get ready, people with uteruses. It's worse than that. Way, way worse."

As the flash eased and the sweat slowed and her breathing returned to normal, Clem started to shiver. This, she was learning, was the irony of a hot flash. Start out hot, end up freezing.

She wrapped a blanket around herself like a cape, hit "End," and stumbled out of the closet into bed. Propped on a pillow, she added captions and a sticker of a hammer pounding a nail into a wall—her heartbeat. Finally, she added hashtags and clicked "Post." She pulled the covers up to her neck when another shiver traveled up her spine, and at that moment, Tor snored. This time it was the kind of rumble that could carve a new gorge in the Grand Canyon. The kind that burst forth when he was in the deepest of sleeps. Clem shined her phone's flashlight at his nose and cursed it.

She reached over and turned on the heated mattress pad. It warmed delightfully fast, but once she started to relax, she began to worry that she might get electrocuted. She was a perimenopausal woman swimming in a puddle of sweat, lying on an electronic device. Did mattress pad companies test for this eventuality? Did they pour a cup or two of water onto the pad and turn it on while a woman lay waiting to see what happened? Had any women died in the testing of this mattress pad?

Good god, the things humans with uteruses had to consider.

But finally, Clem began to ease into sleep. She sighed and turned away from the schnoz. She was warm and cozy. If she was going to be electrocuted post–hot flash, so be it. The comfort was well worth it. Her muscles softened. Her shivers settled. Her breathing steadied. Her heart rate slowed. At 3:33 AM, she noted that if she fell asleep right then, she'd get nearly 2.5 hours of sleep. She closed her eyes. The kids were sleeping. Hagrid was on the floor at the foot of the bed. What would she do without Hagrid? The giant hairy nugget who filled their house with love and fur and drool and happiness.

She fell asleep this way. Somewhere between delight and anger. So deeply that she didn't even hear the *crunch, crunch, crunch* as the beast passed once again in the night.

CHAPTER SEVEN
Buttercup

Books set in winter! Go!

The next morning, Clementine saw Meghan's text a second too late, and Samantha pounced first: The Snowy Day by Ezra Jack Keats.

Keisha was right on her tail: Smilla's Sense of Snow by Peter Hoeg.

Clem plopped onto the sofa in front of the fireplace for a speed round of Snowstorm Lit. She started with an Irish writer.

John Banville's Snow.

Jade jumped in: Beartown by Fredrik Backman.

Clem paused. Was it okay to play Snowstorm Lit with so much going on? It seemed too frivolous.

Walter made a play: Isabel Allende's In the Midst of Winter.

Victor: Hello? Anna Karenina.

Of course, Tolstoy was an excellent choice, but excellence didn't matter if you forgot to include the author's name—one of the five rules of Snowstorm Lit. Meghan texted a gong emoji. Translation? *You're out, Victor.*

Victor sent a trail of facepalm emojis. Going out on the first round was an embarrassing blow.

Jing, Jade, and Samantha simultaneously sent the title of the same book: Run by Ann Patchett.

Meghan must have seen Jing's first, because Samantha and Jade got gonged. (Rule number two: Book titles can't be repeated.)

Jing: A Christmas Carol by Charles Dickens.

Clem: *Ali Smith's Winter.*

The third rule in Snowstorm Lit was that once you were out, you were out. No private messages to other players. No sharing book titles. No cheating. Honor's code. Victor was the only one who'd ever tried it, after which he'd lost Snowstorm Lit privileges for an entire month.

In came Keisha: The Snow Child, Eowyn Ivey.

Then Walter: The Children's Blizzard by Melanie Bettle.

Gong! Meghan followed up the gong emoji with the author's correct name: Melanie Benjamin.

Clem knew how hard it was for Meghan not to play, but the fourth rule in Snowstorm Lit was that the initiator couldn't join in.

The thread zipped and zinged for five or six minutes:

Washington Black by Esi Edugyan.

The Lion, the Witch, and the Wardrobe by C.S. Lewis.

Winter in the Blood by James Welch.

Then, as it got harder and harder to come up with titles, the game slowed. (Rule number five: No searching for answers on the internet or bookshelves.)

Clem: *How the Penguins Saved Veronica by Hazel Prior.*

Keisha got three gongs when she said *The Shining* was written by Michael King. Horror was not her genre. Later she insisted it was a typo—"Even I know Stephen King wrote *The Shining*"—but rules were rules.

It was down to Jing and Clementine.

But as Clem was about to send in a zinger, three reminders from her to-do list popped up on her phone. Order a ring light. Make snickerdoodles for the hockey team's bake sale. Print out a list of ingredients to accompany the snickerdoodles so no one keels over from an allergic reaction.

Jing leaped: Sister Souljah's The Coldest Winter Ever.

And with that gem, Meghan awarded the trophy emoji. Game over.

Clem opened her to-do list and took a breath:

1. *Order a ring light.*
2. *Make snickerdoodles for Anna's bake sale.*
3. *Make a list of ingredients to accompany the cookies so no one dies from an allergic reaction.*
4. *Venmo Evan's tutor.*
5. *Reschedule Hagrid's vet appointment.*
6. *Print photos from last summer's vacation.*
7. *Remember which vacation photos Anna liked and which she said she'd barf on if I printed them.*
8. *Wash sheets.*
9. *Update Evan's school forms with the proper pronouns.*
10. *Look for Tor's sweater.*

On and on it went.

When Clementine got to number thirty-five, she paused.

Stop.

That's what it said.

35. Stop.

Stop what?

No matter how hard she tried to remember what she'd meant to come next, she couldn't. Stop fantasizing about moving to Costa

Rica? Stop thinking about the woolly mammoth? Stop worrying about Georgia? Stop delivering Anna's left-at-home crap to school?

She texted a screenshot of her list to Georgia. *What do you think stop means here?*

What do you think?

Could be anything, I guess.

You wrote it.

I know, but I can't remember.

What would you like it to mean?

That was an entirely different question.

At first, Clem believed *stop* was part of a longer statement: Stop working out, stop making stew because the kids hated it, stop trying to solve the snoring problem, stop thinking about applying to *House Hunters International*. But what if it was literal? What if it literally meant *stop*? Stop everything.

When Clementine was ten, she'd vowed never to repeat the dreadful mistake her mother and grandmother had. "I will only marry a person who does not snore," she'd declared, thinking not of her heart but of her father's thunderous snores, the ones that shook shingles from their roof.

The look her mother shot her in response fell just short of a smirk. "Good luck," she said. The dark crescents under her eyes told stories of the generations of wives, lovers, and mistresses who had come before her. Generations of women who'd fallen in love, then slept—or tried to sleep—next to snuffling ogres.

"I'll do it. You'll see," Clem told her.

"My dear," her mom said, "it's an admirable goal, but how will you accomplish it?"

"I will observe my potential mate while sleeping. If he doesn't snore, I'll marry him. If he does, I'm out of there." She was studying the scientific method in fifth grade, and this seemed like the perfect opportunity to put it into practice.

It all seemed so logical and precise. So doable. And at ten years old, Clementine hadn't understood the depth of her mother's sigh. Nor had she believed her words. "I hope that works for you, sweetie, but by the time you're comfortable enough to observe someone sleeping, you'll likely already be in love. You will marry that person—snore or no snore—believing love will conquer all."

"I will not!" Clem had shouted.

But she had.

Since marrying Tor, Clem had spent an inordinate amount of time researching anti-snoring devices and remedies, and one recent night, while enduring a particularly intense hot flash, she discovered that the 1960s were as revolutionary for anti-snoring devices as they were for women's rights.

"Hey," she said to Georgia the next day, dropping food flakes into Frankie's punch bowl, "did you know that a number of patents for anti-snoring gadgets were filed in the 1960s?"

"Really?" Georgia said. She sipped a cup of chai, her current favorite.

"Yup, do you remember hearing anything about them?"

Georgia shook her head. "I remember a lot of things from that time. Go-go boots, the Civil Rights Act, Apollo landing on the moon, the Beatles, miniskirts—but anti-snoring devices? Those don't ring a bell."

"You were probably too young to think about such things."

"True," Georgia said. "I turned twenty in 1962 and didn't meet Henry until 1963. I was probably busy doing the mashed potato to pay attention to things that helped people sleep better."

"Well, my friend," Clem said, "while you were out dancing, it seems some very pissed-off wives were inventing some very serious machinery. Check out this shock collar." Clem held up a picture on her phone.

"Yikes," Georgia said.

"And this mouthpiece is even worse." Clem scrolled through her photos until she found the diagram that showed the snorer's tongue in a death grip, then held it up for Georgia to see. "It was designed to latch on to your tongue to hold it in place."

Georgia's eyes got big. "Wouldn't that make you gag?"

Clem nodded. "Which may be why this particular device never came to fruition."

"And the shock collar?"

"As far as I can tell, it never got past the design stage either."

Patents for two specialty alarms were also filed: one that buzzed when the snorer slightly opened his mouth while sleeping and another that jolted the head of the snorer if it detected even the softest rumble. Both elicited small tremors of excitement in Clem's heart.

It was impossible not to draw conclusions about the relationship between anti-snoring devices and women's rights. She could find no proof, but even so, Clem knew in her heart that as women's demand for greater personal freedom and legal rights had surged, so had their demand for a peaceful night's sleep. It was a fight that continued to this day.

"Have you talked with Tor about a CPAP machine in the past few months?" Georgia said.

Clem shook her head. The CPAP machine—the holy grail of snoring remedies—required a sleep test to prove apnea. If proven, the snorer was gifted a CPAP machine from their insurance company and from then on wore a mask while sleeping to which a steady flow of air was delivered through a tube, keeping the snorer's airway from collapsing. Tor would never submit to such an experience. He'd said so many times.

"Maybe you should give it another shot."

"Nope," Clem said. Before this day, she would have refused because he'd rejected this suggestion so many times, but now her *nope* was bigger than that. Why should *she* have to talk to *him* about this? Shouldn't *he* be concerned that his snoring was causing his wife to suffer? Shouldn't *he* be talking to *her*?

"Why not?"

"Georgia, I've complained about Tor's snoring for years. If he were going to do something to help the situation, he'd have already done it." Clem looked out the window as if she were nonchalant about the whole thing, but that bubble of anger was once again rolling around in her middle. She used to feel hopeless and sad. Now she was also pissed.

Georgia picked up the teapot and refilled Clem's cup. "I understand."

"You know," Clem said, "my grandmother and mother *had* to put up with snoring. Women didn't have options in their day. But things are different now. It's not 1960. It's not even 1980. Women in this country have rights. I have rights. Sleeping rights." She rubbed a circle of frost from the window with her elbow, then peered down into their yards.

"All that is true," Georgia said, "but what's the alternative? Are you going to divorce over a snore?"

"Lots of people do."

Georgia raised her eyebrows.

"They do. Snoring is the third leading cause of divorce in this country."

"It is?"

"Yes, and do you want to know the name for the charge against the guilty party?" She paused. "Snoring spousal arousal syndrome."

Georgia chuckled. "Well, that's not the right kind of arousal, is it?"

Right then, Brewster knocked on the closet door.

"Mom?"

"Brewster, Georgia and I are having tea."

"So?"

"So, you can't come in."

"But I want to. I like tea."

"It's hot, not iced."

"I like hot tea."

"Not this kind. It's spicy."

"I like spicy."

"No, you don't."

"But I need you."

"For what?"

"I have a question."

"It can wait."

"No, it can't."

"Then ask your dad. He's in the basement."

"Mom?"

"What?" She could tell Brewster was pressing his mouth to the doorframe.

"Moooooooooom?"

"What, Brew?"

"Mom. Mom, Mom, Mom."

"What?"

"I need you, not Dad."

"Why?"

"Dad never has answers. He doesn't know anything. Let me in." He jiggled the doorknob. This was exactly why Clem always locked it.

"Not now, hon. We'll wrap up soon."

"What are you doing?"

Clem sighed. "Talking."

"About what?"

As tempted as Clem was to answer *periods* or *sex* so that Brewster would go away and give her fifteen minutes of peace, she couldn't. That boy was so sweetly sensitive and so easily embarrassed these days, it could mar him for life.

"Girl stuff," she said.

"Is Anna in there?"

He was relentless.

"No, she's at the rink already. Now go on, Brew. Find your dad and ask him whatever it is. He may surprise you."

When the bedroom door slammed, Frankie's punch bowl shuddered and a bit of water splashed out. While blotting the spill, Clem said, "Her name is Buttercup, you know."

"Whose name?" Georgia said.

"The woolly mammoth whose DNA is being used to help create the new and improved woolly mammoth. They found her in Siberia."

"Why Buttercup?"

"When they studied her feces, they discovered that she ate a lot of dandelions and buttercups."

"Her feces?" Georgia grimaced.

"Yeah, they found lots in her intestines."

"How long ago had she lived?"

"About forty thousand years."

"They were able to study her feces after forty thousand years?"

"Yup."

Georgia was quiet for a moment. "Science is fascinating, isn't it?"

"And weird," Clem said. "Buttercup is the freshest specimen they've ever found, so they know all kinds of things about her."

"What else?"

"She was in her mid-fifties when she died. She'd weaned eight calves and lost one."

"Wow," Georgia said.

"Right?" Clem said. She checked her watch. "All right, my friend," she said. "Time for me to head back to work."

Georgia reached for her cane.

"You stay put," Clem said. "Finish your tea. Head home when you're ready but lock this door behind you. I don't want Tor or the kids to discover Frankie." Her phone pinged.

Brew and I searched the basement. No sweater.

"Tor?" Georgia said.

Clem nodded. "He roped Brew into his search for the sweater, but they didn't find it. The mystery continues."

"Hm."

"Don't look at me like that, Georgia Mark. I did not take the sweater. He must have misplaced it."

"Clementine, your husband is fastidious. He doesn't lose things."

It was true. Torvald was fastidious. Fastidious about his clothes, food, driveway, and yard, just not so much about his marriage.

"I swear I didn't touch Tor's sweater. Am I okay with that hideous thing being gone? Yes. Am I okay that Tor is suffering its absence? Yes. But I didn't take it."

Georgia pulled the blanket over her legs and picked up her mug. "Okay, okay. Hey, before you go, do they know how Buttercup died?"

Clem nodded. "She got stuck in a peat bog, and the part of her hind end that was sticking out was devoured by a predator. Likely cave hyenas or a sabertooth cat."

Georgia looked astonished. "What a horrible way to go after such a fruitful life!"

Clem unlocked the closet door. "The woes of females are as old as time, my friend." And she was gone.

After dinner that evening, Clem stared at Tor's nose. Though his nostrils were a bit odd, bubbling out more than most, it was still a decent thing. Not too big. Not too small. Relatively central on his face. He scoffed when she speculated that his bubbly nostrils might be why he snored so loudly.

"What are you talking about?" he said.

"I'm talking about your alae," she said.

Tor sighed. "What is an alae?"

Clem pointed at her nose with both fingers. "These. These are alae. The wing-shaped structures that make up the outside wall of your nose."

"And you know this because?"

"I'm studying noses."

"Why?"

"Because I've had it with your snoring."

"Clem."

"Tor."

"Little lark."

Clem seethed.

"What is going on?" he said.

"I'm saying that your alae are bigger than most people's alae."

Tor rolled his eyes, then reached up and gripped the wings of his nose between his thumbs and index fingers. "My alae, dear wife," he said, wiggling them at her, "are exactly like everyone else's."

"No, they're not," Clem said. "Look at mine." She reached up and tugged on hers.

"They are just like mine."

"No, they're not. Mine are petite, and yours are humongous, like your father's." This part was true. Clem had studied their photographs. They had identical snouts.

Right then, the kids walked in. Clem and Tor were still gripping their noses and staring intensely at one another over the table.

"What's going on in here?" Anna said.

"What are you two doing?" Brewster said.

Evan smirked. "Must be some wacky grown-up sex thing."

"Shut up, Evan. Don't say that word," Brewster said.

"Sex?" Evan said. "What's wrong with the word *sex*?"

"Stop it!" Brewster said. The blush started to build on his cheeks.

Clem let go of her alae and looked at her youngest. Being thirteen was so hard. Everything embarrassed him. "Leave your brother alone," she said, then picked up her tea. "Dad and I are simply comparing our alae."

"Alae?" Anna said.

"Yes, alae. These things right here." Clem pointed at the wings of her nose.

"Where do you get all these bizarre facts?" Anna said.

"Your mom does work in a library, Anna," Tor said.

She rolled her eyes. "As if I could forget."

"Want another nose fact?" Clem said.

"No," Anna said, and she ducked out of the room with Evan and Brewster close behind.

Tor looked at Clem. "What are you now, some kind of undercover nose examiner?"

"No, I'm being observant."

"What else have you learned?"

"Nothing."

"Really?"

"Really."

This was a lie. Through her late-night research, Clem had learned that the straight column of skin that divided your nostrils was called the *columella* and the midline tip of the nose was called the *lobule*. But instead of weighing down the conversation with more anatomical facts, she told Tor that the man with the longest nose in the world lived in Turkey. His nose—an impressive 3.46 inches long—had earned him the nickname Schnoz growing up (in Turkish, of course). And while this would have cut many kids to the quick, he was undaunted because his nose was not only big, it was talented.

"This guy's nose can pick up smells almost as well as a bloodhound's," Clem said.

"Impressive," Tor said. "Does he snore?"

"I don't know yet, but I'm going to find out."

Years before when the kids were young and Clem had complained that the wee bit of rest she got was constantly interrupted by Torvald's snores, he gave her a set of earplugs for Christmas. "If I snore as loudly as you say, these will help you sleep."

That night, she'd stuffed them deep into her ears and slept straight through until morning. It was the best sleep she'd had since Evan's birth. "These are amazing," she'd told Tor the next morning, "but I can't wear them."

"Why not?" he'd said.

"Who's going to hear the kids?"

"Hear them what?"

Ah, the luxury of fatherhood. Of sleeping like a hibernating bear after a hearty season of berries and bugs. Of turning off the self completely. Of having hours upon hours to rest and rejuvenate. Of knowing that Mom would be there day and night, for the kids, the house, the friends, the family, the neighbors, the teachers, and anyone else who needed attention.

Clem had laughed when he'd said that, even though there wasn't anything funny about it. "Hear them what?" she said. "For god's sake, Tor, hear them call for water or cry out after having a nightmare. Hear them throw up. Hear them holler about a monster behind the curtain. Hear them sneak into each other's beds and giggle their butts off. Hear them come to our room and whisper, 'I'm too hot,' when they're burning up with fever. Hear them yell, 'I have to pee!' And everything else."

"When do they do all that?" Tor said.

Clem looked at him, flabbergasted. "When you're sleeping."

CHAPTER EIGHT

I Prefer Not To

The next afternoon, when Clem spotted Anna and her friends draped on the beanbag chairs in the teen room at the library, she jumped back, tiptoed behind the graphic novel shelf, and pressed a cheek to the row of best-loved books. Depending on how many copies of *Laura Dean Keeps Breaking Up With Me* were checked out, she'd long ago discovered it was the best spot for getting a peek at the teenagers. Being the parent of a fourteen-year-old girl—especially after the COVID years—was like playing a guessing game. Was Anna happy? Was she frustrated? Did she have a crush? Was she doing her homework? How were her friendships? Was her mental health okay? Spying for a couple of minutes now and then seemed like a fairly innocuous way to check on the well-being of her kid.

Anna, stretched on the floor, was combing her fingers through her friend Laila's hair. Laptops, binders, phones, papers, bags of candy, water bottles, and coats were scattered in piles around them. It looked like they'd been living there forever. Another friend, Janna, was reading aloud from a book cracked open on her lap. Her voice was intense and dramatic.

"'But I waive,'" read Janna, "'the biographies of all other scriveners for a few passages in the life of Bartleby, who was a scrivener of the strangest I ever saw or heard of.'"

A scrivener? Clem's heart started to sing. There was only one story she'd ever read about a scrivener: Herman Melville's "Bartleby, the Scrivener: A Story of Wall-Street."

"What's a scrivener?" Anna said.

Janna shrugged.

"I'll look it up," Laila said, typing on her phone. "Someone who works for a lawyer and copies legal documents by hand."

"By hand? Why would anyone copy anything by hand?" Anna said. "When was this story written?"

Janna thumbed to the copyright page. "Eighteen fifty-three."

Clementine grinned. The date confirmed it. It had to be "Bartleby."

"Eighteen fifty-three?" Laila said. "I thought only dinosaurs lived in 1853."

Anna rolled her eyes and tugged Laila's hair. "Keep reading," she said.

Janna continued for a few paragraphs, eventually getting to a description of another scrivener in the lawyer's office. A guy named Turkey, whose face, the narrator said, "flamed with augmented blazonry, as if cannel coal had been heaped on anthracite."

When she read that description, Anna laughed out loud. "My mom looked like that this morning."

Clem let the insult slide because, holy hummingbirds, Janna was reading "Bartleby, the Scrivener: A Story of Wall-Street." One of the best stories ever written.

At first the girls looked distracted, but after a couple of minutes, they put down their phones and leaned in. Janna was a natural reader who emphasized the right words and lingered on sentences that demanded lingering. This wasn't a learned skill. It was instinct.

Clem closed her eyes and listened too. This had been one of her favorites as an undergrad. Many of her classmates had written it off as boring and monotonous, but Clem had loved Bartleby's gradual refusal to do any work—his unexpected strike, passive defiance, and refusal to comply—all accompanied by the phrase "I would prefer not to."

One of the kids' phones pinged, then another, but in a shocking turn of events, not one kid looked. Instead, they shifted closer to Janna and listened more intently. It was a phenomenon Clem hadn't witnessed in a long time.

She wanted to stand there and continue listening too, but an older man in a red hat was waving to her from the circulation desk. She stepped away, escorted the gentleman to the poetry section, then returned, her cheek to Tamaki and Tamaki's *This One Summer*. For her, listening to this story read out loud was like listening to a symphony.

As Janna was finishing up Melville's introduction of Ginger Nut, a ball of paper flew over the bookcase and beaned Clem in the head. Anna. Through a gap in the books, Clem saw her daughter glaring and pointing at her phone. Clem checked hers.

mom i c u

move away

i told you no more spying

no one elses mom spies at the lbry

also this story is gd

Move away hurt in the way that being a mom to a teen often hurt. Clem hadn't realized it was coming when Anna was little, clingy, and loving. But her daughter's follow-up, *also this story is gd*, reconnected them just enough.

Clem acquiesced and moved back a few feet. While she waited for her favorite moment in the story, she caught up on her texts. Several were from Tor.

Don't forget to pick up Indian for dinner.

Indian for dinner?

Yes, boys and I are starving.

She must have missed his earlier text telling her to order the food, because it was nearly 6:00 and she hadn't done it yet. If you didn't order from Delhi Garden by 5:45, the wait was unbearable.

Too late.

Clementine, we're ravenous.

Clem considered yesterday's lasagna, the weekend's stew, and all the other leftovers in the fridge. Not to mention the chicken legs and premade meatballs waiting to be cooked.

Heat something up.

We want takeout.

Bake the chicken.

I'm still working.

Clem gritted her teeth. *Fine. I'll order now.*

At that moment, Janna read the sentence Clem had been waiting for: "'Imagine my surprise, nay, my consternation, when without moving from his privacy, Bartleby in a singularly mild, firm voice, replied, 'I would prefer not to.'"

The words rang in Clem's head the same way they had when she'd first heard this story years before, but this time, she understood why.

A few sentences later, the narrator challenged his employee: "'Prefer not to,' echoed I, rising in high excitement, and crossing the room with a stride. 'What do you mean? Are you moon-struck? I want you to help me compare this sheet here—take it,' and I thrust it towards him.

"'I would prefer not to,' said he."

And just like that, Bartleby was standing up to something. To everything.

Thirty minutes later, after reading the entire story out loud, Janna's voice cut through the bookcase and interrupted Clem's thoughts. "But what is this story really about?" she said. "You know that's what Ms. Nguyen is going to ask tomorrow."

Ms. Nguyen was their very demanding English teacher. They had a love-hate relationship with her.

"I'll do a search," said Laila.

"Don't," Anna said. "We can figure it out ourselves."

Clem smiled.

"It's about boredom," said the curly-headed friend whose name Clem didn't know.

Another friend rolled onto her back and opened her eyes. "I agree. I slept for the last fifteen minutes of that story."

"Spoiler," Janna said. "Bartleby died."

"I don't think it's boring," Anna said. "I think it's about human relationships and being done with shit."

Janna nodded.

"Got it!" Laila said, looking at her phone.

Anna groaned.

"Listen," Laila said. She stood, shook her hair out, and read in an announcer-type voice, "This site says Bartleby is about the 'decremental extinction of a human spirit.'"

The kids sat quietly for a moment.

"What does *decremental* mean?" the curly-headed friend said.

"It's a gradual decrease in something," Anna said.

"Think about that," Laila said. She repeated the line.

"Whoa," Anna said.

"Whoa is right. That's some serious shit," Janna said. She pounded her chest a few times. "The decremental extinction of a human spirit."

When Clementine heard it said like that, something inside her shifted. Her brain sizzled. Unable to restrain herself, she jumped and sucked in a breath, knocking six copies of Robin Ha's *Almost-American Girl* off the bookshelf. Anna and her friends whipped around to look at her.

"Mom!" Anna hissed.

But Clementine ignored her. "That's it!" she said out loud.

"That's what, Mom?"

Clem's eyes got big as she looked from kid to kid.

"Your mom is scaring me," Laila whispered. "She's so weird."

"Shut up," Anna said. "Yours is worse."

"Kids! That is it," Clem said. When she clapped and grinned wildly, Anna folded over and buried her head. "Bartleby," Clem continued, "is about being a woman. You've hit the nail on the head."

Laila looked dubious. "We did?"

"Yes! And this is exactly why I've always loved this story so much. I finally understand," Clem said. "Herman Melville's 'Bartleby, the Scrivener' may seem like it's about some scrivener guy named Bartleby, but, in fact, it is about being a woman."

The kids' mouths dropped open. They'd never heard Anna's mom talk like this. Usually, she was lecturing them about cleaning up, not snickering, or the importance of reading a book instead of playing Minecraft all the time. Normal mom crap.

"Mom," Anna said, "you're embarrassing me. What are you talking about?"

"I am talking about the decremental extinction of a woman's spirit, my dear child. It's what happens to women over time . . . women with kids and needy husbands and bosses who don't listen and periods and hot flashes and lost dreams and sycamore trees." Clem's voice grew louder as her list got longer, and, as it did, she noticed a couple of women poking their heads around the New Fiction bookshelf.

"I don't even know what you're talking about, Mom."

"Not now, Anna, but someday you will." Clem spun in a circle. "All of you will." She sidestepped a few fallen copies of *Almost-American Girl* and moved among the kids. "So tomorrow, when Ms. Nguyen asks what 'Bartleby, the Scrivener' is about, tell her that it documents a forty-four-year-old woman's desperate response to a life in which the daily demands, the mental load, a husband's snores, and hot flashes all got to be too much."

"Mom, please stop!" Anna's voice was sharp.

Clem looked at her daughter, then each of her friends. "I would prefer not to," she said, repeating Bartleby's famous catchphrase.

The women in the New Fiction section stepped around the bookshelf and moved close to Clem. One was nodding, and the other had tears in her eyes. "I know that Melville story," the teary one said. "And you're right! I've never thought of it that way, but it absolutely is about women. It is about us."

Clem noted that the women looked as tired as she felt. She didn't know their names, but she'd seen them in the library many times—had even tracked down a novel set in Italy for one of them. She held out her hand. "I'm Clementine Crane, Connector of People to Magical Things."

"Nova Johnson," the teary woman said. "Forty-year-old woman with hot flashes and anger spilling over the edge."

"Rose Kirby," said the other. "Sorry for eavesdropping, but we were talking about our husbands just moments ago."

"Cursing them, actually," Nova said. "Hearing you and Bartleby has to be destiny."

Anna scoffed. "Destiny? Seriously?"

Nova turned to her. "Yes, seriously. Your mom is right, you know. Reread the story. You'll see."

Bathsheba appeared at the top of the stairs. "Clem, I'm not sure what the hubbub is," she said, "but Meghan needs you downstairs. Now."

"Can she come up here?" Clem said. She'd been avoiding the children's room as much as possible. Seeing Frankie's empty tank and the hundreds of notes and hand-drawn pictures that wallpapered the room was excruciating.

"No, the kids have something they want to ask you."

Oh geesh. That couldn't be good.

"Can I get your contact information?" she said to Nova and Rose. "I'm building an"—she glanced at Anna, then leaned close to the women and whispered—"an empire. We need to connect."

Anna shot darts at Clem with her eyes. "Why are you whispering, Mom? What are you building?"

Clem waved her off, took the women's contact information on her phone, then rushed down the stairs. "I'll be in touch," she called back.

On the first floor, she ran past Frankie's empty tank, trying not to think about what could be so wrong with her that she'd kidnapped a beloved community pet. She was partly worried that some malevolent virus was growing within her, but she knew that wasn't true. She was simply a woman who'd been bottle-fed on the rules and regulations of a patriarchal society, nurtured into being a people pleaser who couldn't say no. And while she'd played the role beautifully for forty-four years, things were changing.

"Hi, Ms. Clementine," Meghan said when Clem got close.

"Hi, Ms. Clementine," the children echoed. They were seated around the table like a board of directors.

"Hello, everyone," Clem said. "Ms. Bathsheba said you have something you need to ask me. How can I help?"

Meghan nodded to the kids. "Take it away."

Little Miss Blue Hat cleared her throat and stood. "Ms. Clementine, we need a GoFundMe page."

"A GoFundMe page?" Clem said. "For what?"

"For Frankie."

Clem's heart thumped. "Frankie?"

"Yes," Meghan said, "the children want to offer a reward for her return. Ms. Bathsheba said the library would provide the funds, but the kids want to raise the money themselves."

Clem closed her eyes and bit her lip. Good god, a GoFundMe when Frankie was right at home in her closet. She knew how wrong this was, but she also knew she couldn't yet return the fish to the library. "How much would you like to raise?" she asked. She had no idea what the going reward for a celestial goldfish might be. It was unlikely anyone did.

"The children were discussing that. Ben suggested twenty dollars," Meghan said.

Ben waved.

"And Kalisha," Meghan continued, "proposed two million."

"Frankie is worth it," a girl wearing polka dots said.

"We compromised and settled on two hundred," Meghan said.

"Two hundred dollars?" Clem asked. It seemed like a lot for a fish that cost no more than ten.

"Yes," said Little Miss Blue Hat. She was quite businesslike. "Can you help us?"

Clem looked at the hundreds of pictures of Frankie taped to the walls. "Of course."

The kids cheered.

Little Miss Blue Hat cleared her throat. "When you make the GoFundMe page, please use lots of photos of Frankie from before she was fish-napped. Ms. Meghan has a ton. My mom says people respond to images. She's an art director."

"Got it," Clem said. "I'll create it this afternoon and have it go live tomorrow."

"Perfect," Meghan said. "Everyone, say thanks to Ms. Clementine."

The children stood and gathered close to Clem. "Thank you!" they yelled.

On the way back up the stairs, Clem's phone rang. Georgia.

"Hey, you okay?" A phone call was unusual.

"Mmm," Georgia said.

She clearly was not.

"Georgia, what's going on?"

"I'm not feeling quite right, Clementine. Can you come over?"

"On my way." Clem got her purse, then ran back down the stairs and through the children's room. She averted her eyes once more as she passed Frankie's tank, then grabbed her coat from the closet and headed for her car. From there, she texted Bathsheba.

Back in a bit. Emergency. Clem could have told Bathsheba why she had to race out, but the last thing she felt like doing was giving private information to her boss. "I would prefer not to," she said out loud.

All the way to Georgia's house, she practiced Bartleby's catchphrase.

"I would prefer not to," she said, sliding through a yellow light at the corner of Main and Green.

"I would prefer not to," she said, speeding up when a road sign advised her to slow down.

"I would prefer not to," she said when asked via text to confirm Evan's upcoming podiatry appointment.

She said the same when the radio host prodded her to donate ten dollars a month. The last thing she needed was another tote bag.

And when her trainer's text reminded her to warm up her buns because it was glute day, Clem used voice commands to send a reply—*I prefer not to*—this time dropping *would* from the statement. Without that conditional word, Bartleby's catchphrase felt more contemporary, more powerful, more her. Melville would approve.

As Clem navigated the icy roads, she thought about how much nonsense girls suffered as people with uteruses. The periods. The bleeding, cramping, and moods. The money it took to buy supplies. Stained sheets. Stained underwear. Stained pants. Embarrassment when you leaked. Even learning about its impending arrival had been stressful. She remembered way back in fourth grade when stupid

Wallace Wright had snuck up behind her in the elementary school library and sneered, "I bet you don't know what a period is." He was the class bully who spent his free time poking fun at fat kids, smart kids, Black kids, shy kids, Asian kids, and the one kid already big enough to play the tuba.

She'd been in the shy-kid category, the nerdy-reader type, an easy target. Why wouldn't you tease the girl who idolized Harriet Tubman and Susan B. Anthony? Mocking her was way better than admitting you'd lost to her in the class *Jeopardy* competition three times in a row.

On that day in the library, Clem knew from the way Wallace was looking at her that he wasn't bluffing. He knew something she didn't. She'd known this boy since preschool.

And he was right. She didn't know what a period was. Not the kind he was referring to. Her mother hadn't yet talked with her about it. Her friends hadn't yet gossiped about it. That unit in health class wasn't taught until fifth grade. All Clem knew was that a period signaled a hard stop at the end of a sentence.

Her obvious naivete on this matter pleased Wallace Wright immensely. He grinned and pushed a clump of greasy hair out of his eyes, but as Clem's cheeks flushed with an embarrassment she didn't understand, the librarian approached. Mrs. Porter. She tapped Wallace on the head with her pen, a little harder than would be considered acceptable in today's school environment, and said, "Mr. Wright, move along."

Before he disappeared into the stacks, he reached out and pinched the back of Clementine's arm. "Period," he whispered.

Clem never knew if Mrs. Porter had heard Wallace's words, but she was forever grateful to be rescued from his torment. In the moments after, as she willed her cheeks back to their natural color by studying a photograph of Amelia Earhart with her airplane, she tried to figure out what else a period could be.

That night, after prodding her mother for answers, she wished she could go back in time. "Puberty is coming," her mother had said, then shared the terrifying news that within a couple of years—maybe months—blood would pour from between Clem's legs during a thing called her "period."

Clem had been incredulous. She couldn't wrap her ponytailed head around this shocking eventuality. "Blood? Where does it come from?"

"The lining of your uterus."

"My what?" She knew many things about her body, but this was new territory.

"It's where a baby grows."

"I'm not ready to grow a baby."

"Of course not," her mother explained. "Not now, but someday maybe."

"Does Steve have a uterus?" Clem compared everything to her brother.

"No, boys don't have them."

Aha. This felt like a thing she might be able to flaunt. Clem imagined taunting *I have a uterus and you don't* in the singsong voice that always made her older brother run away.

"But why would I bleed? Doesn't my uterus need its lining?" She imagined her brain not needing its frontal lobe or her heart not needing its ventricles. Impossible.

"You only need the lining if you're ready to have a baby."

Back to that baby thing.

"I am not ready for a baby."

"Agreed," her mother said. "You don't need the lining of your uterus right now, so you'll bleed."

"How long will this period thing last?" She was thinking a few minutes. An hour at the most.

"It will average five to seven days every month."

"Five to seven *days*?"

"Yes."

"Every month?"

"Every month."

"And for how long? Like, until I'm fifteen? Or eighteen? Or twenty?"

"Until you're about fifty or so."

"What?" Clementine had jumped up and thrown her hands in the air. "I'll bleed every month for the rest of my life." At ten, it was impossible to imagine any kind of life after fifty.

"Well, not the rest of your life, but for a long, long, time."

"And it'll be a little bit of blood? Like when I scraped my elbow last week?"

Clementine's mother bit her lip in the way she did when she was about to reveal a hard truth. "No, honey. It will be a good bit of blood, at least for the first few days each time."

Clem stared at her mother.

"Should we keep going?" her mother asked. "Or would you like to continue tomorrow?"

"There's more?"

"There is. It's important you know what to do when your period arrives."

Clementine pictured her big red period arriving like Mary Poppins, floating down from the sky with an open umbrella in hand. "Keep going," she groaned. "Let's get it over with."

Her mother nodded, then reached into a bag Clem had assumed held her knitting gear. Wow, had she been wrong. Instead, her mother pulled out a pad, a tampon, and a weird rubbery cup and explained each as if they were having show-and-tell.

All of it was overwhelming. That this period thing would last for a week or so. That it would show up every month for years and years to come. That there were all kinds of products she could use to collect the blood before it soaked through her clothing and onto the bus seat or her chair at school. And that it would arrive with an undetermined amount of physical pain and emotional woe—cramps, headaches, crankiness, tears, and more.

While her mother sipped her iced tea, Clem tried to envision waddling to the whiteboard at school with a giant pad wedged in her underwear.

"Is there any way to stop this thing from coming?" she asked.

Clem's mother sighed. "Someday you'll be able to take a pill that can stop your periods until you're ready for a baby, but right now, you're too young for that."

"What if I lie down and never get up except for meals?"

"Your period will still come."

"What if I squeeze my legs together super hard?"

"You'll still bleed."

"What if I walk on my hands so I'm upside down all the time?" This felt promising. Gravity was a powerful thing.

"Sounds like a good challenge," her mom said, "but your period will still arrive."

For the next fifteen minutes, the two of them studied the "products" Clem's mother had brought to the talk. The pad, which looked like a humongous Band-Aid. The tampon, which resembled a rocket. And the weird rubbery cup that Clem couldn't figure out at all.

"Do I stay home from school when this is happening?" she asked.

"No, you do all the normal things. Nothing changes, except that you're in pain and you bleed a lot."

Clem stared at her mother. She had to be joking. "I have to go to school in horrible pain while I'm gushing blood?"

Her mom nodded. "You get used to it."

That night Clem dreamed about drowning in cherry lemonade during social studies class. The next morning, she called Lorraine, a friend who wasn't a bestie but was the closest thing Clem had at the time.

"Lorraine?" she whispered into the phone. "Do you know about periods?"

"Of course," Lorraine shot back. "Periods end declarative sentences."

"No, there's another kind of period," Clem said, then whispered all the things her mother had explained to her.

"What the hell?" Lorraine said when Clem finished up. It was her favorite phrase. She'd borrowed it from her mother, who, as the mother of six boys and Lorraine, what-the-helled all day long.

The next morning, Clem pulled her mother aside. "Mom, I have one more question."

"Happy to answer," her mom said.

"What happens to boys at puberty?"

Her mother was quiet for so long Clem was sure she'd fallen asleep. "Mom?"

"I'm here, sweetie."

"Well, what happens to them?"

"Not much, hon. They grow facial hair, and their voices change."

That explained a few things about her brother. "Anything else?"

"They get more erections."

"What's an erection?"

Her mother explained that a boy's penis took on new behaviors once puberty hit. "In its quiet state," she explained, "a penis is soft and smallish, kind of like that sea cucumber we saw at the aquarium a few weeks ago. But when a penis gets excited, it gets hard and grows bigger. Like a banana."

"Excited?" Clem asked. "About what?" This was all very strange.

Her mom sighed and suggested they save that bit of the story for their next conversation.

"Okay," Clem agreed, "but I do need to know if boys bleed from their bananas every month."

"No."

"Do they have any pain?"

"No."

"Do they have to buy products for their erections like girls do for their periods?"

"No."

"What the hell?" Clem said.

Normally, Clem's mother would have called her on the swear, but this time she sighed and said, "You took the words right out of my mouth."

For the next few months, every time Clem noticed that the trash can in her parents' bathroom was filling up with pads wrapped in toilet tissue, she snuck in when no one was watching, unwrapped one after the other, and ogled the bright-red blood in the soaked pad. It was terrifying. "What the hell?" she'd whisper over and over. "What the hell?"

Like most girls her age, Clem was scared, horrified, and curious. But she was also mad. How could Wallace Wright, a human with a sea cucumber in his pants, a human who would never experience this thing called a period, yield power over her using something so inherently female, so inherently *her*? The power should be hers.

As Clem turned into Georgia's driveway, she realized that in the busyness of life, she'd forgotten all this. And now she couldn't wait to post it on TikTok.

"Georgia!" she called as she walked into the house.

"In the kitchen!" Georgia answered.

Thankfully, she was feeling better. The dizziness had passed, as had the numbness in her arm. And although she still had a small headache, no amount of cajoling could convince her to go to the hospital or urgent care. She was as stubborn as Henry had been.

Refusing to leave until she was sure Georgia wasn't going to have another episode, Clem sat at the kitchen table working on the GoFundMe for Frankie, setting the goal at $200. As requested, she added photos and text, then an overly dramatic reenactment video Keisha had filmed. The video was funny and poignant, and it was no surprise that Little Miss Blue Hat played the fish-napper. The scenes flowed nicely into one another. The storyline was complete. And the final frames featured a call to action: "Help us find Frankie. Your generous gift will make a significant difference in bringing our fish home."

Directly after, the film cut to an image of Frankie's empty tank. Love and despair oozed from the screen. A moment later, unexpectedly, the video cut to Justin yelling, "When we catch this fish-napper, we'll put them behind bars forever!" Behind Justin, another kid pounded his fist on the table and chanted, "Slam-mer! Slam-mer!" Pretty soon all the kids had joined in. "Slam-mer! Slam-mer!"

Clem's hand was shaking as *Finding Frankie* went live. Not once had she considered the possibility of going to jail for borrowing Frankie. Now it was all she could think about.

By lunchtime the next day, while Mother Nature pelted Byrock with another six inches of wet, heavy snow, Clem trekked from bedroom to bedroom collecting spoons. She pulled four from under Brewster's pillow. Five from under Evan's. And six from under Anna's (unless Clem also counted the dirty ones in crusty cereal bowls on her desk, in which case there were ten).

Tor, not surprisingly, had seven spoons under his pillow.

That made a total of twenty-two. No wonder it wouldn't stop snowing.

Instead of returning the spoons to their proper spots in the kitchen, Clem headed to her closet and hid them in the drawer beneath Frankie's punch bowl. "You guard them," she told the fish.

Clementine's period had started at the end of fifth grade, a little less than a year after Wallace Wright cornered her in the library. She'd recently turned eleven, and that first time her legs cramped up so badly she couldn't even walk to her mom's bed. She crawled, pulling herself along the carpet with her arms, her spasming legs dragging behind. "Mom! Mom! I'm dying!" she whispered into her parents' dark room.

"I've got you," her mom said as she scooped her up and carried her into the bathroom. Blood had soaked Clem's nightgown and underwear. Her inner thighs were sticky with it. Her head throbbed, and her stomach hurt. "I don't feel well, Mom," she whispered. "Take me to the hospital. I'm dying."

"You're not dying," her mom said. "You got your first period." After giving her a dose of ibuprofen, Clem's mom slid her into a warm shower. While Clem washed, her mom changed her sheets, then laid out a fresh nightgown and clean underwear with a thick pad in place. Shortly after, she tucked Clem back into bed and said, "You'll feel a bit better in the morning."

Hours later, when Clem woke, she did not feel better at all. She felt far worse. Her stomach still hurt, she had diarrhea, and the blood between her legs was thick and brilliantly red. "Can I stay home?" she asked. How in the world would she be able to go to school this way? Sit in class? Eat in the cafeteria? Talk to teachers? Look Wallace Wright in the eye?

"Today, yes," her mom said. "We'll go to lunch and celebrate."

"Celebrate what?" Clem said.

"You're a woman now."

Clem shook her head. "I'd rather be a kid."

"Too late." Her mom smiled. It was a weird smile. Not celebratory. Not happy. It certainly didn't scream *Yay, you're a woman!* If Clem had known the word *resigned,* that's the one she would have used.

Right then, Clementine's uterus clamped down. She doubled over and moaned. "What the hell?" she repeated.

"Rest and lunch today," her mom said. "But tomorrow, it's back to school and back to the normal routine."

Clementine knew her routine would never be the same again.

CHAPTER NINE
Go, Go, Go

One thirty-eight AM, Clem's head:

Were any humans displaced by the ice melt in Greenland?
Did female woolly mammoths have tusks?
My ears are itchy.
I have to call Charlene.
How can a human be this hot?
Who used to feed Frankie when the library was closed?
Does Evan have a boyfriend yet?
Which kid will yell the loudest about the horrendous Valentine's Day pj's?
When will the snow stop?
How do I build an empire?
Where is Tor's green sweater?
How did Samantha hide her hot flashes for four years at work?
Workplaces should have hot-flash rooms.
How do real thieves live with the gnawing guilt?
If I fall asleep right now, I'll get five hours of sleep.

Will the new woolly mammoth have any predators?
I am the Connector of People to Magical Things.
How old was Melville when he wrote Bartleby?
Is Georgia going to be okay?

The last question sent her down a rabbit hole. During Georgia's last neurology appointment, when the doctor had explained the significant risks of the carotid endarterectomy, Clem had zoned out. She was overwhelmed by the thought of losing her best friend. But now, in the night, she couldn't stop thinking about myocardial infarctions, perioperative strokes, postoperative bleeding, intracerebral hemorrhages, and a few risks she made up on her own. The wee bit of space in Clem's chest that wasn't taken up by appointments and to-dos was now filled with the fear of having to live without Georgia. There was a time when Clem would have turned to Tor for comfort and support, but as she lay staring out the window, she realized she was past depending on him for anything.

At 2:01 AM, she began obsessing about why the word *stop* was on her to-do list, then ran through all the things she couldn't stop. The snow. Her periods. Tor's snores. Bathsheba's bullheadedness. Georgia's health problems.

She remembered back when everything felt possible, when her favorite word was *go*. Go to Europe. Go to the moon. Go to grad school. Go to the dance club. Go to yoga. Go to the beach. Go wherever the hell you want. She'd been in go mode when she'd first met Tor, and when they were new and young and falling in like, then lust, and finally love, it was *go, go, go, go, go*. He wasn't her first love—that honor belonged to scrawny long-distance runner Phillip Moss back in eleventh grade—but Tor was her first and only grown-up love. When they met, he was handsome and smooth, muscled and sexy. Selfish, too, in the way most males were selfish. But back then, selfish looked more like confidence. That's the way it snuck in.

She'd been confident too. Lean and energetic, duty-free and able to sit in bars reading books, which was what she'd been doing when she'd met him. Perched on a stool sipping a cool gin and tonic, reading, for the thousandth time, Rilke's poem "Fears." The thousandth time because of a single line: "the fear that this little button on my nightshirt may be bigger than my head." What a notion. What brilliance. So much brilliance that she'd shifted on her stool, tapped the guy next to her on the shoulder, and when he'd turned, said, "Listen to this."

And the guy had. He'd set those green eyes on her, put down his drink, leaned in, and listened.

Moments later, he asked the bartender for a pen, then, on a napkin, drew a sketch. A button on a nightshirt and a head—her head—with a wild mane of curls. He held out his hand. "Torvald," he said.

"Clementine," she said, taking it.

He nodded.

"I've only heard of one other Torvald in my life," she said. "In Ibsen's *A Doll's House*."

"No relation," he assured her, then pointed to his drawing. "Have you ever felt fear like this?" he'd said. "So afraid the button on your nightshirt may be bigger than your head?"

Clem knew she could answer one of two ways: *I don't have that kind of fear* or *I don't wear a nightshirt*, which she knew was more invitation than statement.

Go, she heard in her head.

Go, go, go, go, go.

By the end of the evening, Torvald Crane knew damn well Clem didn't wear a nightshirt. They were in her bed, slick with sweat, beginning the relationship that would carry them through to this very moment in their existence.

But now, all she could think was *stop*.

The next day Georgia nudged Clem with the tip of her cane. "Come on. If you're not going to return Frankie yet, at least we can do right by her," she said. "She needs a filtration system."

Clem looked at the fish. Did she need a filtration system? Clem had no idea. She'd had one at the library but didn't seem to be suffering without one. She was still eating with vigor and swimming brightly around the punch bowl.

"I can't pop into Pet-O-Rama, Georgia. I buy Hagrid's food there every month. Everyone knows me. Knows I work at the library."

"So?"

"So, if I go in there and buy a filtration system for a fish tank, they'll get suspicious. I'm sure they've all heard about the fish-napping. Someone will connect the dots and turn me in."

"Unlikely, but to be safe, we'll go in disguise."

"As what?"

"Do you still have our Halloween costumes downstairs?"

Clem nodded.

"Go get them."

Clem grinned. This was another of the million reasons she loved Georgia so much. The spontaneity. The fearlessness. The determination. She sprinted to the basement, pulled a few costumes from a bin, and ran back up. She pressed a bunny suit into Georgia's hands. "I couldn't find your clown outfit. I got you this instead."

"You want me to wear a bunny costume to the pet store?"

Clem smiled.

"Well, Henry would love this, wouldn't he? What are you wearing?"

"You'll see." Clem disappeared into the bathroom. Minutes later, she stepped out wearing the giraffe costume she'd been wearing when she and Georgia had first met. Her face poked out of the hole in the base of the neck, and the neck stretched another three feet in the air. At the top? The bobbing giraffe's head. "Remember this?"

"How could I forget it?" Georgia said.

An hour later, they pulled into the parking lot at Pet-O-Rama, then strolled in as casually as a giraffe and an elderly bunny with a walker could. When a cashier did a double take, Clem nodded her wobbly giraffe head, smiled through the face hole, and galloped awkwardly toward the fish aisle.

"You know," Georgia said, flouncing along with her walker, "we wouldn't need to do this if you hadn't taken Frankie."

"Borrowed, Georgia, borrowed," Clem whispered. "And you can't talk about the borrowed thing here. Not out in public."

"Fine," Georgia said. "Who are you going to ask for help?"

Clem's phone pinged. Tor.

Mexican food for dinner?

She knew, although he asked it as a question, that Tor's not-so-subtle intention was for her to order the food.

Sure, I'll have enchiladas.

Can you order?

Clem halted, causing her giraffe head to bob wildly, then stared at her phone, weighing her options. Say yes to her husband and she'd not only have to order and pick up the food but also set it out on the table, get plates and silverware, call everyone to dinner, call everyone to dinner a second time, and so on.

Say no and her husband would be cranky and whiny, like a boy who'd dropped his lollipop in a patch of dirt.

I prefer not to.

Damn, that felt good.

She started galloping again and, once in the fish area, pointed her hoof at a nerdy guy scooping guppies from a tank. "How about him?" she said, trying not to look too closely because the guy's britches were halfway down his buttocks.

"Does he know you?" Georgia said.

"I don't think so."

"Well, since he hasn't paid enough attention to know his pants are halfway down his derriere, I can't imagine he's going to pay much attention to us," Georgia said.

"Follow my lead," Clem whispered. She pranced over to him. "Excuse me. We need a filtration system for a fish."

Without looking at her, the guy lifted a scoopful of guppies and transferred them to a bucket. "What kind of fish? What kind of tank?" He spoke in a monotone.

"A goldfish in a punch bowl–shaped tank." Both answers were mostly true.

"Goldfish don't need filtration," he said. He squatted to scoop from the lowest tank, exposing his butt cleavage even more.

Clem winced and looked away. "This goldfish does," she said. Her phone pinged. You prefer what?

Clem knew exactly what Tor's face had looked like as he read her text. All scrunched up like he'd gotten a whiff of Evan's wet swim gear after they'd left it in their gym bag for a weekend.

I prefer not to.

Clementine? Is that you?

It is.

Then, order Mexican for dinner?

Clem didn't hesitate. *I prefer not to.*

Georgia nudged her. A crowd was starting to gather. Halloween was long over, and their costumes were garnering a lot of attention.

"Why?" the guy said. "A goldfish is a goldfish."

"My goldfish is special."

This turned out to be the wrong thing to say to *this* fish guy. He stood, turned, hitched up his pants with his forearms, and looked directly at her. "Special how?" he said.

Clem's phone pinged. Tor wouldn't let it go. Clementine? Have I texted the wrong number?

You have not.

What's with "I prefer not to"?

It's like I said. I prefer not to.

Little squirrel, is that really you?

This was Tor's test. If it were really her, she'd coo favorably as she had when the nickname felt sweet and lovey. But it was now so annoying that cooing was impossible. In fact, paired with her hot flashes and the tsunami of crap she and every other woman had to deal with, hearing that nickname disguised as a term of endearment made her want to jab one of those spoons up Tor's nostril. Fuck *little squirrel.*

Tor, she typed, *is that really you?*

Ha ha. Mexican food for dinner? I'll have burritos.

Clem lowered her phone and leaned closer to get a look at the fish guy's name tag. Douglass. When she did, her giraffe head dipped into the highest tank with a plop. She lifted it quickly, and a bit of water dripped onto Douglass's shoulder. "Listen, Douglass," she said. "I'm in a hurry. I need a filtration system, not a conversation."

"Ms."—he paused, eyeballing her long neck—"Giraffe. It is my job to keep all fish safe. If I sell you a filtration system that causes your goldfish to die, that's on me. Karma sucks. I refuse to suffer in my next life because you can't take proper care of your goldfish in this one."

"Listen," Clem said, "this goldfish has had a filtration system since she was a small fry, so I don't want to alter her life situation."

Douglass pursed his lips. "She *had* a filtration system, but she doesn't *now.* What happened to it?"

"We moved."

"You moved with the fish but not the system?"

"It fell off. In the moving truck." Strangely, lying was getting a little easier for Clem.

Douglass's eyes bulged out. "You put your fish in a moving truck?"

Clem scrambled to keep up with Douglass's increasingly emotional responses. "Only for a moment. The mover set the bowl down in the truck while I made room in the trunk of my car."

Clem's phone pinged. Clem? Come on. Order now?

Keeping up with the emotional antics of two men at the same time was a lot. How in the world had she arrived at this place? A place in which she felt no agency over her own life. Her own decisions. Her own existence. Her own heart. If only she had those cymbals in her purse. This would have been a perfect opportunity to pull them out and clash them together. Instead, she took a deep breath. *I prefer not to.*

Clem, the kids and I are hungry.

Well, there it was. Not-so-subtle male manipulation at its finest. Use the kids. While in recent years, this guilt trip would have worked perfectly, all Clem could think in that moment was *stop*.

But she had no time to ponder it, because Douglass's shock was amping up. "The trunk of your car?" His voice rose in pitch and volume. "You put your fish in the trunk of your car?"

Clem backpedaled. It was surprising to see the guy she'd pegged for nerdy and quiet become commanding when talking about his passion. Lesson learned. "No, no, not the trunk," she said. "Of course not. I put her in the passenger seat."

Douglass looked aghast, and Clem wondered if there were an emergency team behind the red employee door waiting to lock her up for a fish infraction. She needed to get out of this conversation, and fast. She tossed a look at Georgia, who, through bestie telepathy, got the message, turned, and sashayed into the growing crowd, dividing it with deep side swings of her walker. Moments later, a voice on the PA system blurted out, "Douglass Dobson! Please come to the help desk for a life-or-death fish question. Emergency."

Douglass grunted. "Wait here," he commanded. "I'll be back in a minute."

As soon as he disappeared around the corner, Clem targeted the girl taking selfies with the clown fish.

"I need a filtration system for a goldfish in a punch bowl," she said.

The girl looked up and eyed Clem from head to hoof. "I heard Douglass tell you that goldfish do not need filtration, but you be you, lady." She handed Clem a system wrapped in plastic. "This will work for whatever the hell you're up to."

Clem glanced at the package. "I'm not up to anything."

"Whatever," the girl said. She was already looking at her phone.

Taking care not to slide into a ditch on the drive home, Clem wondered if borrowing Frankie would go down in history as a literary crime. Clem had taken her from a library, after all. And if someone discovered that Clem was the fish-napper, would this be the one thing in life she was remembered for? Forget the linchpin. The library work. The magical connecting. The mothering. Wife-ing. Listing. Caring. Healing. Cup filling. Sexing. Remembering. Washing and drying. Supporting. Driving and delivering. Shopping and making and baking. Stuffing-of-everything into her chest. In the end, would the only thing that mattered be that she borrowed a fish that wasn't hers? She imagined her gravestone: *Clementine Crane, Fish-Napper.*

After settling Georgia in at home, Clem slunk into the Crane house. Tor and the kids were at the kitchen table eating peanut butter sandwiches. "You managed to get dinner together after all?" she said.

Tor didn't answer.

"Thanks a lot, Mom," Anna said.

Torvald grunted.

Clem swallowed her response, then turned away. Once upstairs, she added the filtration system to Frankie's punch bowl. As she watched her charge swim a few delighted laps, she thought about the most famous literary crimes around the world—the theft of one of Shakespeare's First Folios from the Durham Cathedral Library in

England and the disappearance of Walt Whitman's notebooks from a box sent from the Library of Congress to Ohio for safekeeping during World War II. The tragic confiscation of Franz Kafka's letters and notebooks by the Nazis in Germany and, more recently, the international phishing scam that had tricked numerous contemporary authors into sharing unpublished manuscripts. Compared to these, would anyone remember her crime?

Only time would tell.

At two fourteen AM, after Georgia had texted her through two hot flashes and a crisis of confidence, Clem sent her final good-night, then signed off to sleep.

Night, G.

Night, C.

Crunch, crunch, crunch.

CHAPTER TEN

Not That Kind of Hot

Craft directions at the next staff meeting read *Make a God's eye.* Clem wasn't interested in religion, but she could get into making an object that symbolized the power of seeing things she couldn't normally see. As instructed, she picked up a popsicle stick cross, chose a ball of variegated yarn, and began wrapping the yarn around and around the sticks. As she did, Meghan explained how the four ends symbolized the basic elements (earth, water, wind, fire) and the four cardinal directions (north, south, east, west).

Ten minutes in, as if they knew the library's management team was gathered together within earshot, the protesters outside the building began their daily chant. "What do we want? Frankie! When do we want her? Now!" A jingly tambourine and a few drumbeats accompanied their cry. Clem saw Meghan's eyes get a little shiny, then felt her own do the same. If only she could shut them up. Send them on a march to town square. Dump a load of snow on them from the roof.

To camouflage her sorrow, Meghan asked, "What are some other things that come in fours?" She was using the singsong voice usually reserved for patrons under five.

"Four-leaf clovers," Samantha said. "The four seasons."

"Sweet, sour, salty, bitter," Victor said. He was alternating between black and red yarn so that his craft was beginning to look more like a devil's eye.

"Four is an unlucky number in Chinese culture," Jing said. "In Mandarin, the word sounds very much like the word for *death*." She wrapped both hands around her own neck, tipped her head to one side, rolled her eyes, stuck out her tongue, and made some kind of *I'm dead* sound. It pulled everyone's attention away from the enthusiastic protesters outside the window. She was good that way. "Eight, on the other hand, is lucky," she said, and she held up her God's eye for all to admire. She'd lashed two crosses together at the center so hers had eight sticks.

"The Beatles," Keisha offered. "John, Paul, George, and Ringo."

Walter immediately began to hum "Ob-La-Di, Ob-La-Da," a crowd favorite. Bathsheba cut him off with a dismissive wave of her hand, then cleared her throat and delivered the news Clem had been dreading. "I know this isn't going to please any of you," she said, "especially you, Clementine. But the board met, and the members decided there would be no changes to titles here at the library."

The entire team looked at Clem, whose brain suddenly felt like a fireball being shot from Venus during a lightning storm. "What?" she said.

Bathsheba cleared her throat. "Titles are staying the same," she said, moving nothing but her eyes as she spoke. In this way, she was kind of like a deer that froze when spotted by a hunter, thinking that if it didn't move, it could become invisible. But you couldn't go backward like that. Once you were seen, you were seen. And there was no mistaking the fact that Bath had been seen.

Clem bit the inside of her cheek. Silently, inside her own head, she repeated Bath's words in the most mocking voice she could muster: *The members decided there would be no changes to titles here at the library.* She couldn't find the courage to say it out loud, even though she'd recently made that comment about Bath being the Director of

Dramatic Sighing and Nodding. Courage, she was learning, took time and practice, and just because she'd demonstrated it once didn't mean she was ready to do it again, especially when she was feeling so vulnerable.

As she tried to find words to respond, the "What do we want? Frankie!" chants coming from outside began to match the pace at which she felt her rage ratcheting up. The maddening jangle of the tambourine started blending with her thoughts, and although half of her was about to fling her God's eye at Bath, the other half—the pushover Clem had always been—wouldn't allow it. This internal wrestling match was as infuriating as Bath's statement about titles. Why was it so hard for Clem to express herself? Why had she never been taught to question things, stand up for herself? Why hadn't she been encouraged to handle banana-pants Wallace Wright all those years ago? If she had, she'd have been able to deal with director-from-hell Bathsheba Wheaton right then.

"No Connector of People to Magical Things?" Clem managed to say.

"No, Clem. I told you it was unlikely. You shouldn't be surprised."

"I'm not surprised," Clem said. "I'm disappointed. What about the other titles we proposed?"

Bathsheba shook her head. "The board is satisfied with our team's titles as they are."

"No Feelings Teacher?" Meghan said.

"No."

"No Mad Scientist?" Samantha said.

"No."

If this had happened a year before, Clem would have cried. Waited until she was alone, or with Georgia, then sobbed her eyes out. She never would have told Bath anything about what she thought. But now she took a deep breath and said, "This isn't fair, Bath. We deserve to have a say in our titles." Then she picked up her God's eye and began to wrap the purple yarn tighter and tighter, imagining the center of the cross was Bath's scrawny neck. It wasn't very Godlike, but it felt damn good.

After the meeting, Clem tiptoed into the children's room at the library. The rest of the team was still down the hall, and the early-bird kiddos, whose moms were either outside banging tambourines or getting a caffeine fix at Brenda's Bakery, were outside in the garden. They were supposed to be fine-tuning their pronoun-positive snowpeople—*he/him*, *she/her*, *they/them*—but instead, with Little Miss Blue Hat at the helm, Clem could see they were building a fish. An egg-shaped, bulgy-eyed celestial goldfish. The kids were building a Frankie. Could this get any more heartbreaking?

Clem stood in front of the empty tank. It had been drained and cleaned. A photo of a resplendent Frankie was taped to the glass. On the floor around the tank, there were even more tributes to Frankie than there had been the week before—cards, paper flowers, stuffed fish, rubber fish, and hand-drawn pictures of Frankie. Happy Frankie. Silly Frankie. Swimming Frankie.

Clem picked up the kids' messages one by one and whispered them out loud.

Wi miss yu!

Swim home!

C you soooon.

Swim back to the books.

Ware r u?

Come back pleeze.

Say hi to Nemo!

Clem needed to reassure the children that Frankie was okay. She glanced around, making sure no one was watching, then scrawled a note in purple crayon on a piece of scratch paper. It read: *Frankie the fish is fine. I promise. Do not despair.*

After dropping the note onto Meghan's desk, Clem tiptoed up the stairs. At first, she was sure she'd gotten away with no one seeing her, but when she got to the landing, she turned and caught Little Miss Blue Hat staring at her from the garden through the full-length window.

How long had she been watching? Had she seen Clem write the note? Had she seen her put it down?

Of all kids. The one who could put two and two together. The one who was four going on forty.

Clem gave Little Miss Blue Hat a small wave and continued up the stairs.

That night, Clem locked herself in her closet with a cup of chai, Frankie, and her laptop. It was time to build an empire. Within an hour, she'd changed the name of her TikTok account to I PREFER NOT TO. She uploaded another hot-flash video to it, added trending hashtags, and created a new one: #iprefernotto. She then organized the collection of names and contact information for all the women she'd connected with. Charlene. Nova and Rose from the library. The women from Dr. Sheffield's waiting room. A woman from the grocery store named Riley whom Clem had saved from hot-flash hell by pressing a bag of frozen peas to the back of her neck at a critical moment. Samantha. Meghan. And, of course, Georgia.

Putting her communications skills to use, she created an email newsletter, also called *I PREFER NOT TO*. In the first issue, she wrote an introduction about who she was and why she was writing to them. The salutation read "Hello, hot-flashers, overwhelmed moms, mental-load managers, and pissed-off people with periods." She knew her audience. In it, she invited the women to follow her on TikTok. She hit send, fed Frankie, then crawled into bed next to Tor.

At 2:32 AM, Clem sent her final text of the night.

Night, G.

Night, C.

She was relaxed and ready for sleep, but after curling into a ball and settling into her pillow, she felt Tor's hand slide across her hip. "Hey, babe," he whispered, "are you still on fire?"

"What?" Clem whispered back. She had to have heard him wrong.

"On fire," Tor said, moving his hand to her thigh. "Are you still hot?" He squeezed and pulled her toward him.

Clem's eyes shot open. This man—this man who had been asleep for hours and who would awake rested and ready for the day—could not seriously be thinking about sex? "Hot? What kind of hot?"

"You know what kind of hot," Tor whispered. He trailed his fingertips across her stomach.

Clem shoved his hand off her body and flopped onto her back. "Geesh, Tor, I haven't slept more than an hour tonight thanks to your snoring and my hot flashes. I've nearly drowned in my own bodily fluids three times. I am not *hot*. I am having hot flashes."

"It's kind of the same thing, isn't it?" Tor whispered. He rubbed against her.

Same thing? How could he think the heat she was suffering might somehow be transformed into lust? "It absolutely is not the same thing," she said.

"We could pretend."

Clem turned and kicked him in the knee.

"Ow," Tor whispered. He nuzzled her shoulder. "Come on. Sex will make you feel better."

In their early years, this would have been true. Clem had loved middle-of-the-night sex. Sex while the kids were sleeping. Sex while she was only half awake. There was something so lovely about that particular orgasm. But today?

"Get the hell away from me!" she said. "You have no interest in my life and no empathy for what I'm going through. And on top of that, you caterwaul in your sleep like a belligerent elephant seal. Get your banana penis away from me."

"My what?" he whispered, still groping for her. "Oh, come on, Clem. Don't be mad. I have lots of empathy."

She turned her back to him.

He tapped her on the shoulder. "Really? No sex?"

"No, Torvald," she said. "No sex."

When he rolled away and stuffed his fist under his pillow, Clem heard the rattle of spoons.

"Are you kidding me?" she said, flipping over to face him. She made a note to add *spoon collector* to the list of titles she'd held throughout her life.

Tor turned and glared at her. "Oh, I'm sorry, Clem, but some of us like snow. And some of us like to encourage snowfall as often as possible. You may think that putting spoons under a pillow is frivolous and strange. An old wives' tale. But the kids and I believe in it. Heather of the Weather believes in it. We've witnessed its power. In fact"—Tor leapt out of bed—"at this very moment you are witnessing it too." He threw open the curtains but paused when he saw the amount of new snow that had fallen. It was piled halfway up the window frame.

"Holy crap," Clementine said. She climbed out of bed and gazed out at the sycamore tree. The balls were so coated with ice and snow that they were now the size of baseballs. It was only January 23.

"Whoa," Tor said. "Those look too heavy. Do you think the tree might tip?"

Clem thought about what the Keeper of Living Collections had said about sycamores. "No, I don't. That tree is made for challenges just like this."

She needed to sleep, but who could sleep in perimenopause? She tossed, turned, shined the light of her phone on the stack of how-to-sleep-during-perimenopause books she'd checked out of the library, and finally fell into a brief middle-of-the-night nap. An hour later, when she woke to that now-familiar thrust of breath, she rolled onto her side, grabbed her phone, and opened TikTok. She hit record, and in the seconds that followed, a blistering heat spread like wildfire from her middle to the top of her head. Color rushed to her chest, then climbed to her neck and spread onto her cheeks. Within minutes, she was glowing like an incandescent plum. While she did, she thought about the sixth-grade social studies teacher who'd mocked her for blushing while giving a speech, as if being in sixth grade as a shy kid hadn't been hard enough. Back then, she'd taken it. She hadn't called him on it, just lowered her head and smiled sweetly, dying inside.

If he were here now, she'd kick him in the shins. Or the balls.

Channeling that anger, she glared at the camera and recorded the rest of the hot flash. She edited it down to fifteen seconds, then added an arrow pointing at the bead of sweat hanging from the tip of her nose.

Finally, she wrote a caption, added hashtags, and tacked on a call to action: "Follow me. I'm sweaty."

When she checked her account in the morning, she had a thousand followers and forty-five comments. Most were supportive and encouraging. A few were offered by men who were irked about her "crappy content." She smiled. Not bad for a single night's work.

CHAPTER ELEVEN
Endangered Species

"Do you know there's a man who was recorded snoring at a hundred and eleven point six decibels?" Clem said.

"Is that a lot?" Georgia asked.

"Georgia, that's louder than a jet plane flying low to the ground."

"Seriously?"

"Yes, and the average snore ranges between fifty and sixty-five decibels."

"How loud is that?"

"It sounds like people talking, somebody typing, kids playing. At ninety decibels, a snore starts sounding like a lawn mower or a drill."

"And this guy hit one eleven?"

"That's what the article said."

Georgia nodded appreciatively. "Is he married?"

"Yup."

"Do they sleep in the same room?"

"Supposedly. The article said that sometimes one of them moves to another bedroom, but for the most part, they sleep together."

"His wife must be a saint."

"Has to be." Clem wondered if, like her, she'd come close to exploding into a billion little pieces.

Georgia looked up from her lap of yarn. "Still thinking of a snore divorce?"

"Maybe."

"Clementine."

"Tor's snoring has tortured me since the beginning of our marriage. He's been denying it for as long. But now with these hot flashes and night sweats, I'm exhausted. Beyond exhausted, Georgia. I'm done."

"But divorce? You love Torvald."

Clementine looked at Georgia but didn't answer. She didn't know how to. Did she love Torvald? In her head, she scrolled back through the lengthy list of roles she'd played for so many years in their marriage and family, landing once more on the almighty linchpin. She felt like she'd been on autopilot for years, fulfilling all expectations but rarely taking even a moment to consider love. But now? She wasn't sure.

"Georgia, do you know that noise levels over seventy decibels can damage your hearing, and I am one hundred percent sure most of Tor's snores exceed that limit."

"Impossible."

"It's not much different than me sneaking a bullhorn into bed with us, then yelling into it after Tor falls asleep."

"That would be cruel, Clem."

"Is it any crueler than refusing to address your own snoring issue when it's kept your wife from sleeping well for years?"

Georgia might believe that if Clem used a bullhorn in bed, Tor would simply roll over and grumble, *Stop the nonsense. I have to go to work in the morning.* But Clem knew better. Her husband would never put up with it. He'd move to the couch, camp out on Evan's floor, or go to a hotel. And she knew damn well he'd consider divorce much more quickly than she had.

The next day, Yahoo picked up the story about Frankie.

"Beloved Fish Disappears From Children's Library," the headline read.

Likened to the event a few years before when a man had kidnapped an endangered lemur from the Santa Ana Zoo in California, the fish-napping became the oh-my-god story of the week.

"Absurd," Clementine said to Georgia. "This is nothing like what happened to that poor lemur."

They were holed up in Clem's closet. Georgia stopped knitting. She shifted her eyes from Clementine to Frankie and back. "Are you sure?"

"I am," Clem said.

Georgia clacked her needles together.

"Georgia, Isaac was a lemur. His species is endangered." She found the story on her phone. "According to this, there are fewer than two thousand five hundred lemurs in the world. The entire world."

"And?" Georgia said.

"And," Clem continued, "Frankie is a celestial goldfish. Celestial goldfish are not endangered. There are millions of them swimming around."

"Millions?" Georgia said.

"Yes, millions. Fish-napping Frankie does not put the entire future of a species at risk. You can buy one at Pet-O-Rama for ten dollars."

"But she's not a run-of-the-mill goldfish. She's unusual."

"I agree. She's super cool. Celestial goldfish were originally bred in China, and their Chinese name translates to *dragon that looks to the sky*."

"That's beautiful, Clem, but it isn't the point."

"What is the point?" Clem said.

"It's that like Isaac, Frankie is beloved. And while the impact on the species may be different, the impact on the people who love Frankie is exactly the same."

Clem blew out a breath and hung her head. When she saw that the Yahoo article had shared Frankie's GoFundMe, she knew it wouldn't be long before the kids had the support they needed. She also knew it wouldn't be long before Boston reporter Amanda Chen reached out for the bigger story. She'd already left a message at the library.

From somewhere in the house, Clem heard Anna holler, "Mom? Mom?"

"I knew the quiet couldn't last."

Georgia grinned.

Anna's voice got closer, and Clem heard the bedroom door open.

"Mom? Are you in here? Moooooooo-ooooooooom! I need a ride."

"Sshh," Clem said, "don't give us away." She watched Frankie swim round and round in the punch bowl.

The bedroom door closed, and Anna's voice trailed off down the hall. "Dad? Dad? Are you here? I need a ride."

"Now," Georgia said, "let's think about how and when you can quietly return Frankie to her tank at the library."

Clem shook her head. "Not yet, Georgia. I'm not ready."

Georgia cleared her throat. "Then when?"

The bedroom door opened again.

"Mom! Are you in the closet? I need a ride to practice." Anna rattled the closet door.

Georgia stood, unlocked the door, and pushed her way out of the closet without letting Anna in. "Hello, dear Anna. I was having tea with your mom."

"Georgia, what in the world do you two do in there all the time? There's got to be secret treasure or something, right?"

"Yes, it's called peace and quiet. Someday you'll understand."

"Well, all I understand right now is that I'm going to be late for practice if someone doesn't drive me to the rink."

Clem stepped out of the closet and locked it behind her.

"Mom, can you drive me? Dad said he's too tired."

"Too tired?"

"Yes, he's resting on the couch. Can you take me?"

Clem took a deep breath. "Actually, Anna, I prefer not to."

Anna rolled her eyes. "Mom, I hate to burst your little fantasy, but you are not Bartleby," she said. "This whole 'I prefer not to' thing is ridiculous. You're not some character in an ancient story who can sit around and do nothing all day. Bartleby didn't have kids or a spouse or a home. He wasn't even real, Mom. He was a made-up character. You are a real person with a husband and a home. You are my mother, and you have responsibilities like getting me to hockey practice."

And there it was. Anna had nailed it. Clem *was* a real person. A living, breathing person who hadn't felt like one in a very long time. The new and improved analysis of her favorite story rang in her head: the decremental extinction of a woman's spirit.

With Anna shooting lasers at her from her eyes, Clem felt the pressure to give in. It's what she'd done her entire married, mothering life. Driving Anna to practice when she demanded a ride at the last minute wouldn't be hard. Except that it was. Clem took a breath. "Anna, someday you'll understand. But I prefer not to."

She turned, unlocked the closet door, went in, and shut the door.

"Daaaaddddd!" she heard Anna yell.

It was snowing.

Later that evening, from her nest in the closet, Clem texted Georgia.

I'm a wretch of a mother.

Nonsense. You're amazing.

I said no to the simplest thing. A ride to the rink.

We hit limits. You've hit your limit.

Other people hit limits. Mothers are not supposed to.

That's a myth.

I am not supposed to.

That's another myth.

Clem watched bubbles breaking on the surface of the water in Frankie's punch bowl. *I feel horrible. I'm a failure.*

You're the farthest thing from that. Take a breath.

Be Frankie, Clem thought. *Be Frankie.* She closed her eyes and imagined she was swimming in a warm pool in Costa Rica. The sun was shining down, warming her from the inside out. *I am Frankie,* she thought. *I am Frankie.*

Better?

A bit.

I'm getting sleepy, Clementine. I'm going to call it a night.

Clem looked at her watch: 10:30 PM. It was early. *Everything ok?*

Nothing that a few hours of sleep won't fix. Now stop beating yourself up. You are an incredible mother and wife. You are an amazing friend. You are a beautiful human.

Clem smiled. She didn't feel incredible, amazing, or beautiful, but Georgia's words made her feel a little better than wretched.

When you wake, we might have another six inches.

Think of it as a blanket.

Night, G.

Night, C.

CHAPTER TWELVE
Cold Tea

The next morning, Georgia was dead. After not hearing from her after breakfast, Clem rushed over and found her friend curled tightly under her favorite floral quilt. Her *Besties Forever* mug was sitting on the nightstand. The tea was cold.

It wasn't as if Clem hadn't expected this. She had. Ever since the doctor had delivered the news that Georgia's carotid artery was stuffed like a sausage, she'd known. But she'd figured they'd have at least another year. Maybe two. Especially if they made it through the endarterectomy.

But very little in life ever went the way you thought it would. Sometimes things turned out better than expected, other times worse. And with that in mind, she sat on the edge of the bed, holding Georgia's hand, wishing she could travel back in time for a few more minutes. Back to the moment they first met on Halloween. Back to a barbecue when the kids were small. Back to the night when she, Tor,

Henry, and Georgia had dressed up in their finest and eaten osso buco at one of the best restaurants in Boston's North End. If only she could spend a few more minutes sitting next to Georgia on the porch on a summer evening, watching the sun set with a gin and tonic in hand. Henry's death had been the signal that things were changing. The ring of the bell. The *things can't stay this way forever.* Georgia's death was the coming down of the hammer. *Things are different. They will never be the same. The shape of your day will change. The sound of your day will change. You will change.*

Death sucked.

Clem stroked Georgia's hair. "I'm going to miss you," she whispered. She looked at her phone. It was January 28. Then she looked at their most recent text exchange.

Night, G.

Night, C.

It was their very last good-night.

An hour later, she called Tor, who called the funeral director, who arrived to take charge of Georgia's body. Tor arrived to help Clem. They turned off lights, set the heat to sixty-eight degrees so the pipes didn't freeze, and poured a carton of milk down the drain. Clem dumped the tea from Georgia's bestie mug into the sink.

"Ready?" Tor said.

Clem nodded. She put on her coat, then tucked the mug into the enormous pocket. "Ready."

Tor took her hand, and together they walked out of Georgia's house into the snowstorm. It wasn't the last time Clem would go in and out of this house, but she knew it would never feel the same. She turned. Even through the sorrow, the lemon-yellow house made her smile.

Back home, Clem and Tor called the kids to their bedroom and told them the news about Georgia. For an hour, they all sat together—crying, telling stories, and comforting each other. When the kids wandered off to process things on their own, Clem stood, unlocked her closet, stepped in, and turned to close the door.

"Wait," Tor said, "stay out here with me? I'd like to help. Make things easier for you."

Clem knew her husband had loved Georgia. She knew he loved her too. But love couldn't fix the things that were out of alignment in their marriage. It was going to take more than that. A lot more. She shook her head. With Georgia's death came an unexpected clarity. "I prefer not to."

CHAPTER THIRTEEN
I Am Greenland

One thirty-eight AM, Clem's head:

Is reincarnation a real thing?
I miss Georgia.
If I could come back in another life, what would I want to be?
I miss Georgia.
A celestial goldfish?
I miss Georgia.
A sycamore?
I miss Georgia.
An Andean condor?
I miss Georgia.
A wayward moose?
I miss Georgia.
A woolly mammoth?
I miss Georgia.

As 2:06 AM, Clem leapt out of bed. In the sadness of the day, she'd forgotten to feed Frankie. She ducked into her closet and flicked on the small lamp. Like Clem, Frankie was awake. She swam to the glass and puckered her lips.

Clem dropped a few flakes into the punch bowl. Frankie swam up to get one, then dipped down, as if she were moving to music.

Clem plopped into her chair. Surprise, surprise. It was snowing. Chubby flakes scooting past the window so quickly she was sure they were trying to avoid her.

"*That one* hates us," Clem imagined one flake saying to another.

"Warm, snowless places are all *that one* talks about," another said. "Costa Rica, Thailand, Bermuda."

Clem opened the window and leaned out. "Oh, shut up," she said, swatting a few flakes out of the air.

She looked across the yards at Georgia's now-empty house. It was impossible to believe that her best friend was no longer sitting in her rocker, texting Clem, and offering her thoughts about the world. All day, as Clem had moved through the steps it took to take care of someone who had passed away, she'd managed not to burst into sobs. Yes, she'd teared up when she told the kids, called Meghan, talked with Georgia's cousin Astrid, and signed the paperwork for the funeral director. But with each task, she'd held strong.

But when she spotted the enormous hoofprints dotting the snowbank on Georgia's side of the fence, she gasped, then gulped. Once she did, all the tears she'd been holding back poured out of her eyes and down her cheeks, soaking the neckline of her nightgown. The prints in the snow were fresh and massive, and even though Georgia had doubted the woolly mammoth theory, Clem was surer than ever.

"Beast!" she called out the window, wiping tears with the backs of her hands. "Where are you? What are you?"

When her sobs subsided, Clem remembered the rain that had fallen in Greenland—a key indicator of the world's climate system—and the 337,000 square miles of ice sheet that had begun to melt.

Because of ocean currents, deep convection, the process of stabilizing global temperatures and rainfall, and other geologic factors she didn't quite understand, any change in Greenland's weather had worldwide implications. She was beginning to understand that the same thing was happening to her. Each storm that struck—hot flashes, lack of medical support for perimenopause, marriage, rage, itchy ears, titles at work, Frankie, Georgia's death, woolly mammoths—was causing a similar melt within her, and each would also have Clem-wide implications.

What would the world do now that rain had fallen on Greenland's highest peak? What would Clem do now that her body—once a well-regulated machine—was heating up like Greenland?

At 2:25 AM, she said good-night to Frankie, hopped onto her phone, and ordered a T-shirt with *I AM GREENLAND* emblazoned on the front.

CHAPTER FOURTEEN
The Funeral

A thousand spoons under a thousand pillows couldn't have stopped the sun from shining on the day of Georgia's funeral. That's the way the universe worked. While the temperature remained below freezing, the clouds broke up and the sky was a bright cerulean blue. Georgia would have loved it.

The stone church Georgia had attended for close to fifty-five years was overflowing with people who'd loved her. Parishioners, a gaggle of book clubbers, shop clerks, her favorite Apple store genius, Henry's fishing buddies, a few players from her canasta group, her team of mall walkers, and so many more. Samantha, Meghan, Jing, and Keisha arrived early to give Clem a hug. Victor and Walter stopped by to offer their condolences. Bill and Oliver Weston stayed from beginning to end, welcoming people at the door and ushering them in. Charlene paid her respects. A lady in a striped dress introduced herself as Elizabeth Gibb, a high school friend Georgia had mentioned once or twice. A set of elderly twins explained that they'd gone to elementary school with Georgia. And a man in a wrinkled suit who smelled like garlic told Clem that Georgia had been the one that got away.

Ran away is more likely, Clem thought. Georgia had hated garlic.

Astrid, Georgia's only living relative, sought out Clem the moment she arrived. "Oh, dear, Clementine," she said, "whatever shall we do without our Georgia?"

This oddly formal, overly dramatic, fake-southern-accented way of talking was Astrid's norm, and it had driven Georgia so batty that she'd avoided Astrid as much as possible. "Hide me!" she'd yelled to Clem every time her cousin arrived for a visit. Even so, she'd left her the house. Astrid was single and on a tight income. "She'll sell it to a sweet, young family," Georgia had told Clem when she'd set up a living trust after Henry died. "Then she'll have a nest egg, and you'll have lovely new neighbors to build memories with."

Georgia had worked out all the details of her passing, leaving nothing to chance. She was to be embalmed, dressed in the lilac frock she'd been wearing when she met Henry, laid out in a shiny coffin, and celebrated during an afternoon service at her church. "Stories and lots of laughter," she'd told Clem while planning it out. "I know you're going to cry, but you have to promise you'll laugh just as much."

Once the service was over, Georgia's body would be cremated. Her ashes were to be planted at the base of a seventy-five-foot-tall sugar maple in western Massachusetts. Henry's ashes had already been planted at the base of the neighboring tree. From the tops of both, you could see a delicious pond so full of fish they were practically leaping out on their own. A simple, round memorial marker would be placed in the earth between the trees. Their names would be imprinted on it, along with something Henry used to say every time they had pancakes with maple syrup: *Always remember to tap into your dreams.*

So far, everything had gone as Georgia planned. The weather, the frock, the coffin, the church, the friends, the stories, and the laughter. When Clem couldn't hold in the tears any longer, she retreated to the back of the church. The pew was perfectly hard and uncomfortable, and when Tor asked if she wanted to take a walk, she responded the way she was responding to most of his requests these days: "I prefer not to." She knew he expected Georgia's death to soften things between them, but, in fact, it did the opposite.

When Clem saw Nova and Rose walk through the side door of the church, she got up and met them at the coffin. "You knew Georgia?" Clem said.

Both women nodded, looking down at Georgia's peaceful face. Nova had tears in her eyes. "We're members of this church," she said. "Georgia was a gift from God."

Clem wasn't sure about the God bit, but she knew they were right about Georgia being a gift. "She was my dearest, dearest friend. I'm not sure how I'll go on from here." She was considering curling up at the base of Georgia's sugar maple in the Berkshires, but she knew Georgia would fuss if she did such a thing.

Moments later, when Nova swallowed hard and looked at Rose, Clem recognized the signs. "Hot flash?" she said.

Nova nodded. Sweat was gathering on her temples and cheeks.

"Let's get outside," Clem said. "The cold will help." On their way, they extricated Charlene from a conversation with Astrid, and once outside, the foursome sat on a quartet of stone chairs under a tree and quickly agreed they each needed one in their own yard. Stone held the cold like no other material, and Charlene speculated that the chair had been designed by a woman in the throes of perimenopause. Nova set her cheek on the cool armrest. "You see this?" she said, running her finger across the shallow area between her chin and lower lip.

Clem nodded and rubbed the area on her own face.

"This is your labiomental groove," Nova said. "And while I'm pretty sure no scientist or doctor has ever confirmed what I'm about to say, I believe this part of the body evolved to collect sweat during hot flashes."

Clem's eyes got big. "Nova, yes!" she said. "You are so right!"

Rose nodded too.

"What's it called again?" Clem said.

"Labiomental groove," Nova repeated.

Clem closed her eyes. Was she really sitting around in the snow talking about hot flashes with women going through the very same thing? A few weeks ago, she'd felt completely alone in the experience. Yet here she was, trading stories with women like her whose husbands snored, whose souls were cracking under the weight of the mental load, and whose hot flashes were threatening to do them in. Who knew this kind of camaraderie could exist? As sad as she was about Georgia's passing, she also felt a warm happiness beginning to take root deep inside. It was small. Much smaller than the sad. But still, it was something.

After sending the kids home from the church with Tor, Clem took a side trip to Pet-O-Rama. It was an unorthodox post-funeral detour, but Clem felt close to Georgia at the store where they'd purchased Frankie's life-giving filtration system. She could hear Georgia's laugh, see her swinging her walker back and forth through the snow, feel her hand on her elbow. Death was confusing. So was life.

After navigating the heaps of snow that had been plowed into the corners of the parking lot and the giant mountain of dirty ice looming in the center, she pulled into one of the few open spaces, turned off the car, and promptly fell into a deep sleep.

Thirty minutes later, when she woke, the windows were fogged up and the air inside the car was quite crisp. She rubbed a porthole in the windshield just in time to see Douglass trudging out of Pet-O-Rama.

"Aha," she said, "there you are!" And right then, she realized that while, yes, she was sitting in the Pet-O-Rama parking lot because it made her feel like her bestie was at her side, she'd also been waiting for Douglass.

Clem slunk deeper into the seat, bowed her head, and peered at him over the dashboard. If Douglass spotted her, she was doomed. Georgia would say she was being paranoid, but Clem was pretty sure that the whole episode about the filtration system had raised his suspicions about Clem's role in Frankie's disappearance.

Douglass stepped off the sidewalk, and as he passed her car, she studied how the hems of his oversized pants dragged in the slushy puddles and the hood of his giant orange parka was yanked up over his head. He looked like a goldfish. Like Frankie. Was this intentional? Was it a sign of what he knew? Was he sending a subliminal message to others? To her?

Clem's phone buzzed. Tor.

Little squirrel, where are you? Home soon?

She ignored him. When Douglass rounded the snow mountain and disappeared from sight, she took a breath, sure she was in the clear. She sat up, started the car, blew into her icy hands, and waited for the engine to warm. But as she was about to put the car into drive, Douglass poked his golden head around the snow mountain and looked right at her. He'd known she was there all along.

When their eyes met, he stepped boldly in front of her car, gave her the peace sign with one hand, then with the same two fingers pointed first to his eyes, then to hers. There was nothing peaceful about his message. She knew exactly what he meant. *I see you.*

Heart thumping, Clem put the car in reverse and hit the gas. Her tires spun wildly before catching, but when they did, she cleared the mound behind her, shifted into drive, and fishtailed out of the parking lot. In the rearview mirror, she glimpsed Douglass's golden glow dimming in the distance.

Later that day, when Georgia's body had been returned to the funeral home and the clouds had begun to gather, two significant things happened. First, Clem's I AM GREENLAND T-shirt was delivered. It was a rich, deep green with white letters. And second, Amanda Chen called. Ever since they'd first been introduced because of a mysterious library book years ago, Amanda had proved to be a tenacious and ever-curious reporter. Clem liked and respected her, but there was no way she was going to talk to her about Frankie. She hit "Decline call."

To distract herself from sorrow, Clem began to research anything that might cast doubt on Heather of the Weather's "knowledge" about how to make it snow. While digging, she discovered Luke Howard, known in weather circles as the Namer of Clouds. Howard was the guy who'd named many of the cloud types referenced today—cumulus (*heap* in Latin), stratus (*layer* in Latin), nimbus (*rain* in Latin), and cirrus (*curl* in Latin). Clem pulled a long, wet curl from her frizzy ponytail and let it bounce in front of her eyes. Cirrus hair.

Howard was dead now. Long dead. Nearly 160 years dead. Eighteen sixty-four dead. But he was commemorated, Clem discovered, with the only English Heritage blue plaque in Tottenham, England—an honor she'd never heard of but figured had to be something special.

Namer of Clouds.

That was the honor he'd achieved, and that plaque celebrated it.

With her damp head resting on the kitchen table, Clem considered the plaque that would hang in Byrock after she'd left this world.

Namer of Children.

Namer of Dogs.

Namer of Hamsters That Escaped and Died in Heating Ducts.

Namer of Dolls, Stuffed Animals, and Dinosaurs.

Namer of Random Birds, Snakes, and Bugs in the Garden.

Namer of Events and Workshops at the Byrock Public Library.

Namer of Invisible Friends.

Namer of Lost Teeth.

Namer of Little Plastic People.

Namer of Monsters Under the Bed.

Before Howard declared his system for naming clouds, Clem read, Europeans referred to them as "essences floating across the sky" and believed them to be impossible to categorize or name.

What a load of bullshit. Clem knew this was a rewriting of history intended to massage the ego of yet another man. She knew damn well that some woman in 1742 England had all kinds of good words for clouds:

drenched-my-laundry clouds
ruined-the-picnic clouds
blocked-the-sun-and-so-my-bean-crop-died clouds
drowned-my-husband clouds
made-a-mess-of-the-dirt-road clouds
flooded-the-apple-orchard clouds

And before this woman, what about the Incas? And the Romans? How about those Greeks?

Surely they all had names for clouds. But they were names, Clem figured, that the Europeans did not acknowledge or know how to pronounce. They wanted their own.

When she dug a little deeper, she learned that Indigenous people in the Americas named important members of their communities after clouds.

Red Cloud, a chief of the Oglala Teton Dakota tribe. Sioux.

White Cloud, a chief of the Ioway people.

Touch the Clouds, a chief of the Minneconjou Teton Lakota. Sioux.

What about Indigenous women named for clouds? Were there any of those? Revered women who commanded such respect?

Though none came up in a quick search, Clem did discover that the Diné Nation of the Southwest had separate words for soft, helpful "female" rain clouds and violent, damaging "male" thunderstorms. Sexist, of course, but still proof that many, many humans had experienced, thought about, and named clouds before Luke Howard, the man who got all the credit. And the plaque.

The kettle whistled. Clem poured steaming water into her mug and carried the tea to the kitchen door. She stared out at the sycamore and the dense snow clouds dominating the sky. Nimbostratus. For a moment, Clem could feel life the way it would feel if she were a deciduous tree, and she thought about the Keeper of Living Collections at the arboretum and his responsibilities for bugs and birds and bark.

If Meghan asked her to name her big feeling right now, it would be impossible to give only one: warm happiness, deep sadness, strange peacefulness. *This is how a tree feels,* Clem thought. *This is how my sycamore feels. This is how Georgia's sugar maple feels.* This fleeting moment of solidity made her remember that she *could* feel this way, that she'd once felt this way, and that she might—perhaps with great effort and immense change—feel this way again.

That night as she lay in bed, Clem used *labiomental groove* as her sleeping meditation.

"Labiomental groove."

She whispered it into the dark room.

"Labiomental groove."

"Labiomental groove."

"Labiomental groove."

She almost dozed off, but then she got distracted by the never-ending to-do list stuffed into her chest.

"Labiomental groove."

She worried about the library kids missing Frankie.

"Labiomental groove."

She worried about her kids missing Georgia.

"Labiomental groove."

She seethed at the fact that Tor never forgot to pick up the two grocery items that mattered most to him: wine and his ridiculously expensive granola. Everything else fell to her.

"Labiomental groove."

And finally, she panicked about all the things she'd had to postpone because of Georgia's passing.

"Labiomental groove."

Slowly, the mantra nudged Clem into a woozy, relaxed state that almost felt like floating, and she sighed. But as she was about to tip into a gloriously hypnotic slumber, flames shot from her belly button. Another hot flash. Within a minute, she was splashing in a sea of scorching lava. Sweat pooled in her labiomental groove and her hair expanded.

Holy fucking hummingbirds.

Rather than waiting for it to pass, she sat up, stepped into her slippers, and went to the kitchen to make snickerdoodles for Anna's bake sale.

When the kitchen heated up, she cracked the window over the sink.

It was not enough.

When sweat beaded on her lip, she opened the window all the way.

It was not enough.

She opened the doors to the patio. Wind blew in with a puff of snow.

The buzzer went off. The first batch of cookies was done.

As the second batch baked, Clem made the required list of ingredients. *No peanuts. No tree nuts. No fish or shellfish. No wheat. No soy. Does contain milk and egg.*

She printed the list, put it in a protective plastic sleeve, and set it with the cookies out of Hagrid's reach.

Even with the doors open, sweat was pooling under her breasts and dripping to her waistband. She slid her pants down and left them in a puddle on the floor. The relief was astounding.

Minutes later, when the kids ran downstairs to catch the school bus, Brewster came to a screeching halt at the bottom of the stairs. "Mom," he said. "Where are your pants?"

"I'm hot, Brew," she said.

"It's snowing, Mom," he said. "In here." He waved at the flakes of snow accumulating on the stone floor.

"I'm having another hot flash. Leave the doors open. I'll put pants on in a bit."

Evan eyed her, then gathered their things. "Whatever, Mom."

Anna stepped into the kitchen. "Mom! What are you doing now?"

"Cooling off."

"Why? No one else's mom is cooling off like this."

"Don't bet on it."

"They're not, Mom. I know they're not."

"They want to," Clem said.

"No, Mom, they don't!" Anna was mad.

"Sweetie, I know you don't think other moms want to strip off their pants and walk around with the doors open during snowstorms, but I promise you, they do. Every one of them who is having hot flashes is longing to do this very thing. And maybe even some who aren't. I am simply brave enough to follow through."

"This isn't brave, Mom. This is loony tunes!"

"It's not, Anna. I'm going through something significant."

"Mom, I realize you are going through something, but if you plan on coming to the bake sale, you better wear pants." Anna glared so hard that Clem was sure her eyeballs were going to leap from their sockets and knock Clem in the head.

Clem nodded, but it was more of an *I hear you* nod than an *I'll do as you ask* nod.

"Seriously, Mom. I'll die if you come into the gym with no pants. Literally die. Do you want that?"

"Of course not, especially from something as ridiculous as embarrassment."

"Mom?"

Clem nodded.

"I mean it, Mom."

"I know you do." As the kids gathered their things for school, Clem began to recite her sleep meditation. "Labiomental groove. Labiomental groove. Labiomental groove."

Brewster stopped in front of her. "Mom."

"What?"

"Stop saying that."

"Saying what?"

"That thing you've been repeating for the past five minutes."

"Labiomental groove?"

"Mom!" Brewster covered his ears with his hands.

"What, Brewster, what?"

"Stop!"

"Why?"

"Because!"

"Because why?"

"Because it's gross! It's inappropriate!"

Anna and Evan stared at their brother.

"Labiomental groove is inappropriate?"

"Mom!" He was becoming hysterical.

"Brewster, I'm confused. What are you talking about?"

Brewster took his hands off his ears and shook them at her. "Mom! It's a private part! A woman's private part. Stop saying it over and over!"

"A private part?"

"Mom! Stop!"

When Clem realized that Brewster had confused *labiomental groove* with *labia*, she chortled. She tried to hold in the laughter, knowing how embarrassed her youngest would be, but she couldn't. She gripped the edge of the island and belly laughed. She howled and bent over the stool.

"What is so funny, Mom?" Brewster said. "Stop laughing at me!" He was standing between Evan and Anna, staring at his mother like she'd lost her mind.

"Mom?" Anna said.

Clem opened her mouth to explain but instead laughed so hard tears dribbled out of her eyes.

"Mom! Stop it!" Brewster was irate.

Clem took a breath and stood. "This, my dear boy," she said, reaching out and rubbing the indentation between his bottom lip and chin, "is your labiomental groove. You confused it with something else."

Anna whacked Brewster in the head with her bagel. "Idiot."

Evan chuckled. "Labia, dude, labia. Come on. Even Mom isn't going to sit around repeating *that* all day."

Brewster's cheeks blared as red as Clem's during a hot flash. Mortified, he grabbed his backpack and ran for the bus. "Well, you shouldn't say it anyway. It's confusing!" Then he was out the door. Anna and Evan followed.

Clem plopped onto the couch and laughed until she heard Tor walking down the steps.

"What was all that about?" Tor was blizzard ready in his shorts and blue seersucker shirt. He looked handsome and, as always, well groomed.

Clem got up to pour another cup of coffee. "Something about the fact that I'm not wearing pants."

Tor stopped, looked her up and down, and nodded. "I see that."

"Long story," she said. "Aren't you late for work, Torvald?"

"I am, but I was hoping we could talk."

They needed to talk. Really, Clem needed to talk, and he needed to listen. But Clem knew they were very far from that. She sipped her coffee, looked at him, said, "I prefer not to," and then walked away. Twenty minutes later she heard the front door close.

Clem remembered what Georgia and Henry had always said about life being full of surprises. Clem knew that being a woman was full of surprises. One day, years before, she'd been climbing trees in her backyard, and the next she was having to go in to change her pad or tampon because she was bleeding. Once she got used to the rhythm of that—the monthly pain, the need to be prepared, replacing jeans when she bled over—she got pregnant. What a whirl that had been! Time passed, and without warning, these hot flashes arrived. And from what she'd learned in recent weeks, there was still much more to come.

CHAPTER FIFTEEN
Abracadabra

Exhausted and pinned to the couch by sorrow, Clem lay watching Hagrid frolic in the snow. Even through the double-paned windows, she could hear the joyful *boing, boing, boing* of his massive paws. How was she going to move forward without Georgia? Who would she complain to, giggle with, lean on, and whisper secrets to? Having a bestie had been worth the eventual loss, but now what?

Her phone pinged.

mom

mom

mom

Evan. Not Anna.
Thank goodness.

mom

mom

mom

$$ for driving class was due last week u didnt pay

Driving class? What driving class?

You're taking a driving class?

mom you filled out the forms

She did?

I did?

mom quit messing around

can u pay online rn

please

How in the world could Evan be old enough to drive? And how could she not remember filling out the forms?

MOM

Evan, ask your dad to pay.

MOM

Your dad. Text him.

MOM HAVE U LOST YOUR MIND

I have not. I remain of sound mind.

MOM

Clem opened the door to let Hagrid inside. Heather had promised more of the white stuff that day. The weather wackadoodle was right.

MOM

DAD WILL NEVER BE ABLE TO DO THIS

Evan, please stop shouting.

IM NOT SHOUTING

MOM PAY

Clem sighed.

I can't, Evan.

WHY

MOM THE BILL PLEASE

THEYLL GIVE MY SPOT TO SOMEONE ELSE

Clem thought about how many decisions she made every day. From morning to night—decisions, decisions, decisions. Bartleby's words echoed in her head.

"I prefer not to," she whispered. "I prefer not to." But how could she let Evan down? Her eldest. Her first baby. The child who'd been waiting to drive since they'd climbed behind the steering wheel when they were three years old and refused to get out of the car. How did you say no to your own kid?

Hagrid set his wet, icy head on Clem's knee. "Hey," she whispered. "I prefer not to."

MOM IF YOU DONT PAY RIGHT NOW ILL NEVER BE ABLE TO DRIVE IN MY WHOLE LIFE

Brewster wasn't the only Crane capable of drama.

That is unlikely.

MOM

Clem took a breath. This was it. A defining moment. *Evan, I love you, but you need to text your father. I prefer not to.*

Later that day, not long after lunch, Clem heard a shriek from the children's room at the library. Then a whoop and a bunch of giggles. "We did it!" she heard Little Miss Blue Hat yell. That know-it-all voice was unmistakable.

Figuring the kids had finished building their replica of Frankie in the garden, she continued her work. But then her phone pinged. Meghan.

Clem, please come down. The children need to see you!

Clem glanced at the staircase. *Busy. Later?*

Now, please! It's good news!

Clem grunted. Nothing good could come from being near Frankie's empty tank, but how could she say no? This was her job, and she needed to feign innocence for as long as possible. *Fine.*

As she made her way down the stairs, she heard the telltale jangle of tambourines. The protesters had gathered for their daily rally. Didn't these people have jobs? Children to tend to? Hobbies?

Little Miss Blue Hat met Clem at the bottom of the steps. "Ms. Clementine, come on!" she said. "Hurry!"

Clem did hurry, right past Frankie's tank, which was now covered with so many drawings and love letters from the kids that the glass was no longer visible. Just past Meghan's desk, she saw the kids gathered around a computer.

"What's up, Ms. Meghan?" she said.

"Kids?" Meghan said.

"Ms. Clementine, we have awesome news!" Kalisha said. "We've raised all the money we need from Frankie's GoFundMe!"

Clem gritted her teeth so hard that shock waves reverberated through her head. She hadn't checked the account since before Yahoo shared the story, and she'd done a fine job avoiding it.

"What?" she said evenly. "It's raised over two hundred dollars?"

"Way more!" Ben yelled.

"Look!" said Little Miss Blue Hat, pointing at the computer.

Clem stepped around the table and leaned toward the screen. When she saw the total, she gasped. "You've raised two thousand eight hundred thirty-two dollars?"

"We have, Ms. Clementine," Meghan said, putting her arm around Clem. "Thanks to you."

The children cheered.

Clem leaned closer. The list of donors was long. Most had given small amounts—five or ten dollars. But someone called Local-Fish-Guy had given five hundred dollars.

"Holy cow!" Clem said.

"Now we can offer a reward!" said Kalisha.

"And send that fish-napper to the slammer!" Ben said, slapping his hand on the table.

Clem jumped.

"Ben," Meghan said, "please don't talk like that. We know nothing about the person who took Frankie. There may be a story there. Something we don't know."

This was the kind of response Clem needed to hear. When she did come clean—*if* she did come clean—would anyone be willing to hear her out? Or would she be turned over to that bloodthirsty herd of tambourine-jangling hyenas?

"The only thing we need to hear is the sound of a cell door slamming," Ben said.

Clementine stared down at him. Was this kid serious?

"Kids, two thousand eight hundred thirty-two dollars is a lot of money," Meghan said. "The reward will be a good incentive, and

I'm positive someone who knows something may very well step forward."

Clem's heart seized, but she nodded as if this would be a good thing. Subterfuge, she was discovering, was a fine art.

"Ms. Clementine, can you put the reward on our social channels today?"

"Yes," Little Miss Blue Hat said, "we need the information out there as soon as possible!"

"Absolutely," Clem said, knowing damn well she was going to put off doing so as long as possible.

"Everyone, say thank-you to Ms. Clementine!" Meghan sang.

As Clem turned and started up the stairs, she heard the kids yell, "Thank you!" She knew she should wave and say, *You're welcome!* but she was too preoccupied with trying to figure out if Local-Fish-Guy could be Douglass.

Who else could it be?

Within hours, Clem received another call from Amanda Chen, but when the name popped up on the phone screen, Clem whispered, "I prefer not to," and hit "Decline call."

From there, the frequency of "I prefer not to" increased daily. When the FedEx deliveryman rang the doorbell and said, "Sign here," Clem looked at the package, recognized it as yet another set of architectural plans for Tor, and said, "I prefer not to."

"You prefer what?" the man said.

"I prefer not to."

"Really?" he said with a quizzical look.

"Really."

The man was holding the package in one hand and the scanning device in the other. He pulled both to his chest.

Clem turned and walked inside.

"Ma'am, I can't leave this without a signature," the man said.

Clem nodded and closed the door. Seconds later, she panicked. What kind of behavior was this? It wasn't the FedEx man's fault she was tired of signing for Tor's five thousand monthly deliveries. The dynamics of their marriage didn't interest him. He was doing his job.

Clem opened the door. The man was already halfway down the sidewalk. He turned.

"I'm—" Clem started to say she was sorry but then remembered the promise she'd made about no more disingenuous apologies. She sighed and shrugged instead.

He shook his head and continued on to his truck.

Her phone buzzed. Amanda Chen.

> Clementine, is this still your number? Trying to reach you to get some information on the fish-napping. What's a good time to connect?

Clem deleted the text.

Throughout the day, she discovered that "preferring not to" was a helpful antidote to the hourly punch of anxiety she usually felt.

Make an appointment with the foot doctor.

I prefer not to.

Pick up Hagrid's boo-boo balm.

I prefer not to.

Fill the dishwasher.

I prefer not to.

Brush Hagrid.

I prefer not to.

Replace a lightbulb in the bathroom.

I prefer not to.

Call the epilepsy foundation to schedule a donation pickup.

I prefer not to.

Check in with Astrid.

I prefer not to.

Replace the mailbox that was run over by the plow driver.

I prefer not to.

Find a new plow driver.

I prefer not to.

Weeks before, when she'd just begun using the phrase, the words had felt clunky and uncomfortable, as if she were running new lines with Brewster for a play. But with repetition, they rolled more easily off her tongue every day, in the same way *otolaryngologist* had so many years ago. As she practiced, she thought about her story—*her* story—the deeply personal one she woke with each day, breakfasted with, made decisions with, presented to people she'd recently met and people who'd known her for years. That story went like this:

I am the "good kid."

I am a follower.

I support others.

I always say yes.

I am afraid.

This last one surprised her. Afraid? Afraid of what?

She didn't quite know, but to get closer to an answer, she headed out to the backyard. There, in thigh-high snow, she clicked on TikTok, then filmed herself staring placidly at the sycamore. She added the five statements of her story with the fifth—*I AM AFRAID*—in all caps. Then music, a call to action, and a few hashtags. She posted it at 5:15 PM, and because there's nothing TikTok loves more than a pattern, the video blew up. By 9:00 that evening, it had nearly thirty thousand likes and thousands of comments. This one hit hard. By morning, women all over the world were telling their stories in five statements with the fifth being the vulnerable one that surprised them. They tagged Clem in their stories.

A woman in Idaho: *I am employee of the month. I am the "yes, ma'am." I give my all. I clean up the mess. I am angry.*

A woman in Paris: *I eat my vegetables. I cook for my family. I sleep five hours a night. I pack everyone's bags. I am sad.*

Another in Toronto: *I am an enthusiastic wife. I am an enthusiastic mother. I am an enthusiastic data analyst. I am enthusiastic. I am exhausted.*

The videos went on and on:

I am an observer. I stay on the periphery. I see everything. I hear everything. I long to jump into the mix.

I am a perfectionist. I crave a clean moral slate. Mistakes cripple me. I feel guilty for things I did forty years ago. I am broken.

I am the "do it all" girl. My house is spotless. My hair is smooth. I vacuum every day. I am frustrated.

I am the breadwinner. I am the house cleaner. I am the laundress. I am the organizer. I am done.

I am the boss. I make rules. I set boundaries. I work out at 5 AM. I want to sleep.

I am a people pleaser. I adhere to all social expectations. I RSVP to every invitation. I smile at everyone in the grocery store. I want to scream.

As Clem watched TikTok after TikTok, she acknowledged four things. First, women all around the world had similar experiences. Second, people with penises had the upper hand. Third, penis people would prefer to keep the upper hand as long as possible. Fourth, a winged fairy was not going to swoop down, say *abracadabra*, and magically make things better for women. Right then, Clem realized that if she wanted the world to be different, she was going to have to change it herself.

CHAPTER SIXTEEN
Snickerdoodles

You better wear pants.

Anna's warning echoed in Clem's head as she carefully chose an outfit to wear to the hockey team's bake sale. After much consternation, she pulled on a pair of lime-green linen trousers that nonperimenopausal women would only wear in July and her new *I AM GREENLAND* T-shirt. The greens clashed, but she didn't care.

At 3:00 PM, she packed up the snickerdoodles, pulled on her boots without socks, trudged outside, and cleared four inches of dense, wet snow from the windows. Then she hopped in the car and, even though she was running behind, drove directly to Pet-O-Rama. Still in the ugly-cry stage of grief whenever anything reminded her of Georgia, she started to sob. With snot gathering on her upper lip, she asked herself the question that would drive the rest of her life: *What would Georgia do?*

In this case, the answer was easy. She pulled the giraffe costume from the black hole, tugged it on, and galloped through the doors of her and Georgia's favorite pet store.

As soon as she entered, all eyes turned. Clem greeted the cashier with an exaggerated nod of her giraffe head.

"Sorry," the cashier said, grinning, "we don't groom giraffes here. Only dogs, cats, and certain types of birds."

Clem smiled. "Good thing I'm a well-groomed giraffe."

"How can I help you?" the cashier said.

"I have a question about my fish."

"I know as much about fish as I do giraffes," the cashier said. "I'm only the checkout girl."

"Then why do you say, 'Can I help you?' when people enter the store?"

The girl shrugged. "I'm supposed to."

"Says who?"

"My manager."

Clem tsk-tsked. "The next time your manager tells you to do something that doesn't make sense, say this." Clem leaned close to the girl's ear and whispered, "I prefer not to."

"I prefer not to?"

Clem nodded.

"Won't that get me fired?"

"It could, but sometimes you have to risk something to gain something."

The girl looked dubious. "I'll think about it."

"That's a good place to start." Clem looked around, pretending she'd never been in Pet-O-Rama before. "Can you point me to the fish section?" she said, feigning ignorance. "I assume there's someone there who can help me."

"That I can do," the girl said. "Head straight down aisle five." As she pointed toward the back of the store, three young teens tumbled in with snow coating their heads and shoulders. They stomped, laughing, but stopped when they saw Clem.

"Well, look at that!" the tall one said. "I didn't know Pet-O-Rama sold giraffes."

The other two fell onto each other, cackling as if this were the funniest thing they'd ever heard.

"Shouldn't you be in school?" Clem said. "Don't pick on giraffes."

"We graduated last year," the tall one said.

"Shouldn't you be at your job or in college?" Clem said.

"Shouldn't *you* be in a zoo?"

The rage in Clem's middle surged. "Ha-ha."

"Ma'am," the tall one said to the cashier. "I want to buy this giraffe."

The cashier smirked. "We do not sell giraffes at Pet-O-Rama," she said in a monotone voice.

"Why not?" the kid said.

The cashier caught Clem's eye. "We prefer not to," she said.

Clem turned and trotted down aisle five as instructed, and when she rounded the corner, she spotted what, or rather who, she was looking for. Douglass. He was kneeling in front of a large tank, ladling something from a cup into the water.

She moved down the aisle until she was next to Douglass, then cleared her throat.

He didn't look up.

She tapped an empty fish tank.

Nothing.

Finally, she said, "Excuse me. Do you work here?"

Douglass grunted. "How can I help you?"

"I have a fish problem."

Douglass must have caught sight of Clem's hooves because he looked up and said, "You again."

"You remember me?" Clem said.

Douglass worked his way into a standing position, then used his forearms to hoist up his pants. "You're not easy to forget. And if I remember correctly, the last time I saw you, you needed a filtration system."

Clem bobbed her head. "Good memory."

"For a goldfish," Douglass said. He stared at her.

Clem's phone buzzed in her purse. "And if I remember correctly, you didn't want to sell me a filtration system because you said goldfish don't need such things."

Douglass set the cup and ladle on a nearby shelf and wiped his hands on his pants. "They don't, but you had a dramatic story about a moving truck and a passenger seat."

"It wasn't a story," Clem said.

"Whatever," Douglass said, and turned back to the tank. "How's your fish?"

"Fine," Clem said. "Very pleased with the filtration system your coworker suggested to me."

"She only lasted here a few weeks."

"I'm sorry to hear that."

"She didn't know a damn thing about fish."

"She was very helpful to me." Clem's phone buzzed.

Douglass sighed.

When Clem's phone sounded a third time, she dug it out of her purse. Anna.

mom

mom

u there mom

u coming to bake sale

started 15 min ago

"Ma'am," Douglass said, "do you need something today?" He paused by a wooden post, upon which the local newspaper article about Frankie was hung. It featured the photo of Frankie from the GoFundMe page. Full color. The headline? *Let's Find Frankie.* "Have you seen this?" he said, pointing. "A real tragedy."

Clem hadn't planned on this development, but she wasn't surprised. Ever since she'd seen that $500 donation on Frankie's GoFundMe from Local-Fish-Guy, she'd been suspicious. "I have seen it," Clem said in a mournful voice. "It's shocking. Who would steal a goldfish?"

"Someone with no soul," Douglass said. "Those poor children at the library. They must be heartbroken."

Clem smirked. She knew he was baiting her, trying to get information.

"You should put your money where your mouth is," Clem said. "Did you donate?"

Douglass shrugged. "Maybe." He was noncommittal. Purposely, Clem was sure. "I'm a pretty passionate fish guy. Getting that goldfish back to the kids at the library matters." He stabbed a damp finger at the newspaper article and looked at Clem. "As the owner of a goldfish, what do *you* think about this fish-napping?"

Clem ignored him, hoping he'd move on to a different topic. She focused on Anna.

I'm on my way. Be there soon.

"Ms. Giraffe," Douglass said when Clem didn't look up, "did you hear me? Any thoughts on the kidnapping of this local goldfish?"

"Why would I have any thoughts about it?" Clem said.

"You're quite zealous about your own goldfish."

"So what?"

Douglass stood taller. "I thought you might have something to add to the story." He looked directly in her eyes as he spoke. It was disconcerting.

"I'm here for a castle," Clem said. "Not chitchat about heart-wrenching fish tales."

"A castle?" Douglass said.

"Yes, my goldfish used to have a castle, so I want to buy her a new one."

"*Used* to have?" Douglass said.

"Yes, *used* to have."

"Did that get lost in the moving truck along with the filtration system?" he said.

"That is none of your business. All I need is a castle. A turquoise one."

Douglass peered closely at the newspaper article. "Turquoise?"

"That's what I said."

"Like this one?" he said, and he pointed to Frankie's castle. It was turquoise.

Crap, Clem thought, *I should have said yellow.* If Georgia had been there, she wouldn't have slipped up.

"No, something a little more extravagant," she said. "That one looks quite small."

Douglass stared deeply into Clem's eyes. "Your very special goldfish needs a filtration system *and* a fancy castle?"

"What my goldfish needs is none of your business," Clem said. "I'm pretty sure your job is to help me find what I'm looking for. Can you please point me to the castles?"

Douglass grimaced. He clearly had more to say but was holding back. "Over there," he said, pointing. "Make sure you don't get one too large for the bowl. You don't want to overwhelm the fish. Especially if that fish is accustomed to a certain castle in a certain tank." His eyes went to the article one more time.

"Understood," Clem said, and she trotted to the next aisle.

While she looked through the available castles, Clem tried to figure out what exactly Douglass knew. She was sure it was something, but what? And what should she do about it? What would Georgia do?

The answer came loud and clear. *Buy the damn castle and get the hell out of there.*

As Clem searched the offerings, she caught Douglass peering at her over the rack. She had to hurry, but then she heard, "Hey, giraffe lady! Over here!"

She grabbed a glittery yellow castle, hoping it would throw Douglass off the track, then spotted the teens heading toward her via aisle seven. "Calling all giraffes," one muttered into a pretend speaker.

Clem gripped the castle as she cantered toward the checkout girl.

"Hey, giraffe lady! Where are you going?" one of the teens yelled.

Clem ducked, trying to hide. Not easy when your giraffe head reached three feet into the air.

"We see you, giraffe lady!"

Clem paused and surveyed the area. She spotted Douglass two aisles away, heading the opposite direction but obviously still looking for her. She bolted into a checkout line. There was one person in front of her.

"There she is!" one of the teens yelled.

Clem heard Douglass's voice call to her. "Hey, giraffe lady! Wait! I have a question."

"I prefer not to," Clem called back, then handed the castle to the checkout girl, who winked and leaned toward the speaker on her register. She hit a button, then said into the mic, "Emergency in the fish department! Emergency in the fish department!" Clem watched Douglass stop short. She knew he cared too much about the world's fish to ignore a call like that.

He looked at Clem over a display of dog food and called out, "I'll find you!" Then he turned and headed back toward the fish department to manage the emergency.

"Thank you," Clem said to the cashier.

Outside, she jumped into the car, tossed the bag onto the passenger seat, revved the engine, and backed up as the three teens ran out the door. "Giraffe lady!" they yelled, laughing. "Giraffe lady!"

She waved and skidded out of the parking lot. Another inch of snow had accumulated while she'd shopped. More cars were on the road, and visibility was so low it felt like she was driving through a shaken snow globe. When she finally got to Anna's school, she parked and made her way into the gym, which was already packed with hockey supporters.

When she spotted Anna at the girls' team's cookie table, she saw her daughter's eyes fill with relief. Like every other mom in the gym, Clem was wearing pants, a shirt, boots, and even a coat. Yes, the greens clashed, but overall, she looked normal. Beautifully normal. Anna stood, rounded the table, and flew into Clem's arms. "Thank you, Mom," she whispered, burying her head into Clem's shoulder. "Thank you for wearing pants."

Hugging Anna like that felt so good. There was no anger in her daughter's body, no teen-mean, no worry or resentment. Just sweet Anna all wrapped up in her arms, the way she used to be when she was small. It was the best feeling Clem had had in months. But as she stood holding her daughter, she realized that the only way she'd be able to maintain this peaceful coexistence going forward—this equilibrium—would be to sacrifice her own growth as a human. To keep Anna happy—to keep everyone in her world happy—Clem would have to go back to accepting all that was given to her and asking for nothing more. She'd have to stop riding her husband about his snoring and accept that the maintenance of the emotional and life needs of every human in her family was her responsibility. She'd have to tell Bathsheba that Director of Media was a perfectly fine title. She'd have to let go of her need to be Connector of People to Magical Things. To keep Anna—and all others—happy, she'd have to say *Of course*, as she always had, instead of *I prefer not to.*

What a strange and horrific realization. Years before when she was on the brink of motherhood, she'd had no idea that one day she'd have to make decisions about how to be true to herself without risking her relationship with her child. Was it possible for Clem to continue moving forward in her own journey without instigating anger in Anna? Without alienating her? Why hadn't anyone told her about this aspect of mothering?

She squeezed Anna close and looked over her shoulder at the other mothers in the gym. Some she recognized from the rink or school functions; some she didn't know at all. Laila's mom was there, leaning over the baked goods, clearly struggling to figure out which cookie to buy. A gaggle of moms was chattering under the basketball hoop. They didn't *look* tortured or miserable, but women were so good at masking their agony and discomfort that Clem couldn't say for sure. It was likely that at least half of them felt like her—pissed off, fiery with rage, on the brink of exploding. With Anna's head resting on her shoulder, Clem tried to pinpoint which were squelching their own needs in order to be the best possible human to everyone else and which were wondering how to stay scrunched up in a ball when all they wanted to do was unfurl.

Her phone pinged.

Evan.

Thanks mom. Dad didn't pay the fee for driving class.
Now I have to wait 3 more months.

As Clem suspected, Tor hadn't been able to figure it out. Still, she was sad Evan had to suffer for the lesson.

I'm sorry, Evan.

Whatever.

And he was gone.

Clem had read so many articles in parenting magazines about the guilt moms felt leaving their children at day care or a sitter's to go to work. Fuck that. What about the anger, the resentment, the I've-had-enough-ness moms felt because always putting someone else's needs first sucked every last drop of life from their exhausted bodies? Especially when their husbands didn't jump in to help?

Clem was at a crossroads. If she behaved, deleted her TikTok account, kept her pants on, stopped talking about her hot flashes, continued without complaint to stuff her chest with appointments and payments and whatnot, Anna would be satisfied. Tor would be satisfied. Evan and Brewster would be satisfied. Bathsheba and Dr. Sheffield would be satisfied. The entire world would be satisfied.

But if she did all those things, the world would not be any different for Anna, and in twenty-five years or so, her daughter would be facing the same things Clem was facing right now. Doctors who refused to listen, a medical industry that didn't prioritize research on women's health issues, husbands who didn't understand or care that wives were cracking under the weight of the mental load, lack of treatment for hot flashes, and so much more.

Clem knew she could no longer behave in the way Anna needed her to, and, slowly, she was making peace with something Georgia used to say: *Sometimes things have to break before they get better.*

When she got back to the car, she opened Instagram, clicked through to her DMs, and saw a message from an account called Local-Fish-Guy. I see you.

What the hell? Was it Douglass? Had he found her online?

She hit delete without even clicking through to the account.

Crunch, crunch, crunch.

That night, the wandering beast returned. And when she heard it, Clem sat straight up in bed. Her chest heaved. A few appointment reminders tumbled out. The kids' wisdom tooth removal. Brewster's haircut. Car maintenance. She reached to put them back into place but then stopped.

"I prefer not to," she whispered.

Crunch, crunch, crunch.

Tor rolled over as she, for the first time ever, let those appointments and reminders slip away, gone forever unless someone else decided to pick them up.

"I prefer not to," she whispered a little more firmly.

Something large was moving into Clem's life.

Crunch, crunch, crunch.

Why not a woolly mammoth?

Clem swung her legs out of bed and slipped her feet into her boots. This time she'd planned and prepared.

Crunch, crunch, crunch.

She ran down the stairs, paused to pull on a coat, and then flew out the door. She plowed into the snow and pushed her way along the fence. When she got near the corner, she peeked through a space in the panels. Sure enough, on the other side, fresh tracks dotted the snow. Tracks as big as the moon.

Clem heard Georgia's voice in her head. *It's a moose, Clementine. It's got to be a moose.*

But maybe Georgia was wrong. Maybe it *was* a woolly mammoth. Perhaps the investors with deep pockets and big dreams had flooded the scientists' coffers with enough money to bring their passion project to fruition. Perhaps the scientists' had managed to scrape enough DNA from Buttercup's bones to make it a reality. Perhaps the new and improved woolly mammoth had broken free and made its way to Massachusetts. Perhaps Clem was right, and if she was, she was looking at the tracks of the very first woolly mammoth in the twenty-first century.

Her chest heaved with excitement, and a few more appointment reminders slipped out and fell plop-plop-plop into the snow.

"I prefer not to," she whispered.

The woolly mammoth cometh.

She imagined the tusks of such a creature. Long and curled. The small, fur-lined ears designed to conserve heat.

With frozen fingers, she searched her phone for an image of the regal beast, and once she found one, she wished she could send it to Georgia, like she would have done just weeks before. Now she stared at it all by herself, thinking first about Georgia's death and then about Henry's the year before.

"How do I go from having my husband for nearly sixty years to him being always and forever gone?" Georgia had confided after Henry's funeral.

Now Clem was asking a similar question. *How do I go from having my bestie for sixteen years to her being always and forever gone?*

As she looked at the picture of the Pleistocene behemoth, Clem felt another hot flash beginning to roll through her. She tried to imagine the same happening to a female mammoth. Heat trying, but failing, to escape through the three-foot-long fur and those fuzzy ears. Maybe this was the root cause of poor Buttercup's untimely death. Maybe she'd jumped headfirst into that peat bog trying to cool her fiery body, putting herself at the mercy of sabertooth cats and hungry wolves.

Feeling the rage boiling in her middle, Clem grabbed an ice-covered ball from a limb of the sycamore and drew back her arm. "What are you?" she yelled into the night. "What are you?" Then she pitched the ball as hard as she could in the direction of the disappearing beast.

At breakfast the next morning, looking from one child to another and finally at her husband, Clem declared, "I will no longer be saying, *I'm having a hot flash*."

"No?" Tor said.

Clem knew she was giving off a different kind of energy, and she could see he was hesitant to say more.

"No," Clem answered. She plunked a plate of pancakes onto the table.

"Who cares?" Anna said.

Evan elbowed her.

"I imagine no one," Clem said, "but I'm letting you know."

"Are you going to stop talking about it?" Anna asked. "Because that would be ideal."

Evan elbowed her harder.

"No, I'm not going to stop talking about it, Anna."

"What are you going to say instead?" Tor asked as he took a pancake from the stack.

"From now on," Clem said, "*hot flash* is a verb. I'm simply going to use it that way. Instead of saying, *I'm having a hot flash*, I'm going to say, *I'm hot flashing*. Using it as a verb makes it active, alive, purposeful." She sat down, rolled a pancake into a tube, dipped it in a puddle of maple syrup, took a bite, and thought about Georgia, whose ashes would soon be ready to be carried to the Berkshires for burial under the sugar maple in the woods.

Tor nodded. "That's great, hon," he said.

Anna rolled her eyes.

Brewster hid his reddening face behind a napkin. "Are we done talking about this?" he said.

"For now," Clem said.

"Good," Tor said. "By the way, any sign of my green sweater?"

Four hours later, Clem was standing knee-deep in snow near the founder's statue in the town center, surrounded by twenty or so women. Some she knew—Charlene, Nova, and Rose, as well as a few add-ons from Georgia's funeral, including Astrid, who was wearing a bright-yellow jacket. Some she didn't recognize at all. To get everyone's attention, she raised her hands in the air.

"Hello, hot-flashers, overwhelmed moms, mental-load managers, and pissed-off people with periods," Clem said. "Thank you for joining me here today."

She was nervous. Her legs were shaky, and her heart was racing. She'd pulled this gathering together so quickly, with little thought about what she was going to say once she got here. She'd sent a few emails with "I PREFER NOT TO" in the subject line to the women she knew: "Meet me in the town center at noon. Bring anyone with a uterus." That was it, but now that she was here, there was great clarity in Clem's brain. She took a deep breath, sucked in the cold air, and said, "I'm here because I've had enough. I suspect you have too. I'm here because I'm about to crack under the weight of the mental load I'm carrying for my husband and kids. I suspect you are too. I'm here because I've tried to maintain the status quo for women and mothers, but I no longer can. I suspect you can't either."

Some of the women laughed nervously. A few nodded and cheered. One sobbed out loud. And when Clem told them the story about Bartleby and her new anthem—*I prefer not to*—a woman in a red hat nearly tumbled backward into the snow. "I could never say that to my husband," she said.

"I didn't think I could either," Clem said. "Come on, I live in a house of cards. I believed that if I said *I prefer not to* and I stopped making sure each card stayed in place, everything would come crashing down." The women were nodding. Each had her own house of cards. "But I'll tell you what, now that I have started to say it to my husband, I know something I didn't know before. Yes, it's the thing he's needed to hear all his life, but more importantly, it's the thing I've needed to say for just as long."

The women chuckled.

"Let's practice," Clem said. There was power in togetherness. "On my count. Three, two, one." She paused and pointed at the women.

"I prefer not to," they whispered, although one woman in the front belted it out like she was the lead singer in a band.

"Now, come on," Clem said. "I know these four little words are terrifying, but we're here to build our power."

The women nodded vigorously.

Clem repeated the exercise four more times. "On my count. Three, two, one."

"I prefer not to!"

"Once more!"

Each time, the response grew a little stronger. And when the women were loud enough to draw the attention of the men shoveling in a nearby parking lot, Clem asked each to share one thing to which they'd most like to say *I prefer not to*. This part was predictably easy.

"I forgot my book. Can you bring it to school?" one woman said.

"Can you wash my white shirt by tomorrow?" said another.

"We're out of peanut butter," a third said. "Can you run to the store?"

"I need you to work on Saturday."

"I'm hungry. Feed me."

"Can you unclog the sink?"

"The deadline is tomorrow."

"Can you drop this off at the post office?"

Astrid surprised Clem. "I have to admit," she said when it was her turn, "I almost didn't come to this gathering today because I don't have a husband or wife. I don't have a partner or kids. It's only me, so at first glance, it would seem I have no one to whom I need to say *I prefer not to*. But, Clementine, as I sat with your email, I realized how much I need to say this to myself."

The fake southern accent was gone from Astrid's voice, and the other women were leaning in to listen exactly as Anna's friends had when Janna was reading "Bartleby, the Scrivener."

"I realized," Astrid continued, "that when my internal voice says, *Hide*, because I believe I shouldn't take up space, I need to say, *I prefer not to*. When my internal voice says, *Keep your mouth shut*, because I believe I don't deserve to participate in the conversation, I need to say, *I prefer not to*. And when my internal voice says, *Astrid Green, you need to stay on the sidelines*, I need to say, *I prefer not to*."

When Astrid finished speaking, the women began clapping. One even said, "Amen."

Recognizing the power of the moment, Clem went right into another call-and-response. "On my count," she said. "Three, two, one." She paused and jabbed her finger at the sky.

"I prefer not to!" the women yelled, this time so loudly that one of the men in the parking lot dropped his shovel with a clatter.

Right then, Clem caught sight of the Channel 5 TV van cruising past the park. Amanda Chen was in town. *Damn.*

At first Clem figured she was looking for her, but then she saw the van pass without pause. They must be heading for the library.

Clem ended the meeting by having each woman promise they'd use *I prefer not to* at least once that week. Her jitters were gone. Her purpose was becoming clearer as she realized the enormity of what she was doing. Clementine Crane was going to change the world.

CHAPTER SEVENTEEN

The Dangers of Dodgeball

The next morning, with all five Cranes around the breakfast table, Clem plopped a jug of milk in front of Tor and tried out her new verb. "I am hot-flashing," she said.

She hoped by now he would feel, or at least feign, a bit of empathy for what she was going through. How could he not? Her suffering was dripping from her temples, right there in front of him.

Tor smirked, obviously more annoyed than empathetic. "Is there toast?" Any softness he'd shown after Georgia's passing had worn off.

Clem wiped her forehead with a dish towel, then smirked back. "Sure, honey," she said. She yanked a piece from the toaster, smeared enough butter on it to make Tor's heart clench, and wondered if there was a way to poison toast.

"Here," she said, handing him the plate.

Tor took it and walked out of the room. Moments later, when her stomach started to roll, Clem cleared her throat and repeated her words. "All right, everyone, I'm hot-flashing," she said. Sweat was dribbling into her eyes, and her armpits were soaked. She checked her reflection in the toaster. Red cheeks. Red nose. Red neck. The boys recoiled and dropped their eyes.

Clem fumed. Why didn't anyone care? Was this hot-flash thing too personal? Too revealing? Did it prove she wasn't invincible? Did it show her vulnerability?

When the flush crawled from her cheeks to her forehead, Clem groaned and whispered, "Help." She leaned her forearms on the counter.

"Mom!" Anna said. "Stop the drama! We do not need to experience this *with* you. Go to your room if you need to 'hot-flash.'" She made air quotes above her head.

Why in the world had society made this thing something to hide? If Clem had pulled a muscle, the kids would be helping out, jumping up to get the toast or pour the juice. That had been proven. She'd pulled all kinds of muscles over the years, even broken her wrist. The kids had been more than happy to lend a hand. But now that this perimenopause thing was unfolding, they were dismissive, unkind, and unwilling to help.

"Mom," Anna said, "does every single thing have to be about you? Do we really need to focus all our attention on you? Could we, for once, focus on me for a single brief moment?"

The irony of this statement eluded Anna, but Clem laughed out loud. When she did, Anna hopped up, muttered something under her breath, then stomped upstairs, raging on about her parents, the unfairness of the world, the horribleness of her family, and the degradation she suffered at the hands of all.

"Good god," Clem said.

The boys finished their breakfast in silence, then pushed away from the table. "Homework," they both said, but Clem knew that was a big fat lie. They were going to spend their Saturday gaming on their computers with their buddies. Clem often intervened, enforcing the homework-first rule, but she was out of energy. Let Tor handle it. "I prefer not to," she whispered.

With a cup of coffee, she checked on the *Finding Frankie* fundraiser. They'd now raised nearly three thousand two hundred dollars. Without reaching out to Bathsheba for direction, she turned off the donations. Enough was enough.

Minutes later, Clem's phone rang. It was the funeral home. Likely calling to tell her that Georgia's ashes were ready. She stared, letting it ring until the call went to voicemail. She wasn't ready to pick up Georgia in an urn. She wasn't sure she ever would be.

Then her phone pinged. Tor. From upstairs.

Help me look for my green sweater?

I prefer not to.

Later that day, Dr. Sheffield nodded when he entered the exam room. "Clementine, you're back. And on a Saturday."

"I am."

"Still having hot flashes?"

Clem stared. "Still? I was here only a few weeks ago."

"And?"

"And you told me hot flashes are likely to last two to ten years."

"And?"

"Two to ten years have not passed."

"And?"

"Why else would I be here?"

"So, you are still having hot flashes?"

Good god. Why hadn't she ever noticed what a moron this guy was? "Yes, Dr. Sheffield, I am still having hot flashes. Would I be here if I weren't?" Her phone buzzed, but she ignored it.

"I don't know the answer to that, Clementine. I don't read minds."

Condescending prick.

"Do your hot flashes continue to be as intense as you described?" he asked.

Clem huffed. "Yes, Dr. Sheffield, my hot flashes are as hot as they were a few weeks ago. In fact, I'd say they're hotter."

Dr. Sheffield typed a note on his computer. "Any specific questions?"

"Absolutely," Clem said. "Is there a name for that feeling I get right before a hot flash?" Her phone buzzed, but she didn't take it out of her purse.

"What feeling? Describe it."

"Do you remember playing dodgeball in elementary school gym class?"

Dr. Sheffield looked up from his computer. "I do."

"Well, there was this kid in my fourth-grade class. Max Walden. He hated me, and every time we played dodgeball, he maneuvered himself onto the opposite team, then spent forty minutes pelting me with balls as hard as he could. He was strong. And relentless."

"He had a crush on you."

Clem imagined pulling her cymbals from her purse. *Clang, clang, clang.*

"He didn't have a crush on me, Dr. Sheffield. That is not why boys are violent to girls. Max Walden hated me."

"Why would a fourth grader hate you so much he wanted to hurt you?"

"There are a lot of possible reasons. Because he was a bully. Because no one told him to cut the shit. Because that behavior was modeled for him by his father or grandfather or uncle or some other outstanding man in his life. Because he saw it on television. Shall I go on?"

Dr. Sheffield shook his head.

Clem's phone buzzed. She continued to ignore it.

"One day I got distracted, and Max Walden took that split-second opportunity to hurl a ball at me from only a few feet away. I wasn't prepared, and when it hit me in the stomach, I flew backward and slammed into a couple of kids behind me. We all went down like dominoes. The air was knocked out of me, and I couldn't take a breath until the gym teacher whacked me on the back. When I was finally able to breathe, I couldn't get up off the floor for twenty minutes. I lay there with balls whizzing over my head and Max Walden howling with laughter."

Dr. Sheffield nodded absently. "And what does this have to do with your hot flashes, Clementine?"

Boy, this guy sure needed things spelled out for him, didn't he? Had he heard a word she'd said?

"Let me connect the dots for you, Dr. Sheffield. I get the same feeling right before a hot flash. It's like Max Walden has hurled a ball at my stomach and turned me into a heaving lump."

The look on Dr. Sheffield's face made Clem feel like she'd told him she'd given birth to a cactus.

"Clementine," he said slowly, eyebrows slightly raised, "you should probably see your PCP for this. There could be something else going on."

"I don't think so. I'm pretty sure this feeling and my hot flashes are directly related."

When her phone buzzed again, Clem yanked it out of her purse. Anna.

MOM

MOM

MOM

"Impossible." Dr. Sheffield looked at his watch and stood.

MOM

MOM

MOM

MOM

MOM

"Listen," Dr. Sheffield said, "I've had patients describe a buzzy feeling they get before a hot flash, and I call this an aura. Sure, women experience these differently, but I've never heard anything like what you've described."

MOM I NEED 2 TALK 2 U

"*Aura* is way too pretty a word for what I feel," Clem said.

MOMMOMMOMMOMMOM

"What do *you* call it?"
"A Max Walden."

MOM I NEED 2 TALK 2 U

"One minute, Dr. Sheffield. My daughter is having some kind of emergency."
Clem texted back.

Anna. What's the matter? Is everything ok?

MOM CHECK TIKTOK NOW

"This all seems a bit extreme, Clementine."
"It absolutely isn't," Clem said. "I thought that after I was done birthing children, I'd only be bothered by periods and the great joys that come along with those. This hot-flash thing is a horror all its own."
"Clementine, I have never in all my years practicing medicine heard any woman describe the feeling before a hot flash this way."
"Then, Dr. Sheffield," Clem matched his condescending tone, "you clearly have not talked to enough women, asked the right questions, or listened attentively. Because I am damn sure I am not the only one feeling this way."

MOM

Clem clicked on her TikTok app. When it opened, Clem swiped past the ad and saw the red number on her profile icon. It was over a hundred thousand.

"What the hell?" she said.

DO U C IT MOM

Dr. Sheffield looked at his watch. "I need to move on to my next patient, but I'd like to make a few suggestions."

"Finally!" Clem said, looking up from her phone. "What can I do to make this better?"

"Let's go over lifestyle changes," Dr. Sheffield said.

Clem rolled her eyes. "Lifestyle changes?"

"Yes, these are the best ways to mitigate the issues."

Clem bit her cheek.

"First, avoid alcohol."

"What?" Clem said.

"Avoid alcohol."

"Like rubbing alcohol?" She was confused.

"No, wine and beer and hard liquor. Booze."

Clem stared at him. "I have three teenagers, Dr. Sheffield. Four if you count my husband. There's a massive animal clopping around outside my house. I don't know what it is. A wayward moose. An alien. A woolly mammoth. Heather of the Weather has promised we will get at least—*at least*—a few more feet of snow this season. My best friend in the whole world recently died. And you—Dr. Sheffield—are suggesting I avoid booze. Is that all you've got for me?"

"Not at all," Dr. Sheffield continued. "Instead of booze, drink cold liquids when you feel you're on the verge of a flash."

Clementine stared at him. Avoid alcohol? Drink cold liquids? "Lemonade, perhaps?" she said.

"That would be a very good choice," Dr. Sheffield said. He was serious. She was not.

Clem wanted to spit at him like one of those deadly vipers Evan was studying in biology.

"And," Dr. Sheffield continued, "consider taking up a cold sport."

"A cold sport?"

"Yes, a sport you do in the cold. Bobsledding, skating, skiing. That kind of thing."

Clementine looked left and right. "I'm still in a medical doctor's office, correct?"

"Excuse me?"

"You're still a doctor, right? You didn't lose your credentials in the last week, did you?"

"Where are you going with this, Clementine?" Dr. Sheffield stood.

"When I come here, I expect medical advice, not lifestyle suggestions. I can get those on the internet. I expected *Let's try a hormone supplement*, not *Drink lemonade and join the bobsledding team.*" Clem stood too.

"Clementine, hormone replacement therapy is known to cause cancer. There is not enough research available to make it a viable option."

Clem grunted. "First of all, Dr. Sheffield, you never even presented it as an option. If I hadn't done my own research, I'd know nothing about it."

"I'm the doctor, Clementine."

"And I'm the woman living in fiery hell." She could tell from his expression that Dr. Sheffield was not convinced.

"And second?" he said.

"From what I've read, that cancer theory has been proven wrong for most women. I think it's time you jump more deeply into the newer research that is available."

Dr. Sheffield cleared his throat. "And I, Clementine, think it's time for you to choose your clothes more wisely." He waggled a hand at her sweater. "Buy breathable fabrics and avoid heavy sweaters."

Clem looked down. She was wearing her favorite black pullover. The same one she'd worn every winter for the past ten or so years. The one she loved as much as Tor loved his hideous green one. It had a high neck, shaped waist, and shiny silver buttons at the wrists. It was the softest, warmest sweater she'd ever owned, and it fit perfectly. The kids always said they knew it was truly winter the first time she put it on each season. "Are you at all embarrassed," she said, "that this is the only advice you have to offer your patients?"

"I can also tell you," Dr. Sheffield continued, "that many of my patients have successfully reduced the intensity of hot flashes by being on time."

Was he sneering at her?

"Are you serious?" Clem said.

"Yes, I am," Dr. Sheffield said. "Being on time instead of racing to an appointment or a meeting. Women in the throes of hot flashes need to make sure they leave enough time to get to where they're going without rushing." He looked pointedly at her, knowing that she'd been late to numerous appointments over the years, including the one they were currently wrapping up.

Clem scratched her head dramatically. "Who, Dr. Sheffield, are these magical women you reference? Fairies with no children? Wives who've secretly devoured their husbands? Witches with the ability to wave a wand and make their lives orderly?"

"No, Clementine, there's nothing magical about these women," Dr. Sheffield said. "They are simply organized."

Clem's rage was building, and she knew she had to get out of there before she did something illegal. "What?" she said. "You can't be serious? Most women I know, including myself, run like maniacs from one obligation to another. Not because we're disorganized but because we have so damn much to do and so little assistance from our partners and the patriarchal world in which we live. I don't know a single woman who arrives on time for anything."

That wasn't quite true. Bathsheba Wheaton was on time for everything. As was Prudence Smith, the mother of one of the girls on Anna's hockey team. But they had their own issues.

"Clementine, I'm talking about the women who are smart enough to realize they must get an early start on things in order to reduce the intensity of the hot flash."

Clem swallowed hard. "Smart enough?" Her voice rose an octave. "What do smarts have to do with this? All humans with uteruses get hot flashes when they hit perimenopause. Am I correct?"

Dr. Sheffield nodded. "Not all, but yes, most. To varying degrees."

"This includes those you consider smart as well as those you do not. Correct?"

Dr. Sheffield nodded again, more slowly this time. Why had she never noticed Sheffield's audacious pomposity? Why had she let him birth her children? Why had she ever taken his advice about anything? If she could, she'd stuff all three kids back up her hoo-hoo and have another doctor—a female doctor—deliver them.

Clem's phone buzzed. Meghan.

Staff meeting in 30. Hurry. Awesome craft today!

If Clem didn't leave Dr. Sheffield's office in five minutes, she'd be late.

"What I'm saying is," the doctor said, "that there are women who are smart enough to know how to help themselves."

Clementine tightened her fists and eyed the speculum on the desk. Giving this bozo a black eye would be so satisfying. But she resisted. A battery charge on top of a fish-napping charge would not look good in front of a judge. Instead of striking him, she said, "Are you implying that being smart has something to do with whether or not you have hot flashes?"

"Not whether or not you *have* them, Clementine. Whether or not you want to do something to minimize their effects."

There was a knock on the door. Clem knew it was a nurse who'd heard their raised voices.

"But you're saying it's smart women who make the correct choices? The rest of us half-wits who have a glass or two of wine on Friday evenings, refuse to take up bobsledding, and wear sweaters in the middle of the snowiest winter on record in New England are a bunch of dimwits. Do I have this right?"

Dr. Sheffield sighed. "You're twisting my words, Clementine."

"Oh, I'm not, Dr. Sheffield."

Dr. Sheffield's mouth wriggled in a way that let Clem know he was frustrated. She'd seen it numerous times over the past fifteen years. When a nurse flubbed a blood draw, when she'd had to bring one of her toddlers along to her annual exam, when she'd refused an epidural then shrieked her way through Anna's delivery.

"I'm not saying that rushing *causes* hot flashes. I'm saying that by not rushing, you can reduce the effects."

"And how the living hell are most women supposed to stop rushing?"

There was another knock on the door. "Come in," Dr. Sheffield said.

As Clem predicted, a nurse opened the door and stuck her head into the room. "Is everything okay in here? Dr. Sheffield, do you need anything?"

Dr. Sheffield nodded. "I need to move on to my next patient."

"That's fine," Clem said, checking her watch. "I need to move on to my next male blockhead. I'm sure there's one around the corner." Her phone buzzed. "Any other tidbits of wisdom before I try to get to a work meeting in twenty-five minutes?"

"Nothing else."

"It's a good thing you went to school for all those years, Doc," Clem said. "Your advice is priceless." She moved exaggeratedly to the door as if she were swimming through gelatin. "How's this, Dr. Sheffield? Slow enough for you?"

"Clementine."

"Dr. Sheffield."

"I hope you decide to consider my suggestions."

She turned, looked him in the eye, and said, "I prefer not to."

This time as she raced through the waiting room, Clem didn't hesitate. She approached every woman in the place, pregnant or not. She gave a quick description of her mission, explained the I PREFER NOT TO movement, took their contact information, and encouraged them to follow her on TikTok. All women, she decided then and there, needed to know what was ahead for them. In the same way she'd needed to know about periods before Wallace Wright cornered her in the library.

Once outside, Clem's phone buzzed.

MOM

Okay, okay!

Clem finally clicked on her profile. Over 122,000 people had liked her most recent post. She had nearly as many followers.

Holy shit.

CHAPTER EIGHTEEN

Going Live

Inspired, Clem hopped in her car, tuned in to TikTok, and blurted out the experience she'd had with Dr. Sheffield. She told the dodgeball story for the second time that day, then turned it back to her viewers. "So, hot-flashers around the world," she said, "give me a one- or two-word description for the feeling you get right before a hot flash? I'm now calling it a Max Walden."

The responses streamed in:

tidal wave
tremor
foreshock
clarity
vibration
prickle
entry into the abyss

flare
fusillade
hocus pocus
tornado
detonation
rankle
convulsion
witchery

All were good, but the last one really caught her. *Witchery.* The TikToker? Amanda Chen, Channel 5.

Ten minutes late to the staff meeting, Clem had to play catchup. On the table, the sandwich board read *Make a powerful animal*, and the team was already hard at work. Meghan had drawn an outline of Frankie and was gluing orange sequins onto the paper as scales. Keisha was sketching Tripod, her three-legged cat, and Victor was cutting out wings for some horrifying pterodactyl-like creature.

Clem thought about making Hagrid, because, truly, there wasn't a more powerful pup on Earth. He'd been godlike since he was a wee furball. Dragging the kids on the sled. Racing them on their bikes. Leaping over them in the yard. Corralling them when a car zoomed down the road. Barking for Clem if they pushed a dangerous idea too far. Hagrid was the epitome of wisdom and power, but because he was also big, hairy, slobbery, and often drowsy, he had fit into many craft assignments over the years. He'd had his time in the spotlight.

Then she considered the *crunch, crunch, crunch* she'd been hearing in the backyard. The woolly mammoth. But because that was something she'd only told Georgia about, it was still too private. Too tender.

Instead, she searched *cow moose* on her phone, then cut the shape from brown construction paper. Four legs long enough to move easily through three feet of snow. Hooves the size of dinner plates. Muscular body. Humped shoulders. Bulbous nose. Triangular ears that poked out and up.

The moose, she read, was the largest member of the deer family. The Cervidae family, a herd of cloven-hoofed ungulates. Details like this delighted Clem, which was why years before, when faced with the inevitable question of what she was going to do with her life, she'd chosen library work. What could be better than spending all day in a place where questions were asked, explored, and sometimes even answered?

"Come on, Clementine," Bathsheba said, "off the phone. You know the rules. No research for crafts."

"Oh, you come on, Bathsheba," Clementine said. "We are employed by a library. Libraries believe in research."

"I believe in research, Clem," Bathsheba said, "but not for our weekly craft."

"I'm not doing research anyway," Clem said. "Anna forgot something and I'm texting her."

"Liar," Meghan whispered.

Clem kicked her under the table.

Bath interrupted. "Clem, have you gotten any leads from the GoFundMe? Now that the money has been raised, I imagine the perpetrator may be ready to come forward."

Clem cleared her throat. "Actually, I haven't checked the email address I created for that. I'll do it later today."

Bath looked sharply at her. "Clem, this is the most important aspect of your job right now. We need you to do everything you can to find that fish. Please check the account as soon as we finish here."

Clem nodded, then pasted a light-brown piece of paper under the moose's throat.

"What's that?" Victor asked, pointing at the addition.

"A dewlap."

"What's a dewlap?"

"A fold of extra skin."

"Why do they have that?"

"It's a mystery."

Victor got quiet for a moment, then said, "So your moose has a dewlap but no antlers?"

"It's a cow moose, Victor. Not a bull moose."

"Antlers are cool. You should have made a bull."

"Not as cool as what a cow moose has," Clem said.

"Victor," Bathsheba said, "you know the rules. No questions." The team was permitted to make positive comments only, as Bath believed that creativity should be applauded, not critiqued.

Victor pretended not to hear. "What does a cow moose have, Clementine?" he said.

"You'll see." Clem grabbed a piece of white paper from the pile, cut a triangle from it, drew a thin brown line down the center, and pasted it onto the moose's backside. She smiled and held it up. "Ta-da!"

"Ooh," said Victor, shimmying his shoulders.

Everyone's eyes got big. They looked from Clem to Bathsheba.

"Clem," Bathsheba said, "what have you put on the moose's rump?"

Clem knew that Bath was breaking her own rule. "I'm sorry, Bath," Clem said, "is that a question?"

Bath cleared her throat. "Yes, it is, Clem. I'm breaking my own rule. Please enlighten us. What is the white triangle you've pasted on the moose's butt? It looks like a menstrual pad."

Jing giggled.

Clem held up her moose. "This, Bathsheba, is what distinguishes the cow from the bull. It is a white vulva patch."

Keisha burst out laughing, and Victor swallowed audibly.

"And why have you put"—Bath cleared her throat—"one on your moose?"

"That's how she's built, Bath. I didn't create the animal. I'm making a replica. For the craft. You always tell us to depict animals as they truly are. This is how kids learn, you say. Right?" The confidence she'd gained during the gathering in the town center—and during that interaction with Dr. Sheffield—was beginning to show.

Bathsheba sighed. "Yes, but this looks a little—"

"A little what?" Clem said.

"A little too graphic."

"For whom?"

"For our audience."

Three weeks before, Clem wouldn't have dreamed of putting a white vulva patch on a moose during the team craft activity. And she wouldn't have talked back to Bath. Instead, like the well-practiced people pleaser she'd always been, she would have seethed silently, then mouthed a few not-so-nice words behind her back. Now, here she was, making an anatomically correct moose and standing up for her right to do so. What was happening to her? She'd spent so much time trying to make sure others were happy that she'd never actually connected with what she truly thought and believed. Every experience had been filtered through the question *How do I behave or engage so this other person feels comfortable and gets their needs satisfied?* It was such a limited way of existing in the world. Exhausting too.

Of course, this hadn't been intentional. She hadn't woken each day as a kid saying, *Mom, today I will be the golden retriever of the universe.* It just happened.

"Clem," Bath said, "how about taking Victor's suggestion and putting a set of antlers on the moose instead?"

"You don't allow us to make suggestions on each other's work, Bath. We've lived by that rule for years."

"Sometimes it's okay to break a rule," Bath said.

Clem stared at her. "Since when?"

"Since now," Bath said.

Clem shook her head. "The cow moose does not have antlers, Bath. It's female, and its distinguishing characteristic is—"

"I know, I know," Bathsheba said, "the white vulva patch."

When the word *vulva* popped out of Bath's mouth, Clem clapped. "See?" she said. "It's not hard to call things as they are."

"Clementine," Bath said, "I hope you are not planning to show this to the children?"

Clem picked up her moose, trotted it across the table, and wiggled its vulva patch at Keisha. It was silly and ridiculous, but Clem was done with Bath's strict governance. "Don't worry, Bath," she said, "I have no intention of showing my anatomically correct cow moose to the kiddos. It will live in my cubicle, right next to Craft Clem."

That evening, still seething about the moose incident and Dr. Sheffield's bobsledding suggestion, Clem went live on TikTok for the first time, dueting a video of two bobsledders hurtling down a track. Terrified of being judged, she almost chickened out. Going live was a serious step. But when she thought of Georgia sashaying fearlessly through Pet-O-Rama in a bunny costume, she knew she had to be at least as brave as that.

"Hello, hot-flashers, overwhelmed moms, mental-load managers, and pissed-off people with periods," she said to the camera, the salutation that was quickly becoming her signature greeting. "I'm a forty-four-year-old hot-flashing mom with three kids, a full-time job, and a husband who doesn't know what the phrase *mental load* means. Welcome to I PREFER NOT TO."

On one side of her head, Clem's soaking-wet hair was pressed flat; on the other, her curls were poking up like clumps of fresh parsley. Her face, gleaming red, was puffy and bright, and she was huffing as if she'd run up a steep hill. Her blue saggy tank top had sweat stains around the neckline and across the belly. She looked like hell, but because this was the most honest look at a hot flash TikTok had ever seen, people began joining in droves.

"Earlier today," Clem said to the camera, "my gynecologist suggested that in order to manage my hot flashes, I should take up bobsledding." She pushed her face close to the camera and said, "Bobsledding, people!"

She could see comments pouring in, but because this was her first-ever live, she could only focus on talking, not responding to viewers.

"People, look closely at this video," she said, referencing the bobsledding video she'd dueted. "These bobsledders are traveling down this track at approximately ninety miles per hour." Her eyes widened. "The track is one mile long and five feet wide, give or take a few inches. It features sixteen curves and a vertical drop of nearly four hundred feet. Thanks to gravity, kinetic energy, and other physics phenomena I know nothing about, these bobsledders would have covered that distance in less than a minute, except this happened."

She paused, looked calmly at the camera, and waited a few seconds for the video to catch up.

On the next turn, the bobsled flipped onto its side, and throughout the rest of the ride, the sled and its riders bounced upside down and sideways on the icy track, still traveling at full speed. "As you can see," Clem said, "the bobsledders, if they survive this hell, will most definitely suffer the effects of excessive force and vibration, leading to what experts call 'sled head.'" Clem leaned close to the camera. "Also known as concussions," she whispered conspiratorially.

She sat back. "I'd gone to my doctor for medical advice on how to alleviate my hot flashes. I'd done a bit of research and learned about hormone replacement therapy. I wanted to learn more. I needed my doctor to be supportive, empathetic, and smart. All I got was condescension and lifestyle advice."

Clem could see that the number of viewers was now in the thousands. "So, what did I say to Dr. Doesn't-Have-a-Clue when he proposed I take up bobsledding?"

Clem leaned back. Herman Melville, Bartleby, and the decremental extinction of a woman's spirit swished through her brain.

"I prefer not to."

Recent novels that reference food in the title! Go!

Samantha always came up with the best Snowstorm Lit topics.

Victor jumped in first: The Coincidence of Coconut Cake by Amy Reichert.

Meghan was quick to follow with The Lager Queen of Michigan by J. Ryan Stradal.

Wrong state in the title! Minnesota!

Clem: *Sourdough by Robin Sloan.*

That one drew a thumbs-up from Jade, who loved bread of any kind. She then added Charmaine Wilkerson's Black Cake.

It took Clem a moment to think of Jennifer Dugan's *Hot Dog Girl*, but once she did, she knew Meghan was going to be jealous she'd thought of it first.

Keisha leapt in: The Tea Girl of Hummingbird Lane.

A good one, but because she hadn't shared the author, Samantha gonged her, then shared Lisa See!

Jade threw one into the mix: The Dinner List by Rebecca Serle.

That one got lots of clapping hands but then got gonged as well. A reference to dinner wasn't specific enough.

Walter, who'd been quiet at first, popped in: Soy Sauce for Beginners by Kirstin Chen.

Victor: Freedom Stew by Tami Charles.

Freedom Soup, not stew!

It was down to Walter and Clem, but just as Clem was about to send in a winner, she got a text from Tor.

Why do you have fish food in your bedside drawer?

Clem jumped up from the couch. Her bedside drawer? What was he doing in her bedside drawer? *What are you doing in my bedside drawer?*

Looking for my green sweater.

In my nightstand?

Crap, crap, crap. If he was looking in her nightstand, was he also trying to look in her closet? She couldn't remember if she'd remembered to lock the door. Every once in a while, she forgot. The last thing she needed was Tor discovering Frankie. How would she explain that? She thundered up the stairs, yelling, "Tor? Tor?"

"What?" he yelled back.

She burst into their room. "Tor, stop!"

He was standing next to her side of the bed, the jar of fish food in his hand. Every hair in place, no sweat dripping down his temple. Next to her, he looked like a runway model. Clem remembered her mother's quiet shrug when she asked what happened to boys when they hit puberty. The way she explained about erections, voice changes, but little else. Sure, there were developments for boys, but compared to what girls experienced, they were nothing. Was the same true for hitting midlife?

"Good god, Clem. Why are you running up here like some kind of wronged wolverine?" he said. "It's your nightstand."

She snatched the fish food out of his hand. "I don't appreciate you going through my things," she said. "And don't compare me to a wolverine." She added that last bit even though she was feeling very much like a tenacious, territorial mustelid.

"I didn't go through anything, Clem. I opened the drawer and peeked in. The fish food was right on top, and since we don't have a fish, I got curious."

Clem tried to settle her nerves. "There's no need for you to look in my stuff for your green sweater," she said. "It's not there. I don't have it. I've told you that." She eyed her closet door. It was closed, but she couldn't tell if it was locked or not. "I have this"—she waved the jar of food at Tor—"because I miss Frankie, okay? I miss that silly little fish, and this food reminds me of her. It makes me feel better about things."

Tor was looking at her like she'd just landed from Mars. "Fish food makes you feel better about things?"

"You wouldn't understand," she snapped.

Tor moved toward the door. "Fine, Clem. Whatever. But where could my green sweater be? Things don't disappear into thin air."

Clem thought about Frankie swimming peacefully in the closet a few feet away. "I don't know. Maybe some things disappear, then reappear."

"What are you talking about?"

"Nothing," she said. "Nothing at all." She really needed to keep her mouth shut. "In fact, I need to follow up on leads from Frankie's GoFundMe, so if you don't mind—" She gestured toward the door.

Tor huffed out of the room, and a minute later, Clem jiggled the knob on the closet door. It was unlocked. She *had* forgotten. Crap. What if he had opened that door? What if he had continued looking for his sweater? What if he'd kept searching instead of texting her? Her heart was racing so fast she couldn't catch a breath.

She charged into the closet, locked the door behind her, and grabbed her laptop. She pulled up the GoFundMe, sorted through the donations, and saw Local-Fish-Guy had given a second time just before she ended the campaign. It had to be Douglass.

When she opened the affiliated mailbox, she found dozens of emails from kookadoodles who suspected Frankie had been abducted by aliens or was the victim of a government conspiracy. A few suggested the kids were the culprits, or even one of the tambourine-toting protesters. A handful were from "anti-tankers" who didn't have any theories about possible fish-nappers but needed someone to know that fish deserved to be free. Clem had deleted nearly all emails when she saw one from Local-Fish-Guy, the same Local-Fish-Guy who'd donated twice. The subject line read "Inside Job." Clem's heart seized as she opened the email. "If I were investigating this case," she read, "I'd start with the library employees." Clem's finger hovered over the "Delete" button. It would be wrong, but who would know?

She leaned back, stared out the window, and took note of the single candle Georgia had put in her window after Henry died. It was the battery-operated kind that would shine until it ran out of juice. "Georgia," Clem whispered. "I miss you so much."

As she moved her finger away from the "Delete" key, Clem's phone pinged. Samantha had awarded the trophy to Walter. Game over.

CHAPTER NINETEEN
Throw the Rock

As planned, Astrid sold Georgia's house to a young family that had been trying to buy in Clem's neighborhood for over a year. Two moms, two kids, two dogs. The closing was a few weeks out, giving Astrid time to empty the house and make a few necessary repairs. Georgia had been easygoing about many things—"Donate my worldly goods to people who need them most"—but she'd set aside a few special items for the Crane family.

Evan got her Volvo, which they'd be able to drive once Tor figured out how to pay for classes. Brewster got her season tickets to Broadway in Boston. And thanks to Georgia's generosity, Anna would be going to eleven Bruins games a season for the next five years. Tor got Georgia's kayak.

"How about you, Mom?" Anna asked when Georgia's lawyer sent the list of who got what. "What did she leave you?"

Tears welled in Clem's eyes. "Her bedroom set."

Tor smiled.

It wasn't really a surprise. Clem had loved the set since the first time she'd gone into Georgia's house. Mahogany with little gremlins carved into the legs of each piece. It was whimsical and mischievous, like Georgia. "We'll put it in the basement until I'm emotionally ready to move it upstairs," Clem said. She had no idea how long that would take.

After the bobsledding live on TikTok, Clem had nearly two hundred thousand followers and hundreds of comments from men who were morally offended by her words. How dare she? She knew nothing about the challenges men faced in the world, they insisted. And if she were serious about wanting to cool off, they said, taking up a cold sport sounded like sage advice.

Clem was irritated but motivated. It turned out that mocking men for their patriarchal crap was wildly satisfying and refreshingly uniting. Women around the world were supporting her by the thousands and claiming *I prefer not to* as their new anthem.

To prove Dr. Sheffield (and men around the world) wrong, Clem decided to try a cold sport. If nothing else, it would make great TikTok content. Her daughter, however, was not thrilled.

"I'm going to a women's curling class tonight," she told Anna during dinner.

"What? Where?"

"The rink."

"The ice rink?"

"Yes."

"*My* ice rink?"

"Technically not *your* ice rink, but yes, the rink where you play hockey."

"Mom, you can't do that. The ice is mine."

"I'm not playing hockey, Anna. Curling is a totally different thing. This is for amateurs. Not even amateurs. A bunch of moms trying to stand up on ice and push a stone for an hour."

"No, Mom!" Anna's voice ratcheted up. "You can't do this."

"Anna, how can this upset you?"

"Mom, the ice is mine. The rink is mine. You're everywhere else. For god's sake, Mom, you're even in my dreams."

Clem smiled.

"Oh, don't go all gaga gooey on me, Mom. I should have been more specific. You're in my nightmares."

Clem groaned and dropped her head on the kitchen table. Anna's teen-mean was so different from Evan's, whose steady, robust indifference coupled with the cold shoulder was aggravating but reliable. Anna's dagger-sharp and always evolving cruelty never failed to cut in a way that stung all day and into the night. Clem was pretty sure it was a woman thing. Somewhere in the depths of her DNA, Anna knew that someday she'd be right where Clem was, in the throes of perimenopause, drowning miserably in her own sweat. Clem remembered the realization that she'd come to during the bake sale: Things would have to break before they got better.

"I'm going to the curling class, Anna," Clem said firmly. "My gynecologist told me I should take up a cold sport to counteract the hot flashes, and I'm going to give it a try, even though I think it's a bunch of hooey."

Anna rolled her eyes, then glared. "Mom, I do not want to hear about your gynecologist or your hot flashes."

Clem sighed.

"And, Mom, you better not mention me to anyone. Do not tell them you're my mother. Do not tell them I skate or play hockey. Pretend you're new to town, that you recently moved here from Tampa."

"Tampa, Florida?"

"That's the one."

"Why in the world would I move from sunny Tampa to New England? I hate winter."

"Mom"—Anna's voice rose an octave—"you didn't *really* move to New England from Tampa. That's your cover story."

"All right, but nearly every person at the rink already knows me. They've seen me with you for years. I work the concession stand during games."

"Then wear a disguise. A hat. Glasses. That stupid giraffe costume you used to wear with Georgia. Pretend you're someone else. Anyone but my mom."

Clem bowed her head. "They'll never believe me, sweetie."

"Try, Mom. Please." Then she stomped off to her room.

That evening, Clem went to Anna's rink—for herself this time. She changed into running shoes, then slipped a gripper onto the bottom of her left sole as instructed by the guy at the secondhand sporting goods store. It released with a *thwck*. Then she pulled a Teflon slider onto her right shoe and stood. Both felt odd as she walked across the buoyant rubber floor. Just as she was about to step onto the ice, a woman blocked her way.

"Did you read the safety rules?" the woman said.

"No," Clem said. "I didn't know there were any." Good gracious, it was curling. How unsafe could it be?

"Of course there are."

"Who are you?" Clem said.

"The coach," the woman said. "Please read the rules before stepping onto the ice." She turned and pointed to a bunch of women gathered around a poster on the wall.

Clem nudged her way into the group and read quietly, "'One, always step onto the ice gripper-foot first. Never slider-foot first.'"

The first picture in the three-frame illustration showed a person stepping onto the ice, slider foot first, as Clementine had been about to do. The second showed the person flailing—suspended in midair, legs high. And the third showed the person flat on their ass.

Ouch.

"'Two,'" Clem read, "'always step off the ice with slider-foot first. Never the gripper-foot first.'"

Things were starting to make sense.

"'Three,'" she read, "'slider-foot is last on, first off.'" She turned to the woman next to her. "They're serious about this which-foot-first business, aren't they?"

"Are you new to curling?" the woman said.

Clem nodded.

The woman chuckled. "You'll likely be serious about it soon enough too."

Clem walked back to the rink, raised her gripper foot to step onto the ice, and smiled at the coach. "First on, last off."

"Good. Let's get moving," the coach said. "Does everyone have their grippers on?"

All the women nodded. To prove she'd read the rules, Clem stomped her gripper foot. When she did, her slider foot scooted away, and she crashed hard on her bottom.

"You skipped the fourth rule," the coach said, looking down at her. "Wanda, what's the fourth rule?"

The woman named Wanda reached out a hand to help Clem up and said, "Keep both feet on the ice. Avoid running or hopping."

"Or stomping with your gripper foot," the coach added.

"Noted," Clem said. Her butt hurt like hell.

The coach divided the women into five groups of four. "Each of you will play a key role on your team," she said. She assigned positions: lead, second, third, and skip. "Together you're a rink." She paused, anticipating the question from Clem. "Yes, we're on a rink, but a curling team is also called a rink."

So much information to absorb.

"You're the lead of your team," she told Clem. "You throw the rock first."

Clem eyeballed the rock. "How heavy is that thing?"

"Forty-four pounds."

"And you want me to throw it?"

"No, no, no. In curling, to 'throw' means to slide."

Clementine nodded, thinking about the etymology of sycamore and the Keeper of Living Collections.

"Your goal is to slide the rock down the curling sheet," the coach said. "But first, you clean the rock." She knelt, tilted the rock back, and wiped the bottom with her glove. "Then you step onto the hack."

"The hack?" Clem asked.

"The hack is . . ." the coach began, pointing to the foothold embedded in the ice, but as she droned on, Clem realized she didn't care what a hack was. She didn't care about cleaning the rock. She was here to cool off. Nothing more.

Clem watched a woman on another team throw the rock with a smooth gliding motion. "That's what I need to do?" she asked.

"That's it," the coach said.

Clem knelt, dusted off the bottom of the rock, and set her foot on the hack. She was ready to push off and slide the rock, but right before she did, one of those awful gut-breaths grabbed her around the middle. She huffed and felt the heat start to build from the inside out. Dammit.

"Hold on," she said. "It's getting hot in here. I can't throw a rock while I'm this hot."

"Hot?" the coach said. "You haven't even done anything yet. It's actually quite cold in here."

Clem shook her head. "Wait." While she hadn't read the rules before coming to class, she had taken note of the advice to layer up. She stood, removed her hat and gloves, and set them off to the side.

"You're going to freeze," her skip said.

"Pretty sure I won't," Clem said. The skip was in her twenties.

She knelt and readied her foot in the hack but still couldn't breathe. "My god, it's like a sauna in here," she said. "Do they have the heat on?"

She stood, took off her jacket, then pulled her turtleneck over her head. She added both to the pile.

Wearing only a T-shirt, she knelt on the ice. All the women in the class were staring at her. They were bundled up like polar bears.

"Are you ready now?" the coach said. She sounded exasperated.

But as Clem was about to throw the rock, a woman on another team shouted, "Clementine? Clementine Crane? Anna Crane's mother? Is that you?"

Oh, shit.

Clem straightened up and grinned. "It is!" She completely forgot to offer up her cover story about having recently moved to town from Tampa. Anna was going to be irate.

"Hi. It's me. Helen. Angela's mom!"

Angela. She and Anna had been teammates for years.

"Hello, Helen! Good to see you. How's everything?"

"Good, good. Clementine, Anna is such an amazing hockey player. We all talk about how she'll be fighting off the college scouts soon."

Clem grimaced as the women in the group began to recognize her. Every hockey fan in town knew Anna and her stick.

The coach got in on it too. "You should have said something. I've been watching Anna play for years. Are you really her mother?" Her tone insinuated that clearly Anna hadn't gotten her finesse on the ice from Clementine.

But at this point, Clem couldn't answer either of them. Fire was bubbling up in her innards, and sweat was dripping down her stomach. Her elbows were sweating, and she felt oddly weak. With everyone watching, she pulled her T-shirt over her head. She was still wearing a tank top, but after that, only her bra was left. Helen was still smiling, but it was a bit strained now.

"Clementine?" the coach said. "Let's go ahead and get started. Time to throw."

Clem shook her head. "No," she said. "I prefer not to." She didn't give a hoot about throwing that rock across the icy field. All she cared about was cooling off. Ignoring the women jabbering on about Anna and hockey and college and D1 schools, she lifted the tank top over her head and tossed it aside. She stood facing them in her dingy, frayed bra.

"Clementine, what is happening here?" the coach said. "What are you doing?"

Through the hot-flash fog, Clem heard a whistle and a few whoops from the men's team practicing at the other end of the rink, then a jumble of *Is she okay?*s and *What's going on?*s from the women around her. Through the muddle of voices, she heard one thing that made sense: "I think she's having a hot flash."

She nodded, set her hands on her knees, and muttered, "Yes, yes," but still too hot to breathe properly, she did the only thing she could to feel better. She lay down flat on the ice, pressed her cheek to the frozen surface, and moaned. Finally, her body started to cool. Dr. Sheffield might not be such an imbecile after all, she thought. This cold sport was the best thing she'd experienced since the snowbank.

The next afternoon, Anna stormed into the kitchen carrying a bundle of clothes. "Mom," she said, "the ice manager left these for me after announcing over the loudspeaker during practice that my mother's clothes were waiting for me in the office."

"Anna, let me—" Clem said.

Anna threw the clothes at Clem's feet. "Mom," she said, "I asked you. I begged you. I pleaded with you not to embarrass me. And now you are the talk of the rink. Why? Why did you do this?"

"Honey—"

"Mom, don't *honey* me."

"Sweetheart—"

"Don't *sweetheart* me."

"Anna, listen to me."

"Mom, I will never listen to you. Not ever. How could you do this? You took off your clothes in the ice rink. Took them off! All the way off! In *my* ice rink. The place where I spend half my life. The place where every single person knows me."

"Anna, I don't know what you were told, but I did not take off *all* my clothes. I left on my pants and bra."

Anna's eyes popped. "And pants and bra are okay because . . ."

"Because I wasn't naked. Good god, I'm less covered up at the beach in the summer than I was in the rink."

"But you're *supposed* to be less covered up at the beach in the summer. People expect it. Everyone is uncovered. Was anyone else at the rink uncovered? Was anyone else wearing just a bra and pants?"

"No, but no one else was having a hot flash."

"Oh, for god's sake, Mom. Can you stop going on and on about the hot flashes? No one cares. You're hot? So what?"

Clem took a breath and watched her daughter. She could see herself right there, in that same stance, with her own mother years before. Being annoyed, angry, frustrated about the constant complaining. She remembered mocking her with, "Hot flash, hot flash, I'm having a hot flash." Funny how those things were passed from mother to daughter.

"Well," Clem said, "at least no one got a video."

Anna whipped her phone from her pocket. "Of course they did, Mom. Someone in the bleachers filmed you disrobing. They posted the video on the rink's Facebook page and Byrock's Instagram account." She held up her phone, hit play, and showed Clem the video that ended with Clem sprawled facedown on the ice.

"Oh gosh, that ice felt so good," Clem said.

"This is not funny, Mom."

"I know you don't think so, honey. And I'm truly sorry you're embarrassed."

Tor poked his head into the room. "Clementine, have you found my green sweater yet?"

Anna whipped around to face him. "Dad!" she yelled. "No one cares about your hideous green sweater. No one! If it's gone, let it go. You're better off without it. It is the ugliest thing in the world!"

Tor stared at Anna. "Who bit you?" he said.

"Her!" Anna yelled, pointing at Clem. "Mom did! She won't stop."

"Stop what?" Tor asked. He was so oblivious.

"Stop what, Dad? Stop what? How about stop embarrassing me day and night? Stop taking off her clothes in public? Stop talking about her gynecologist? Stop droning on and on and on about her stupid hot flashes?" Anna spun back to face Clem. "Please, Mom. Stop."

Clem looked deeply at her child. There was that word. *Stop.* Stop what? she thought.

Stop picking up the kids?

Stop delivering the kids?

Stop packing lunches and toting forgotten things to school?

Stop scheduling doctor and dentist appointments?

Stop dropping Tor's sweaters at the dry cleaners?

Stop negotiating for the title she well deserved at the library?

Stop being the organizer, the reminder, the person who over-stuffed her chest cavity until it was about to explode?

Stop washing uniforms on cold so they didn't shrink?

Stop saying yes?

Stop being the linchpin?

Stop.

Anna's voice cut into Clem's thoughts. "Mom! Mom? Are you listening to me?"

"Mom!"

"Yes, Anna?"

"Are you listening to me?"

"No, Anna, I'm not. I was, but I am no longer."

Anna's eyes bugged. "What? Why?"

"Because, my dear child, I prefer not to."

After Anna stomped out of the room and before the video was taken down from the town's Instagram account, Clem saved it on her phone.

That evening, the kids were watching Heather of the Weather dancing around in a glow-in-the-dark beanie that a viewer had sent her. "Visibility is everything when the snow is coming down like this!" she yelled gleefully over the roar of the wind. Aside from a snowplow crawling along behind her, the street was empty.

"Raise your hand if you'll be skiing this weekend!" she shouted, her phosphorescent head bobbing this way and that. "Raise your hand if you put a spoon or two under your pillow last night!"

Clem seethed. She despised this woman. "Raise your hand," she muttered, "if you'd like that snowplow to squash the snow maven into a pancake."

"Mom!" All three kids said it at the same time.

"What? I'm not serious." But she kind of was.

When it became clear that the TV station would not be returning to actual news, Clem told the kids to switch it to *House Hunters International*. "Enough of the weather," she said. "Go do your homework." Moments later she was watching a couple and their two high school kids make the move from Caribou, Maine, to Phuket, Thailand. Lucky ducks. Clem had never seen four people prance along a beach quite like these four Mainers.

"We've had it with long, bitter winters," the mother said to the real estate agent. Actually, she sang it, like a blissful banshee. "Thirty years we've been battling ice and snow in New England. We're ready for sun and sand."

"Me too," Clem said, wondering if they'd mind having one more on their tropical adventure. A beach cottage in Thailand sounded perfect.

That night, Clem uploaded the video from her curling expedition to TikTok. Within a few hours, her account heated up to more than three hundred thousand followers, and the new followers offered thousands of comments. They were full of love for her and the story she was telling.

2old4shit: *Thank you for seeing me!*
Warrior1: *You are so honest. Love you!*
JustJessica: *Brave human! Ice princess!*
PeachyTree3: *I'm not alone (sob).*
TheOtherMonica: *I'm too hot too.*
walkingtheearth: *Joining a curling team today!*
WeaverBird77: *I thought I was heating up because I was dying! Seriously.*
SantaMonica4CA: *Keep these great stories coming! xo*
WiskeyOne: *More! More!*

CHAPTER TWENTY
Leader of the Pack

Clem pinged Charlene right after Heather of the Weather announced that Boston area towns were running out of salt.

Leaving in 5! Be ready!

Before heading out, she watched the rest of the report. "Towns are attempting to buy salt and ship it in from states not affected by this winter's fury," Heather explained. "The DPW reports that it will take a week or so to get what each town needs. Until then, please plan accordingly. If you don't have to drive, stay home."

The ticker at the bottom of the screen began to run a list of affected towns. Clem waited to see if Byrock was included.

Acton
Arlington
Bedford
Belmont
Bolton
Boston Proper

Boxborough
Brookline
Burlington
Byrock

There it was. Proof that within days driving in town would become an even more treacherous ordeal than it had been in recent weeks. Drivers would be sliding through intersections and bouncing off the snow mountains in parking lots all across town. In years past, this would have terrified Clem, but now she grinned. Sailing along on the icy streets was becoming fun. Freeing even.

Outside, the snow was light, but a thin layer had already coated the road. The clouds were so heavy it felt like they were sitting on top of her. Clem thought about the Keeper of Living Collections. Were clouds and snow part of his purview? Were they considered to be living things as well? She hopped in her car, and because she couldn't see around the snow piles at the end of the driveway, she blasted her horn as a warning to anyone gliding past. Once she cleared them, she raced to Charlene's house. *I'm outside. Ready when you are!*

Charlene jumped in with two cups of coffee. "Let's get started!"

"Windows up or down?" Clem said.

"Is that even a question?" Charlene said.

Clem rolled them all the way down, letting the crisp winter air blow through. Having a perimenopausal partner made it much more fun than going it alone. At least there was someone who understood the nausea, rolls of sensation, brain zaps, itchy ears, heat, night sweats, anger.

"No salt truck yet," Charlene said.

"Nope, and there likely won't be one. Heather just announced that the town is nearly out of salt."

"How are they going to get us through the rest of the winter?"

"They're trying to borrow some."

"Who is going to give up salt at this point?" Charlene said. "Every town in New England is in the same predicament."

"Pennsylvania."

"Pennsylvania?"

"That's what they said."

"Does Pennsylvania have extra salt?"

"Supposedly."

Charlene nodded. "How will we pay for it?"

"We're going to trade for it. A good old-fashioned barter."

"With what?"

"She said they aren't sure yet. Maybe lobsters."

"Lobsters?"

"I made that up, but if I was employed by the public works of Pennsylvania, I'd ask for lobsters."

Clem put the car in reverse and inched backward. The snowdrifts at the end of Charlene's driveway were even higher than the ones at home—double the height of the car. She blasted the horn.

"I made an I PREFER NOT TO play list. Listen to this," Clem said.

Buster Poindexter's "Hot, Hot, Hot" bounced out of the speakers. Clem cranked it up and danced in her seat. "Our anthem," she called over Buster's voice.

They shouted at the same time, "I prefer not to!"

On Main Street, a plow truck driver stuck his arm out of the window and waved at Clem to go around him. She swerved into the left lane, passed, and swerved back. Then she slowed to a crawl and inched past the stop sign, leaning as close as she could to the windshield so she could see around the mounds of gray snow pockmarked with black bits of dirt and asphalt.

The GPS called out directions to Dr. Sheffield's office. Left, another left, three-quarters of a mile to 93N, a few miles, next exit, right, right, left.

When they pulled up outside the brown brick building, Clem squeezed her car into the last available spot. Either Dr. Sheffield's group didn't believe in paying snow loaders to remove snow from the parking lot or the snow-loading teams were too busy to take on the work. Mountains of the stuff dotted the lot.

"I've been to this office so many times in the past sixteen years," she said. "First, with Evan. Then Anna. Then a miscarriage. And finally, Brewster. I can't even count the number of appointments I've had with Dr. Sheffield." She was quiet. It didn't seem right that a doctor who had shown such compassion for pregnancy, pregnancy loss, and birth was so callous about and dismissive of hot flashes and perimenopause. She couldn't even imagine what he'd be like when she reached actual menopause.

"Me too," said Charlene. "I had two miscarriages, then four kids."

"You have four?" Clem said.

"We were supposed to have three, but the last turned out to be twins."

Clem shook her head. Two of anyone seemed unfathomable.

As if timing were everything, Clem felt a hot flash beginning to build. As it rolled up through her middle, she tried to imagine where it had originated in her body. The confluence of cells and energy that culminated in the flash, the spark. And then the wild surge through the center of her being. Damn, women's bodies were weird. The things they could and couldn't do. The output they could create. The goop, the humans, the juices, the blood, the heat. Infuriating but impressive.

They popped out of the car and learned, as they skidded across the icy sidewalk, that Dr. Sheffield's team believed in shoveling and de-icing the walkways as much as they did in clearing the parking lot.

Clem took video footage of her and Charlotte at the door of Dr. Sheffield's office. "Mission I Prefer Not To," she said into the mic, "is about to begin." She held the camera so that part of the sign—*Obstetrics & Gynecology Associates*—was visible, just enough to give viewers the gist of their destination but not their exact location.

Inside, it was standing room only, and although the two of them did their best to sneak in unnoticed, Dr. Sheffield's eagle-eye admin caught sight of them immediately.

"Ladies," Clem heard her say. She tried to be smaller, more invisible, but it didn't work. "Check-in is this way."

"Do you know her?" Clem whispered to Charlene as they clambered over boots and strewn coats.

"Nope. You?"

Clem shook her head. "I've never seen her before. Must be new. But she doesn't look particularly strong or fast. We can outmaneuver her."

Charlene nodded.

Clem began filming again. "Divide and conquer!" she whispered. She switched off the video, and the two of them pushed through the crowd in opposite directions. Each on the search for women in the middle of hot flashes.

"Ladies! Ladies!" the admin called. "Over here!"

Clem ignored her. She spotted a hot-flasher from across the room. A drowning woman wedged between two radiant preggos. Wet bangs plastered to her forehead. A woozy look in her eyes. No coat. Flip-flops. The sharp edge of anger in her eyes.

Clem cupped her hands around her mouth and called to Charlene. "I've got one! Hot-flasher near the window!"

Clem knelt when she got close. "Hey," she whispered, keeping her eye on the admin.

Both preggos, alert and perky, pointed at themselves. "Me?" they said at the same time.

"No, not you," Clementine barked. "You!" she said, pointing directly at the drowning woman.

The woman was oblivious, deep in the hot-flash state of mind. The shiny, glowing preggo to her right nudged her. "Hey, I think this lady is talking to you," she said.

The woman looked up at Clem. "Me?" she said. Her voice was low and slightly slurry. She wiped her forehead with her palm, then wiped her palm on her shirt.

"Yes, you. Are you hot-flashing right now?"

The woman moved her eyes to the left and right. "Hot-flashing?"

"Yes, are you having a hot flash right now?"

The woman's eyes got big, as if she suddenly recognized one of her own. "Yes, yes, how did you know?"

"How could I not know?" Clem said. "You are my people. Come with me."

As they made introductions and started to move toward the exit, the admin was wending her way through the tangle of legs, boots, bags, and coats. She was stepping over shallow puddles of dirty, melted snow, trying to reach Clem. It was like a chase scene from an old Saturday morning cartoon in which the predator is befuddled and thwarted by obstacles flung into their path.

Clem glanced across the room at Charlene. She had two women in tow. They were following her closely along the back wall toward the door.

"Hey," the admin said, "where are you taking our patients? Ms. Bald? Mrs. Clark? Ms. McLeish? Where are you going? You have appointments!"

Clem and her single hot-flasher made it to the door as another woman was coming in, conveniently providing one last obstacle for the admin. Charlene waved and yelled, "Doughnuts! We're going on a doughnut run! We'll bring your patients back! Promise!" Then the five women pushed out the door and tumbled into the elevator, leaving the preggos and the admin behind.

Outside, they crashed into a snowbank and looked at one another, grinning. They were lovely. The whole lot of them. All in their early forties. A mix of heights, hair, and skin color.

"Well, that was fun," said a woman who introduced herself as Gish, "but what's this all about?"

Charlene and the three women looked at Clem. Clem looked back. Holy cow, this was terrifying. Clem knew that if she was going to change the world, if she was going to successfully lead a movement for women, build an empire, she was going to have to get used to explaining the damn thing. She couldn't expect women to fall in line behind her and chant, *I'm having a hot flash. You, Clementine Crane, are my leader.* Women needed to learn what it was they were falling in line for, and Clem needed to be able to explain it quickly and concisely. But because she'd always needed reflection time before engaging deeply, this on-the-fly discussion was going to take practice. *Practice makes better,* she recited in her head, trying out the same mantra she'd used with the kids every time they had to acquire some new skill. *Practice makes better.*

She took a breath. "I'm Clementine Crane, Connector of People to Magical Things," she said. "Dr. Sheffield has been my ob-gyn for sixteen years. When I started having hot flashes recently, he dismissed my symptoms and my concerns. That, as they say, was the tip of the iceberg." She told them about Tor's green sweater, Georgia's death, TikTok, "Bartleby, the Scrivener," and the mantra she now lived by: *I prefer not to.* "I'm now," she said, "leading a renaissance for women."

By the time Clem finished talking, the women were applauding. After getting their contact information, Clem slid across the parking lot, leaned into her car, and pulled Anna's selfie stick from the back seat. Sometimes her daughter's forgetfulness paid off.

The women lined up in front of a snowbank as Charlene and two others began to flash. Timing was everything. Clem recorded every steaming second, then added their theme song "Hot, Hot, Hot" as well as a few key hashtags—#ifyouknowyouknow, #hotflashmama, #hothothot, #iprefernotto, #perimenopause. She wrote a description: "Mission complete! 3 hot-flashers recruited!" Then she hit "Post."

The response on TikTok was immediate.

LenaLove112: *Yaaaaaassssss!*
OrangeLemon: *Me me me! Recruit me!*

Pivot: *Im at gyn in Tulsa. Recruit me!*
walkingtheearth: *lucky hotties*
KrispiGlover: *wegothot*
I_Drive_A_Fast_Car128: *I will drive the getaway car*
SantaMonica4CA: *All hail the hotties!*
CocoPuffX: *sizzling*
shinystar: *sweatin' here in South Carolina*
pumpingpenelope: *make a stop in the Dakotas!*

Moments later, Gish, Elena, and Jennifer headed back upstairs to deal with the admin at Dr. Sheffield's office. As they walked away, Clem noticed their newfound confidence. The kick in their step.

In the car, Clem logged in to Facebook and went to the local moms page. "Need a new GYN," she wrote. "A woman who is knowledgeable about perimenopause and positive about hormone replacement therapy. No dinosaurs or anti-HRTers. TIA."

Within an hour, Clem's post had over one hundred comments. There were warnings about the geezers to avoid as well as some horror stories. Thankfully, there were recommendations as well, and from what Clem could glean, Dr. Cynthia Parker sounded like a perfect fit.

Thirty minutes later, Clem had an appointment scheduled for the following week.

CHAPTER TWENTY-ONE
The Crime That Almost Was

When the movers pulled into Clem's driveway to deliver Georgia's bedroom set, Clem had to gulp back tears. As long as Georgia's things were still in her house, Clem had been able to pretend that her best friend might be coming home. That she wasn't gone forever. But now she had to face the truth.

"Where to, ma'am?" the mover guy said, stomping snow off his feet on the welcome mat.

"Basement," Clem said. "First door on your right. It's open."

"Yes, ma'am." He and his partner pivoted the pieces of Georgia and Henry's bed so they fit neatly through the doorway.

Clem and Astrid followed them down the stairs. The basement was well organized. Two walls were lined with sturdy steel shelves, and the shelves were stocked with identical plastic bins, each neatly labeled: Christmas decorations, 1st grade art, 2nd grade art, Easter decorations, 1000-piece puzzles, 500-piece puzzles, snow pants, Halloween costumes, etc.

"Wow," Astrid said. "Georgia always said you were well organized."

"She did?"

Astrid nodded. "It impressed her, how you could keep things so orderly with three kids, a husband, and a job."

Clem smiled.

The movers set down the bed, then went back for another load.

"I'll have the furniture moved up to our bedroom once I'm able to clean ours out in the spring," Clem said. "I don't have the emotional capacity right now."

Astrid nodded. "Georgia would be so happy to see these beautiful pieces in your home."

"She'd be happier if they were upstairs," Clem said.

Astrid laughed. "All in good time."

When the movers carried down the dressers, Astrid made sure they placed them with the drawers facing out. "I'm so sorry," she told Clem. "The drawers are still full. I didn't have time to empty them. There have been so many things to coordinate with the sale of the house."

"Perfectly fine," Clem said. "I'll do it when I feel ready. It will be good to go through some of Georgia's things."

As they walked upstairs, Astrid said, "I did have the movers bring one more item for you. A little surprise."

When they got to the top, Clem saw the men holding Georgia's rocking chair with the patchwork quilt folded on the seat. Clem teared up. "Oh, Astrid, thank you," Clem said. "Are you sure you don't want it?"

"Georgia told me all about your sanctuary upstairs," Astrid said. "I think this might be a good addition."

Clem squeezed her in a tight hug, then followed the movers up to her and Tor's bedroom.

"Right here is fine," she said, pointing to the door of her closet.

"Should we put it inside, ma'am?" the man asked, reaching for the knob.

Clem pictured Astrid and the movers walking in and discovering Frankie swimming around in her fancy punch bowl. She didn't know if they knew anything about the missing fish, but she couldn't take that chance. "No, thank you," she said, unlocking the door, "but I'd appreciate if you'd take down another." She slipped into the closet, grabbed one of the two chairs at the window, and handed it out to the mover. Then she carried the rocker into the closet and set it next to hers.

"The closing is in two days," Astrid told her as they walked down the stairs. "The new family will move in after that."

Clem took a breath. This was going to be hard.

"They're lovely people, Clementine," Astrid said. "It's like Georgia handpicked them herself. They're going to make great neighbors."

Clem hugged her. "Thank you for all of this."

"Anything for our Georgia," Astrid said, and she walked out the front door into a flurry of whirling snow. Halfway across the porch, she turned. "Hey, have you heard anything from the funeral home about Georgia's ashes?" she said.

Clem shut the door, pretending Astrid's question got lost in the wind. Pretending she hadn't ignored two calls and an email about that very thing. Through the window, she could see that the rhododendrons—buried deep beneath the snow—weren't even visible anymore. If they survived this, it would be a miracle.

She rested her forehead against the cold pane of glass. Hell, if *she* survived this, it would be an even bigger miracle.

That night at 3:30 AM, Clementine woke shivering. In recent weeks, she'd gotten used to shivering after a hot flash, but this felt different.

She flopped onto her back and reached both hands up to her pillow. It was sopping wet.

She patted her hair.

Soaked.

She felt her forehead and cheeks.

Slick.

She poked a finger into each ear.

Sloshy.

Her labiomental groove was overflowing.

What had happened during the brief hour she'd been asleep?

"Tor," she yelled. "Tor!" She reached out in the dark and batted him in the head. "Help! Help!"

"What?" he yelled back. "What is it, Clem? Is someone hurt?"

She heard him leap out of bed. "I don't know!" she shouted. "I think I'm hurt! My head is covered in blood!" Her voice rose higher.

"Blood?"

"Yes, blood! I think I've been bludgeoned!"

"Bludgeoned? By who?"

"I don't know. Be careful! They might be hiding! Turn on the light!"

"Why is it so dark in here?" Tor yelled.

Usually, a decent amount of light from nearby streetlamps lit the room, especially when the snow was deep. Reflection brightened everything. But now it was pitch black, outside and in.

"There must be a power outage," Clem yelled. Why couldn't she stop yelling? She heard Tor smack into something. Hard.

"Ouch!" he yelled.

She heard him sliding his hands along the wall, trying to find the switch.

"Got it," he hollered, flicking it up and down. "It's not working! The power must be out!"

"That's what I said!" Clem shouted. She shook her head. When she did, wet strands of hair whipped across her face. "Oh my god, the blood! My hair is drenched with it!"

"I'll get my phone and call for help!" Tor yelled. "Hang on!"

She heard him stomping across the floor in the direction of his dresser.

"I'm almost there!" he yelled, but then she heard a horrible crash and the sound of cracking glass. Hagrid keened in the blackness.

"Hagrid!" Clem cried. "They're killing Hagrid!"

"Nobody's killing Hagrid!" Tor yelled. "He ran in and tripped me. Quit worrying about that damned dog. I hit the window and smashed my face on the floor."

"Hurry, Tor! Hurry! I'm think I'm dying!" Clem buried her fingers in her hair, trying to find a cut or bump.

Just as she heard him slam into his dresser on the other side of the room, the lights came on. Both froze in shock and surprise. Tor jumped around, looking for an intruder, a burglar, a bludgeoner.

"The curtain! The curtain! Behind the curtain!" Clem hollered.

"I'll get them!" Tor yelled, and he gripped the pale-orange curtains with both hands as if strangling someone. He bellowed and thrashed them back and forth in a death grip.

Finally, realizing there was no one there, he stopped and took a breath. He turned, looked at Clem, and limped closer, his hand cupped around his nose. "Where's the blood, Clementine? You said you were covered in blood?"

Clem reached her hands up, squished them into her hair, and pushed her pinkie fingers into her ears. When she brought them down and looked at them, there was no blood. Only sweat.

She sat up with a wet *thwck* as her neck and upper back peeled off the mattress. "I don't know," she said. "I'm soaked. I was sure it was blood."

"There is blood, Clem," Tor muttered, taking his hand off his now-swollen nose. "But it's mine, not yours." Both of his eyes were already turning black-and-blue.

Oh my god, Clem thought. This was a night sweat. She'd read about these but assumed one would feel the same as a hot flash. This was no hot flash. Not the kind with which she'd become familiar. This one hadn't rolled up through her middle. She hadn't gotten nauseated or felt floofy or fuzzled. Her brain hadn't zapped. Hell, she hadn't even woken up. And she wasn't sweating from her body. Not her pits or arms or elbows or belly. It was only her head. From the neck up, she was completely soaked, as if she'd been dunked while bobbing for apples. What the hell?

"You said you were covered in blood," Tor said.

"I thought I was!" Clem said.

"You said you'd been bludgeoned," Tor said. His voice rang with anger.

"I thought I had been."

"How do you mistake being bludgeoned for not being bludgeoned?"

"I don't know. It was dark. I was covered in something wet. I thought it was blood."

"You're sweaty, Clem. That's it." He looked in the mirror. "Crap. I have a meeting tomorrow with a new client."

Clem dropped her head into her hands. "I'm sorry, okay? This has never happened before. It's one more trick of perimenopause. You try waking up out of a deep sleep with your head so wet it feels like you climbed out of a pool two seconds before. You'd think you got bludgeoned too."

Tor grunted, and as he squeezed the tip of his nose trying to staunch the flow of blood, the hall light clicked on. Clem heard Brewster's voice. "Mom? Dad? Is everything okay?"

Brewster's hair was tousled in the same way it used to be when he was little. Clem's heart did a little leap.

"We're fine, Brew. We had a misunderstanding," she said.

"We?" Tor said.

Clem shook her head, and sweat dripped from her hair onto her T-shirt.

"Jeez, Mom. You scared me."

"That wasn't my intention."

Anna's voice shot down the hall. "Hey, what is wrong with all of you? It's three forty-five in the morning. I have an early practice. I need sleep."

Good gracious. "I was nearly bludgeoned, Anna," Clem called. "But don't worry about me."

"Clem, you were not nearly bludgeoned," Tor said. He lay down on his back.

"It doesn't matter, Mom," Anna called. "I need sleep. I have an important practice leading to a more important game."

"Brew, can you get me a towel and an ice pack?" Tor said.

"Sure, Dad." Brew padded out of the room.

Clem glared at her husband. "Tor, I'm sorry about your nose. I am. But maybe you can muster up a little empathy for what I'm going through. This was terrifying."

Tor didn't say anything. Instead, he tipped his head back and pinched the end of his schnoz a little tighter.

Fed up, Clem stood, grabbed her phone, put on her robe, stomped into her closet, and locked the door behind her. She added a bit of cinnamon oil to the diffuser and curled up in Georgia's rocker with the quilt wrapped around her. *What would Georgia say?* she thought.

TikTok it, of course.

She went live again and this time was far less self-conscious. She didn't fix her hair or put on lip gloss. She didn't hide the fact that she was still wearing pajamas. She just told the story of her first night sweat, including the thought-she-had-been-bludgeoned bit and Tor's horrible response. She cried her way through all of it. This time, she even managed to answer a few questions that viewers posted.

When she signed off and paused to say good-night to Frankie, she realized that the filtration system wasn't on. The outage.

Oh, shit.

"Frankie?" Clem couldn't find her at first but then spotted her bulgy little eyes poking out from behind her favorite frond.

With the system off, there were no bubbles, so no oxygen was being added to the water. Would this kill Frankie? Would she die? Would Clem be known as a fish murderer instead a fish-napper?

Clem did the math. She'd been awake at 1:38 AM as usual. Probably asleep by 2:30. The outage couldn't have started before then, because she would have noticed. The system had likely been off for no more than an hour and a bit. Was that long enough to cause death in a celestial goldfish? Douglass's words reverberated in her head: *Goldfish don't need filtration systems.* God, she hoped he was right.

Clem unplugged, then plugged the system back in. It started up immediately. When bubbles started to roll through the water, Clem could have sworn Frankie did a fancy fin dance. "Crisis averted," Clem whispered.

When she returned to the bedroom, Tor was sitting up in bed, holding the ice pack to his nose. "Clementine, what exactly do you have going on in there?" he said.

"Nothing. Why?" She crawled into bed and shivered. Her pillow was soaked, and it had already begun to stink. She flipped it over and tugged the comforter up to her chin.

"You never locked that closet door until recently."

Clem slipped the key under the pillow. "Sure I have."

"I'm pretty sure I'd notice if you locked your closet."

"There are many things you don't notice, Torvald."

"Well, I've noticed this. So why are you locking the door?"

"I'm feeling more private these days."

"You're feeling private but you're stripping in the yard and hurling yourself naked into the snow? Taking off your clothes at the rink and lying facedown on the ice?"

Clem sat up and glared at him. This was the first time he'd referenced either incident. "I wasn't naked," she said.

"All right. Almost naked."

Still, he didn't ask why. He wasn't interested in what was happening in her body and her brain. He was feeling at risk himself, so instead of focusing even the tiniest bit of energy on her, he made it about him. If he had asked right then, *Are you okay? What's happening? Can I help?* she would have fallen out of bed with gratitude. If he had apologized for the fact that he regularly interrupted what little sleep she got with his outrageous snores, she would have softened. But he didn't, and she was angrier than ever.

"And the cinnamon scent wafting out of there?" He bobbed his head at the closet door. "What's that about?"

"I like it."

"Since when?"

"Why do you care?"

"Come on, Clem. What is this all about? Are you keeping a lover in there?"

Clem laughed. Good god. A lover. That was the very last thing she wanted. Someone else to take care of. "Yes," she said, batting her eyelashes and putting on a sexy voice, "I've lured a hot man into my walk-in closet with the scent of cinnamon. He's been living there for weeks."

"Clem," Tor said, "you're acting very strangely. The snowbank, the ice rink, the locked door, the cinnamon scent, the fish food in your bedside drawer, the mistaken bludgeoning. I can't even talk to you right now."

"Then don't, Tor," she said. "Don't." The word *stop* from her to-do list popped into her head.

Stop.

Stop what?

Stop talking to Tor? Was that what she'd intended?

Stop.

Stop talking altogether?

Stop.

Stop what?

She still didn't know.

"Well, what are you going to do now, oh bludgeoned one?" Tor grumbled. He lay back down on the bed. "Bludgeon me back?"

Clem turned away and yanked the comforter to her side of the bed. "I prefer not to."

CHAPTER TWENTY-TWO
Sleep Catcher

The next day, after slogging through the exhaustion of another sleepless night, Clem replaced the *Director of Media* nameplate on her desk in the library with one that read *Connector of People to Magical Things*. It wasn't an exact replica, a bit more brass than brown, but it was a close enough match that she didn't think Bath would notice right away. Wrong! Bath removed it so quickly Clem was sure she'd been watching and waiting for this very move.

No matter. Clem had ordered a dozen nameplates. She'd be able to play Bath's game for a good while. She set another on the desk, right next to her well-worn copy of *Complete Shorter Fiction of Herman Melville* with a scrap of paper marking the first page of "Bartleby," then headed for the conference room where Meghan was prepping supplies for the day's craft.

"What are we making today?" Clem said.

Meghan held up the fancy sample she'd finished the night before—a paper plate cut into the shape of a wreath with multicolored yarn threaded across its middle and feathers, beads, and other baubles strung like ornaments. "Dream catchers," she said, then handed Clem a pair of scissors and a stack of paper plates. "Help me cut out the centers of these."

Clem popped the point of the scissors through the center of a plate. "I haven't had a dream in months," Clem said. "Guess I can skip this craft."

"Still having trouble sleeping?" Meghan said.

Clem nodded. "Do you know the horrid things a human suffers when they don't get enough sleep?"

"Besides dream deprivation?"

"That's the least of it. There's memory loss, mood swings, and hallucinations."

"Like that *crunch, crunch, crunch* you've been hearing at night?" Meghan said.

"No, that is a real thing. I hear it as clearly as I'm hearing your dulcet tones right now. Plus, I've seen tracks in the snow from whatever beast is trudging around. Georgia saw them too."

Meghan nodded. "I'm teasing. What else happens when you don't get enough sleep?"

"Forgetfulness. Slow metabolism. And over time? Diabetes, depression, and cardiovascular disease."

Meghan organized plastic charms, balls of yarn, pom-poms, buttons, and whatnots into bowls and set a few near each place at the conference table. "You know what you need?"

"Tahiti?" Clem said.

"A sleep hygienist," Meghan said.

"What's that?"

"Someone who helps you figure out healthy ways to get better sleep."

"Like a dental hygienist?"

"Exactly. I went to one after my divorce because I couldn't sleep alone after ten years with Ben. She was hugely helpful."

"How so?"

"She taught me a sleep meditation that worked beautifully, and I got a white noise machine."

"I don't want a white noise machine. I don't want to bury the sound of Tor's snores under something else. I want *no* noise. That's the point. I want silence." She thought about Frankie swimming quietly in her punch bowl. If only she could replicate that experience for herself.

"Think about it," Meghan said. "I can give you her contact info if you're interested."

Clem shrugged and popped the scissors through the center of a second plate. "Since this craft won't work for me, I'll spend the meeting making faces at Bath."

"Oh, no," Meghan said. "I'm giving you a special assignment. You get to make a sleep catcher instead."

Thirty minutes later, Clem held up her sleep catcher for everyone to admire. It had turned out better than she'd expected, with wee replicas of Tor's nose molded from clay and braided yarn laced densely across the circle.

When Bath questioned the noses, Clem launched into a lecture on the anatomy of the face, including a lesson on alae.

"Why," Bath said, "do you keep making things that are mysterious and uncommon? Things we have to question." She still hadn't gotten over the cow moose.

"Bath, noses are not uncommon or mysterious. Most of us have one. And as for the moose, we live in New England. The fact that you didn't know about the white vulva patch doesn't mean my art is mysterious or"—Clem made air quotes—"'uncommon.'"

Bathsheba raised her hands. "Enough," she said. "We are not getting started on the—"

"Vulva patch," Keisha whispered.

Bathsheba sighed. "Clementine, I hope you catch as much sleep as you possibly can with that thing," she said, pointing at the sleep catcher. "Clearly, you need it."

"Clearly I do," Clem said.

Bathsheba pushed away from the table and stood. "I'm cutting our meeting short today," she said. "Too many points of controversy. Let's regroup and meet next week."

Clem nodded almost imperceptibly. Although her goal wasn't to piss off Bath, she did want to break her resistance and get her to think differently.

By the time she got back to her desk, the second *Connector of People to Magical Things* nameplate was gone. The battle had begun. She stood tall, pulled a third from her bag, and placed it on the desk, this time mounting it firmly into place with Velcro.

A few hours later, Bathsheba asked Clem to write a press release for an upcoming author talk. The request was simple and the task fairly straightforward. But without a second of thought, Clem responded in the same way Bartleby had when his boss asked him to examine a document.

"I prefer not to," Clem said. She liked writing press releases, but as with everything else at her job, she'd been locked into a certain voice, style, and format. Bath had long ago shut down any attempt at originality or artistry, at creating something that might actually grab the press's attention instead of being deleted immediately.

"Excuse me?" Bath said. She was tapping her finger on top of Clem's new nameplate.

"I prefer not to."

At the mirrored moment in Melville's story, the narrator said that he was "turned into a pillar of salt" by Bartleby's refusal and admitted that he should have "flown outright into a dreadful passion, scorned all further words, and thrust him ignominiously from my presence." Instead, he tried to negotiate with him.

Clem swallowed hard. Would Bath turn into a pillar of salt? Would she get pissed and toss Clem out of the library? Or would she, like the narrator, immediately try to bargain with her?

From her peripheral vision, Clem watched Bath's face contort into something that resembled the face of the gargoyle that sat on the east corner of the library's roof.

"You're refusing to write a press release?" she finally managed to say. "You've written hundreds of press releases. You could write it in your sleep."

Clem wanted to yell, *That's the fucking point!* But instead she focused on Craft Clem, who was still pinned, surrounded by flames, to her bulletin board next to the cow moose. Until this moment, Clem had believed she was being destroyed by fire, but suddenly another possibility popped into her head. If she could get through this mess of perimenopause and marriage and constraint, she very well could be the phoenix—set afire, yes, but ultimately reborn from the ashes. Stronger. More radiant. Transformed.

To embody this new possibility, Clem folded her arms into wings and flapped them.

"Clementine, I don't know what that is"—Bath waved her hands at the flapping wings—"but I need you to write this piece. Now." Bath's voice was nearing shrill, and it was beginning to draw a small crowd.

Clem thought about Bartleby's passive defiance. If she gave in now, she'd never fight back. She had to stand her ground. Silently she chanted, *Be Bartleby. Stay the course. Be Bartleby. Stay the course.* And out loud, she said, "I prefer not to."

Bath growled, yanked the nameplate from its Velcro bed, and stomped away.

A minute later, Clem set up her phone on the tripod she'd purchased for this very purpose. And an hour later, when Bath returned, Clem used the remote to start filming. She didn't hide the phone. She wanted Bath to know she was being filmed.

"Clementine," Bath said, "there's a woman up front who's looking for a movie about vampires. One she hasn't seen yet. Can you please help her?"

Clementine smirked, knowing that Bath believed the *please* would nudge her into action. Clem knew she could complete this task with her eyes closed. She knew dozens of vampire movies to which she could magically connect this woman. But she couldn't give in. Instead, she held firm and repeated, "I prefer not to," then pointed to the nameplate on her desk, the one she'd replaced once again. *Connector of People to Magical Things*.

Bath threw up her hands and stomped away.

Clem finished the TikTok with music, a caption, hashtags, and her usual "Follow me. I'm sweaty." Within an hour of posting, it had thousands of likes and even more comments.

The I PREFER NOT TO movement was growing.

By the time she reached Dr. Cynthia Parker's waiting room, Clem was feeling calm and powerful. Still, when she walked in, tears poured down her cheeks. The walls were covered with posters about the symptoms of perimenopause, the stages of menopause, and women's overall physiological health. Above the welcome desk was an oversized photo of a woman having a hot flash. Sweat seeped from every pore, and her hair was spiked like the horns of a triceratops.

"Is this heaven?" Clem said.

The receptionist smiled. "For many, yes," she said. "Welcome."

Clem took footage for TikTok—filming every poster and every photo—and by the time Dr. Parker joined her in the examining room, she was grinning.

"I had no idea a doctor like you existed," she said to Dr. Parker. She was still wearing her clothes because, as the nurse explained, Dr. Parker always chatted with fully dressed patients before asking them to disrobe for an examination. "I'm astonished."

Dr. Parker laughed. "I wish that weren't the case," she said, "but I know from years of experience that most people with uteruses who land in my office have been through a lot with previous practitioners. They're often in a state of shock."

The walls in the examining room were as informative about perimenopause and menopause as the walls in the waiting room. And for nearly twenty minutes, the two talked about all that Clem had been experiencing for the past few months, including the Max Walden effect. Dr. Parker was not at all surprised by Clem's dodgeball description. In fact, she appreciated the detail and comparison. "That helps me understand how to help you," she said.

"I'm coming to live with you," Clem said. She also told Dr. Parker about stripping down in the snow and on the ice rink.

"I get it," the doctor said. She didn't laugh or mock Clem's behavior. "I'm surprised more women don't do the same thing."

When she heard those three words—*I get it*—Clem got up and did a little dance. Thirty minutes later, she left with a prescription for a hormone replacement patch, an order for bloodwork, a nudge to increase both vitamin D and calcium, and a sense of being cared for that she hadn't felt in years.

"Don't be surprised if your phone starts ringing off the hook, Dr. Parker," she said on her way out.

"I'm ready," the doctor said.

That night, Clem went live on TikTok. This time she outlined the steps Dr. Parker was taking to help her be as healthy and comfortable as possible during perimenopause. She even applied her first HRT patch right there on camera. She peeled off the backing, held it up for everyone to see, pushed down the waistband of her pants, stuck the patch to her stomach, and smoothed out the wrinkles—acknowledging the likes and responding to comments and questions as she did. Afterward, it took her a minute to identify the feeling she had, but once she did, she was able to put a name to it. Hope.

CHAPTER TWENTY-THREE
Makeup Lessons

When Clem was twelve, her mother had given her a bag of makeup and a subscription to one of those teen magazines that taught girls how to look good for boys. The first issue featured tips for kissable lips, lessons on goof-proof makeup, a quiz for discovering the "real you," and ten reasons to say no to sex.

Since yes to sex wasn't something she was considering yet, she focused on mastering her makeup. When she emerged from the bathroom three hours later, she looked more like a rabid raccoon than a girl, but her lips were definitely kissable.

Now, staring at herself in the bathroom mirror, she heard her mother's voice in her head explaining how important it was to "look the part." At the time, Clem hadn't understood what part she was expected to play, but she sure did now.

One by one, she pulled items from the drawer and lay them on the counter: moisturizer, concealer, foundation, powder, eye shadow, eyeliner, mascara, blush. For nearly thirty years, she'd successfully played the "hide that, highlight this" game with her face, but finally she'd had enough.

She set her phone on the tripod and hit record.

"Hello, hot-flashers, overwhelmed moms, mental-load managers, and pissed-off people with periods," she said. "This morning I'll be teaching you how to do your makeup when you're having a hot flash. Listen up!" She leaned toward the mirror and fluffed her hair.

"First," she said, "get your hair out of your face. You need clear access to the blank canvas. If your hair is long and belligerent, like mine, pull it up in a ponytail. If it's shorter, throw on a headband.

"Second," she said, "if you're wrapping up a hot flash, swab the sweat from your face." She grabbed the hand towel from the rack and patted her scarlet cheeks dramatically.

"Third, once your face is dry enough, smile. Smile big. Show your gorgeous self some serious love, even if you're not feeling it." She smiled a big toothy smile.

"And fourth"—she gave side-eye to the camera—"toss your makeup back into the drawer and say, *I prefer not to.*"

She paused and got close to the camera. "I'm serious now. See this foundation and concealer?" She held up a couple of tubes. "If I put these on right now, I will sweat them off within the hour. They will bead and smear. And despite all ads trying to convince me otherwise, they will settle deeply into my wrinkles. Worth the time to apply them? Nope." She opened a drawer and plopped them in.

Next, she held up an eyeshadow stick. "See this smoky brown eye shadow? You don't need it, and it won't stay on anyway." She dropped it in the drawer.

"Eyeliner? I prefer not to."

Drop.

"Mascara? Even if it's waterproof, I prefer not to."

Drop.

"Lip gloss?" she said, holding up her favorite tube of Merry Berry. "This is the one thing I suggest you apply every hour, every day, because with all this sweat pouring out of you during hot flashes, you are going to be dehydrated. Once a hot flash starts, you may look like the human incarnation of the Nile River on the outside, but on the inside, you will be a desert—the Sahara, the Gobi, the Kalahari." She pursed her lips, then swished lip gloss back and forth across them. "Carry it with you. Lip gloss is your only friend in this dehydration journey."

She hopped up onto the counter. "And when ads make you feel like crap for how you look and encourage you to invest more money in your makeup, all you have to say is *I prefer not to.*"

An hour later at the breakfast table, Anna glanced at Clem, then grimaced. "Mom?" she said. "What is wrong with your face today?"

Clem wiped her chin. "Do I have crumbs on it?"

"No," Anna said, "your skin is all blotchy, and you have a brown smudge on your cheek. Are you sick?"

Evan elbowed Anna, but she ignored them.

Clem tapped the sunspot on her right cheek. She knew exactly where it was. "Anna," she said, "this is a sunspot."

"Is it new? I've never seen it before."

"No, I've had it for years. I usually cover it with makeup."

Anna made a gagging noise. "You should cover it now."

Evan nudged her shoulder and mumbled something into their bowl of cereal.

"And what's with everything else?" Anna continued, waving her hands in front of her mother's face. "The blotchiness and those dark circles under your eyes. You look like a phantom."

Clem laughed. Better a phantom than a rabid raccoon. "My dear, this is called Mom Without Makeup. I'm tired of taking the time to put it all on only to sweat it off during a hot flash."

Anna growled. "Here we go," she said. "Let's start the day talking about Mom's hormones."

"Anna, you need to get used to this conversation. Hot flashes and perimenopause are an inevitable reality of life for people with uteruses, like you," Clem said. "As are maturing testicles and erections for young males, like your brothers."

Evan laughed, but Brewster spat a mouthful of cereal onto the table. "Mom!" he yelled. "Stop it!"

Clem looked sheepish. "Sorry, Brew, but even you need to get used to it, honey."

Brewster pushed back his bowl and stomped out of the room. "I do not!" he yelled back.

"Are you going to look like this all the time now, Mom?" Anna said.

"If I want to," Clem said.

"Ew," Anna said, then stuffed a bite of pancake into her mouth.

Later that morning, when Clem received the Your package has been delivered text, she groaned, trudged outside, and found it partially buried in the snow beneath the mailbox. Thankfully, the plastic wrapping had held tight. No seals were broken. Every year before, she'd carried that package over to Georgia's house and opened it over a cup of tea. Georgia had loved the Valentine's Day pajamas tradition, waiting each year to see which set Clem ordered.

Now, since Georgia was no longer there, Clem went back into the house, dropped the package into the sink, and wiped off the snow. Strangely, she wasn't even dreading it anymore. She'd accepted the horror of what she was about to see. And somewhere in her head, she was formulating a plan about not celebrating the holiday at all. The plan wasn't fully shaped yet, but it was there, floating around.

Once the package was dry, Clem tore off a corner with her teeth, then ripped the bag wide open. The pj's flew out, along with a wretched chemical smell that reminded her of her grandfather's garage. Worried she was going to poison herself and Hagrid, she opened the door and let in a gust of fresh air. Once her head was clear, she held up a pair of the pajamas. Long bottoms with a ragged hem and a long-sleeved top rougher than a burlap sack. They were worse, even, than the picture on the website from which she'd ordered. The polyester was thin without a bit of stretch. The brown was washed out. The blue was neon. The faces were sneering, not smiling.

She held up the pair intended for Hagrid. They were shockingly enormous. Designed more for a woolly mammoth than a Newfie.

No one was going to wear these things.

An hour later, after Clem had tucked the pajamas under a stack of sweaters in her closet, Anna stormed through the front door. "Mom! Mom!"

From the sound of Anna's voice, Clem knew she'd either lost a game or witnessed a murder. "What is it, Anna?"

"My friends are seeing your TikToks," Anna said. "They're running around telling people *I prefer not to.*"

Clem grinned. That was it? "Good. They're learning young."

"Mom, you need to stop all this. You are embarrassing me."

"Sweetie, embarrassment never killed anyone."

Anna ignored her. "Every time I think it can't get worse, it does, Mom. First, the whole *I'm taking my clothes off everywhere* thing, and now saying 'I prefer not to' like you're some kind of character in Melville's short story. You are not Bartleby."

"Sweetie, I'm not trying to be Bartleby, but learning to say no is an important skill."

"Mom, in math today, the teacher asked Laila to read the paragraphs about the triangle inequality theorem."

"And?"

"And she said, 'I prefer not to.'"

A tiny smile formed on Clem's lips.

"Don't laugh, Mom! It's not funny."

"I'm not laughing, Anna, but that's brilliant!"

"It's school, Mom. When a teacher asks you to read a few paragraphs, you read a few paragraphs. Not a big deal."

"Sometimes, but it sounds like Laila is trying on her newfound ability to say no to something. Saying no to reading in class was exercise for her. She's strengthening her no muscle. You should try it."

"You want me to say no to teachers?"

"If it feels right, yes, yes, I do."

Anna smirked. "Sorry, Mom, I prefer not to."

CHAPTER TWENTY-FOUR

The Big Apple

Near the end of fifth grade, Clementine wrote a monologue for the end-of-year talent show. It was about a classmate, a kid named Ronald Simpson who had been bullying her since kindergarten. Throughout the years, this boy had repeatedly kicked her, stolen her sun butter sandwiches, allied himself with Max Walden in gym class, tripped her, pinched the backs of her arms until they bruised, and many other things. He'd made her daily life in elementary school a living hell. From time to time, she'd complained, but despite closed-door talks with teachers, principals, social workers, and Ronald's parents, the boy's behavior had never changed. Clem decided that the talent show was a perfect opportunity to express her feelings once and for all and hopefully put an end to Ronald's behaviors before middle school. A few days before the show, she rigged a curtain and stage in the basement and put on a dry run for her mother.

Clem was proud of her work. The monologue was poignant and funny. Detailed with a strong through line. And she delivered it with the right amount of drama. But after saying "Ta-da!" and taking a bow, she saw that her mother was horrified.

"Mom?" she said. "You didn't like it?"

"Sweetie, you can't talk about Ronald like that," her mother said. "I know his mother and his aunt."

"So?"

"You can't say these things about him. They'll be devastated."

"But he's horrible to me. And you know it." As she spoke, ten-year-old Clem felt little bits of strength and bravery evaporating from her soul.

"You're not exaggerating a little bit, honey?"

Clem stared at her mom. This was the first, but not the last, time someone would suggest that she was exaggerating about a man's bad behavior. "No, it's not."

"Even so."

Clem's mother didn't say it out loud, but Clem heard her message loud and clear: *You have to put up with it.*

"Mom, this isn't fair."

Clem's mom cocked her head.

"Oh, come on, Mom! This isn't right. He shouldn't be allowed to get away with this."

But he was, and her monologue was nixed from the program. Instead, during Clem's allotted spot, Ronald Simpson juggled apples.

Clem thought about those apples on the day a producer with the *Happy A.M.* morning show called. Clem was in the women's hygiene aisle at the grocery store trying to decide if three boxes of ultra-size tampons would be enough to manage the next Amazon River flow of blood. Maybe four? Perhaps some pads as extra insurance?

After introducing herself, the producer asked if Clem wanted to travel to New York to join Mattie and May for a conversation the following Monday about Clem's I PREFER NOT TO movement. Clem dropped the tampon boxes into the cart. Mattie and May were the most popular duo on morning TV. Women all over the world watched them. They were smart and funny and charming. Of course she wanted to join them for a conversation, but because *I prefer not to* had been popping out of her mouth so frequently and so powerfully in recent days, she almost said it to the producer on the phone. Thankfully she caught herself and instead said, "Absolutely. I'll be there."

After sharing her email address, she hung up. She'd travel by train on Sunday and return to Byrock, via Boston, on Tuesday. *Happy A.M.* would put her up in a cozy hotel right next to Rockefeller Center, where the show was filmed.

Feeling buzzy, Clem settled on four boxes of tampons as well as a set of cooling sheets and an ice pack. She'd been invited to New York City to be on television. To talk about stuff she cared deeply about. If only she could call Georgia and tell her the news. As she was stocking up on tubes of lip balm, she heard a voice call, "I prefer not to!" Then a woman with gray hair popped into the aisle, ran up and hugged her, then disappeared. A few minutes later, Clem heard it again, "I prefer not to!" She grinned. She didn't know if she believed in signs from the "other side," but if they were a real thing, she was sure that was a sign from Georgia.

Not surprisingly, Anna was ticked about the invitation from Mattie and May. "It's not bad enough that you embarrass me daily on TikTok? A platform you're too old for. Now you're going to do it on national television?"

Clem wanted to remind Anna that the only reason she'd even known about TikTok was because Anna had begged her to join, but she decided not to poke the angry critter. "Come with me, Anna," she said. "To New York. It'll be the two of us. Girls' trip."

"No way," Anna said. "I'd rather lose to Northridge." Northridge was Byrock's greatest rival.

That night, while sweating in bed, Clem thought about Ronald Simpson, Max Walden, and Wallace Wright. How could the effects of their crude, unfunny behavior thirty-five years ago still be affecting her? And she wondered how those early experiences led her to her husband, a man whose belief in the traditional rituals of men and women was causing their marriage to crumble. When she talked about it on TikTok, her following ballooned to well over half a million. She was not alone in these wonderings.

A few days later in New York, as Clem was getting hair and makeup done in preparation for her spot on *Happy A.M.*, she made a fashion TikTok about how to get curly hair styled by a professional in the middle of a hot flash. With her curls trending toward broccoli crowns, it didn't seem possible that Clem would end up looking—and feeling—better than she had in months. But the brilliantly talented BetsyQ didn't bat an eye, and when she spun Clem around to face the mirror, Clem smiled bigger than she had in months. Maybe years.

"You, BetsyQ, are a magician."

"An artist is only as good as the materials they're given to work with. It was true for Picasso, and it's true for me. This is all you, hon."

The day before, Clem had hung the red heart-shaped Valentine's Day wreath on the Cranes' front door, then taken the train from Boston to New York City. With two nights on her own in the Big Apple, she did what every American mom dreamed of doing. She slept. She slept for twelve straight hours, and during those hours, no one snored, turned on the bathroom light, or called for a late-night pickup after a game or performance. She did have one night sweat, but because she was all alone in a king-size bed, she simply rolled from the drenched side to the dry.

She also turned off her phone. This one she'd had to think about because she knew the kids would need contact and Tor would need instructions about who had to go where when, what time all the important events were happening, and which items he needed to provide. If she'd traveled alone a year before, Clem would have left him a long, detailed list for each kid. Then another list of the meals and snacks they needed. And finally, a color-coordinated calendar. No ball would have been dropped. But this time, she'd simply packed a bag, called an Uber, and walked out the door.

The only note she'd left read *Have fun, kids! I won't be answering texts or calls so please talk to your dad about anything you need. Back on Tuesday! Love, Mom.*

The texts had begun as soon as she'd stowed her suitcase on the train. Anna:

what is this note on the table

where r u going

An hour later:

MOM
MOM
MOM
MOM
where r u
i need a poster board for a science project
due tmrw
can u take me 2 store
i need to get it or i will fail
do u want me 2 fail
MOM
i need a poster board
u do not care that i will fail

Clem did not text back. Ten minutes later, Anna tried again.

mom
mom
MOM
skate blades r dull
whats temp gng 2b 2day
y don't we have eggs

we shld get chickens then will always have eggs
how old is hagrid
wld hagrid eat chickens
yr not answering texts
where r u
i dreamed abt georgia last night
i miss georgia

When Anna started texting about Georgia, Clem had to sit on her hands to keep herself from responding. She wanted to help her daughter with her feelings about this. Georgia's and Henry's passings were the first significant deaths the kids had experienced. But why did Anna wait until Clem was away by herself? Why couldn't she have talked to her yesterday or the week before? Why hadn't she come along to New York City? Why, as soon as Clem had made and announced the decision to have a full forty-eight hours to herself, did Anna choose to text about the one thing that would grab Clem's heart?

Clem knew the answer. She didn't think her daughter was being intentionally manipulative, but even so, the result was the same.

Clem looked out the window of the Acela. Trees and waterways were rushing by. The whistle blew when a train heading the opposite way roared past. The train slowed as they chugged through another New England town. She wanted to respond to Anna. She wanted to tell her that Hagrid was seven years old. That they didn't have chickens because, yes, Hagrid would eat them. But also because Clem already had enough beings to care for. She wanted to tell Anna that if she'd been listening, she'd know that Clem was heading to New York City to be on TV. She might even remember that Mattie and May—*the* Mattie and May—of *Happy A.M.*, wanted to talk to her about the I PREFER NOT TO movement. She wanted to share her excitement and surprise that anyone was referring to it as a movement. She also wanted to remind Anna that she'd been invited to tag along and said no. Finally, she wanted to tell her how tightly Georgia had held Anna when she'd first come home from the hospital, a wee thing with long eyelashes and an insistent babble. While Clem had rested, Georgia had rocked her, taken her for walks in the stroller, and picked her up when she cried. Missing Georgia made sense. Anna would always miss her.

But Clem didn't respond. She was determined to stick to her no-contact decision. If there was an emergency, she'd be home in a flash, but for anything else—even dreams about Georgia—she needed to stay firm.

It was only three and a half hours to New York on the Acela, but she wished it were longer. It was relaxing to watch the changing landscape through the window with snow as the common denominator. She dozed off somewhere in Connecticut but woke to her phone buzzing with more texts. Tor this time.

Lark, you there?

What should I make for dinner tonight?

Heather is predicting a big storm. Did you buy a new shovel?

Any revelations about where my green sweater might be?

Did you sew the hole in Brewster's costume?

Did you organize a carpool for Anna's away game?

How much should I feed Hagrid?

Tor's texts went on and on until finally Clem did what she'd promised. She turned off her phone. When she got off the train, she went up the escalator and found the car sent by *Happy A.M.* And when she checked into her hotel, she stood at the window looking out over Rockefeller Center, basking in the aloneness. This was the first time she'd been on her own in forever. At home, there was always a child, a boss, a husband, a colleague, another human to think about. Sorting through her thoughts had been excruciatingly difficult, impossible really. But now, alone in her hotel room, no one was pushing or pulling or tugging or begging or complaining. The anxious nerves over the next day's show had subsided, and the anticipation of all that lay ahead was building.

After a quick shower, she headed to a restaurant around the corner. It had been years since she'd eaten alone, so she took her time, reading every item on the menu. She was so relaxed by the end of the meal that she almost called home to check on everyone. But as she was about to hit the green call button on her phone, she remembered that the gym next to her hotel had a sauna. And that's how she finished the evening, basking in the warmth, trying to forget the storm predication, and ignoring her telephone.

She fell asleep in the big bed and woke twelve hours later.

The interview with Mattie and May went beautifully. Mattie was three years into having hot flashes, and May had begun, like Clem, a few months before. Both connected deeply to I PREFER NOT TO. "I've already started using this phrase at home," Mattie said. "May and I want T-shirts."

Clem explained the origin of the movement. The story of Melville's "Bartleby, the Scrivener" and the realization of its meaning that day in the library. On national television she disclosed that this story was really, at its core, about the decremental extinction of a woman's spirit. When Mattie heard that, she tipped backward on the couch, grabbed Clem's hand, and said, "This, this, this!"

They pulled up Clem's TikTok account on-screen to show the number of followers she had. Overnight it had ballooned to 1.25 million. And they played her most recent "hot-flash fashion" video and rolled with laughter.

Through the window of the studio, Clem watched snow begin to fall. Heather of the Weather's prediction had been spot-on.

They closed with "If you're not following Clementine Crane at I Prefer Not To, get on it. This is the account every human with a uterus needs."

That night, a woman in China tagged Clem in a TikTok. She was forty-five years old. Her husband had treated her like an employee their entire married life. Her son now demanded she watch her grandchildren fifty hours a week while he and his wife worked. Her husband snored.

"Walrus," I yell every night, she said to the camera, *"walrus, stop snoring." But he pushes me away and snores on. I've put up with it for so many years, sacrificing my own well-being, my own sanity. And now, like you, I'm having hot flashes. As if the world hadn't made my life as a woman challenging enough. But two weeks ago, I found your TikTok account. When you said, "I prefer not to," my brain lit up. That very night, when my husband told me to put on his favorite show, I said, "I prefer not to." He looked at me cross-eyed, then hollered, but I didn't give in. I've been saying "I prefer not to" whenever he makes a request.*

"Get me dinner," he says. "I prefer not to," I say.

"Draw me a bath," he says. "I prefer not to," I say.

"Do the laundry," he says. "I prefer not to," I say.

My heart feels like it is brand new, and I'm not going to stop there. Clementine, I'm leaving my husband tomorrow. I bought a car and a tent with money I secretly saved over the years. I've packed one bag. He can throw away the rest. I've always wanted to see our country from coast to coast, and now I'm going to. Thank you, Clementine Crane. You have put words to my thoughts. You have given me a voice.

Holy shit. Clem sat on the edge of the bed in the hotel room, trying to process the fact that I PREFER NOT TO was impacting a woman on the other side of the globe so much that she was changing her life in magnificent ways. Leaving her husband. Leaving the things that weighed her down. Setting off on the adventure of a lifetime.

She leaned into the ride home on the Acela and used the time to build a website, make TikTok videos of the train ride, send out an issue of her newsletter, connect with a graphic artist about creating an I PREFER NOT TO logo, and reach out to a company that printed custom T-shirts. By the time the train reached Providence, Rhode Island, she'd already received three invitations to be the keynote speaker at conferences throughout the country. One in Boston, one in California, and one in North Carolina. Things were growing, and when the train pulled into Boston's South Station, she realized that things were bigger than her now. Bigger than Tor's snoring or her own hot flashes. She was now guiding something women all around the world needed. In China and beyond.

CHAPTER TWENTY-FIVE

Puppet or Puppeteer?

"You're home!" Anna shouted when Clem walked through the door. "What took you so long?"

Clem pushed her snow-covered suitcase into the house and shut the door behind her. "I'm home exactly when I said I'd be home. Did you see the spot on *Happy A.M.*?"

Anna smirked. "Yes, Dad made us watch."

"And?"

"It's embarrassing."

"Only embarrassing?"

"And kind of cool."

Clem smiled inside.

"Everyone at school is talking about it. Laila says you're becoming some kind of a goddess to people with uteruses."

"Goddess is a bit extravagant, but I'll take it," Clem said. "Anything exciting happen here?"

"Dad tried to pick the lock on your closet door."

"What?" Clem said.

"Yeah," Anna said, "he's convinced you're hiding his green sweater in there."

Clem's heart seized. Frankie. She tried to be calm and cool. "Was he successful?"

"Nah, Dad would never make it as a thief."

Clem listened to Anna jabber on about this and that, waiting for a quiet moment when she could make a clean break. When Anna got caught up in a text exchange with Laila, Clem dragged her suitcase up the stairs and into the bedroom. She unlocked the closet and ducked in, locking it behind her.

Nothing looked out of place, so she had to assume Anna was right. Tor hadn't gotten in. She lifted Frankie's bowl from the shelf and sat down with it in her lap. "You okay?" she said, dropping a few flakes into the water. It had only been forty-eight hours, but Frankie was ravenous. She shot to the surface and grabbed those flakes like Hagrid stealing steak from the table.

As she unpacked, Clem thought about what Anna had said. The thing about being a goddess to people with uteruses. She didn't want to be a goddess. But the experience on *Happy A.M.* had helped clarify things in her head, and she realized that she was a person who could get and hold the attention of the masses. This was unexpected and surprising.

Before she could move cleanly into the work that was before her, she first needed to figure out why the hell she'd been complicit in her marriage, why she'd played Nora Helmer to Torvald Crane. For so many years, she'd accepted, even welcomed, *little lark* and *wee squirrel.* She'd been a smart, accomplished woman since the beginning of her and Tor's relationship, yet she hadn't presented herself as an equal in their marriage. She hadn't challenged society's gender roles. She hadn't stood up and shouted, *This is wrong.* She hadn't proven herself as an individual woman. She hadn't strengthened women's place in society. Instead, she'd allowed her daughter and sons to learn this dynamic, cementing it in their mushy little baby brains, letting them see that inequality was real, that it was a part of their fabric, so that no matter what, they would believe it and have to unravel it for themselves later in life, if they ever did at all.

Yes, she was pissed at Tor and society, but she was also pissed at herself, and this piece was the hardest to unravel. How could she forgive herself for passively participating? Why hadn't she said *stop* a long time ago?

When Clem thought back to being denied the opportunity to perform her Ronald Simpson monologue, she knew that she too had had this gender-rooted dynamic cemented into her mushy little baby brain by *her* mother.

This internal argument—*They did this* versus *I did this to myself* versus *The world did this*—was both excruciating and enlightening, and by the end of the night, as Clem lay drowning in sweat, she knew it was an intricate combination of the three.

CHAPTER TWENTY-SIX

Let It Snow

On the night of February 12, when Heather of the Weather invoked the specter of the cataclysmic Blizzard of 1978, Clem knew things were getting serious. "Georgia used to talk about that blizzard like it was the storm to end all storms," she said to the kids.

They were gathered around the television, leaning close as Heather did her dance and explained expected accumulations and potential damage.

"The Blizzard of '78," Heather said, "paralyzed the entire state of Massachusetts. In approximately thirty hours, many areas got between two and four feet of snow." Heather paused for effect, eyes wild with excitement. "The accompanying winds were wicked, and they blew snow into giant drifts. Some more than fifteen feet high."

"I've been waiting for this my whole life," Tor said.

Clem groaned.

Brewster whipped around to look at her. "It's okay, Mom. Even if the storm is this big, we've got it. Nothing to worry about."

Tor hushed him. "Heather is still talking, Brew."

Clem rolled her eyes.

Heather continued, pointing to images of the 1978 blizzard on the green screen. "The snow came so fast and so unexpectedly on February sixth that people got stuck on Route 128. It became a parking lot, with hundreds of cars buried in the snow."

The kids looked gleefully at Tor.

"We need to get our sleds and cross-country skis ready," Evan said. "We'll put them just inside the garage where we can get to them easily. We might need to go out and save people who get stranded."

Although there was no way Clem was ever going to let the kids out in a blizzard to save people, she nodded. Anything to keep them occupied. "Evan," she said, "how would you feel about being the boss of blizzard prep this time?"

Evan smiled. "I'm ready, Mom."

"Good," she said. "You're in charge. We'll follow your lead."

Evan sat tall. "Thanks, Mom." Then they instructed Anna to gather batteries, headlamps, and lanterns, Brewster to prep the fireplace, and Tor to put together all other emergency supplies. "Make sure you have everything handy, Dad," they said. "You never know what we'll need in a storm like this. Duct tape, rock salt, plastic sheeting in case a window blows out. Think outside the box." Then Evan looked at Clem.

"Yes, dear?"

"Mom, I know you're mostly preferring not to right now, but how would you feel about going to the store and getting last-minute necessities?"

Clem nodded. Of course she was going to the store. As much for herself as for them. "On my way," she said.

Forty-five minutes later, the woman behind her in the grocery line tapped Clem on the shoulder. "Hey, I know you. You're the I PREFER NOT TO woman, aren't you?"

Clementine turned. "I am," she said. "How do you know?"

"I saw you on *Happy A.M.*," the woman exclaimed. "But I've been following you on TikTok for weeks."

"Really?"

The woman nodded. "It drives my daughter crazy. She says I'm too old for social media."

Clem held out her hand. "Clementine Crane."

"Jessica Whitting. Wonderful to meet you!" She glanced at Clem's cart. "Do you live here in Byrock?"

Clementine nodded. "I do. I work in the library."

"Our library? Here in town?"

"The very one."

Jessica laughed. "I had no idea. Wait until my book club hears this! You're our favorite human!"

"Me?"

"Yes, you. Our members are all around forty years old, so we're collectively starting to hit perimenopause. At our last meeting, we spent half the time cooling down the hot-flashers and the other half watching your TikToks." She laughed. "We all have kids. We're all buckling under the mental load. Most of our spouses snore. We're all ready to snap. You've come along at a perfect moment."

Clem grinned.

The line moved. Clem was next.

"Before we check out, can I get a picture with you? My friends are never going to believe this."

"Absolutely!" Clem said. Then she and the woman wrapped an arm around each other's shoulders and snapped a series of selfies. The woman immediately sent hers to her book club, and Clem loaded hers into TikTok stories.

When Jessica was through the line and on her way out the door, she said, "They are so excited! Will you come to our next book club meeting?"

"I'd love to!" Clem said. They exchanged contact information, then went their separate ways.

Clem texted Charlene. *You are not going to believe what just happened.*

Outside the winds were whipping something awful. Clem looked at the sky and opened her arms. She was ready for anything.

CHAPTER TWENTY-SEVEN

Happy Valentine's Day

By the next morning, snow was piled halfway up the first-floor windows and the wind had blown the cherry-red Valentine's Day wreath into a nearby drift. School was canceled for the ninth day that year. A record. And Clem woke knowing that on this Valentine's Day eve, the house was going be overstuffed with her three stinky, hormonal, self-centered, cranky, hilarious, sometimes wonderful humans. And Tor.

After a good lie-in, the kids decorated the heart-shaped sugar cookies Clem had baked while they'd slept, arguing, as they did every year, about who was hogging the red sugar and who ate too many cookies when no one was looking. (Brewster, always Brewster.)

During a lull in the storm around four o'clock, all five Cranes headed outside to clear snow. The driveway markers had been buried for weeks, so Clem watched Tor maneuver the blower as best he could, trying not to veer wildly into the grass so they didn't have to reseed in the spring. Yet another reason to move to Costa Rica.

As Clem cleared the steps with a shovel, she tried to keep her back to Georgia's dark house. It was sad to be out in a blizzard without running over to Georgia's to clear snow from her porch as well. It was even sadder not to hop into her house for hot chocolate and a slice of pie when she got too cold.

Back inside, they settled around the fire for chocolate-covered strawberries and milk, another Crane family Valentine's Day tradition.

Once she'd polished off the last of the berries, Anna jumped onto the couch and yelled, "Pajama time!"

"Yes!" the boys said in unison.

Clem had been hoping they'd forget about the pj's. Did teens really need Valentine's Day sleepwear? Shouldn't they have outgrown this desire?

"Come on, Mom, let's have them!" Anna said.

Obviously, they hadn't.

"What do you have for us this year, Mom?" Brewster's excitement was oozing. "I could barely sleep last night thinking about this."

Clem sighed. She felt guilty, but there was nothing to do but move forward. She pushed the laundry basket across the kitchen floor with her foot. "Here you go," she said.

The kids looked at her as if she had grown a second nose.

Tor touched the basket with his foot. "In here, Clem?"

"Yes."

"Why in here?" Evan said.

They were used to their pajamas being wrapped in special Valentine's Day paper with big red bows and bags of candy hearts.

"Things are a little different this year," Clem said.

"No kidding," Anna muttered.

Clem yanked the basket back. "We can skip them. I'll return them."

Brewster grabbed it. "No! We can pull them from the basket, right?"

Tor and the kids looked at one another. Clem could tell they were confused about what was happening.

"Fine." Evan picked up the pajama set on top. They stood and unfurled the pants.

Tor chuckled. Brewster grunted.

"What the hell?" Anna said.

Tor laughed. "Hon," he said, "what are those?"

Held up to Evan, the pajama pants looked even more ridiculous than before. They'd shrunk in the wash and barely reached their knees. The colors were putrid, and the grimacing faces more terrifying than cute.

"Is this a joke?" Anna said.

"Clem?" Tor added. He pulled another set from the basket and held it out to Anna, who recoiled as if she'd been offered a sack of rotten meat.

Clem's body tingled. She had never blatantly defied tradition in their home. From the beginning, she'd done as expected, and when she created a tradition, she kept that tradition. At Christmas, they decorated trees in the back and front yards with lights. Every Easter, there was an outdoor egg hunt. And on Halloween, theirs was the scariest house on the block.

Clem was tempted to apologize but caught herself at the last second. No more insincere apologies. "Kids, I ran out of time to order, and this is all they had," she said.

"You ran out of time?" Anna said. "You always order early. What happened?"

Clem looked at her daughter. "Life happened. Cookies for your bake sale happened. Driving Brewster to rehearsals happened. Evan's tutoring sessions happened."

"So what? Those things take a minute."

"A minute," Clem said. She was expanding like a puffer fish. "Georgia's death happened," she said.

Everyone got quiet for a moment, then Anna said, "Don't you think Georgia would be disappointed in these?" She held up a set of pajamas. "Ooh," she said, "they stink too!"

They did stink. After barely surviving the toxic gush a week before, she'd aired the pj's on the back porch, then run them through the wash three times with a fresh-smelling dryer sheet. They still stunk.

"Mom, you didn't try to exchange them once you saw them?" Evan said.

"There was nothing to exchange them with, Evan." Clem looked out the window. Flakes were still drifting down. "Now, since Valentine's Day pajamas are so important to you, please go put them on." When nobody moved, she used her serious voice. "Now!"

As she waited for them to move, Clem realized that she was going to have to disappoint her kids and husband in order to get them to understand the issues. God, it was so painful.

Anna stood and pulled her set from the basket. "What the hell?" she said. "A nightdress, Mom? Seriously?" She hadn't worn a nightdress since she was six.

"Put it on, Anna," Clem said.

Tor held his pair far from his body. "Clem, come on. Is this a joke? Do you have the real pajamas hidden somewhere?"

"It is not a joke," Clem said. "These are your Valentine's Day pajamas. Happy Valentine's Day. Now, go put them on." She turned her back to them, picked up Hagrid's set, and began to stuff him into it, leg by leg.

"Dad!" Brewster said. "What is going on?"

Because the room grew quiet, Clem knew her husband must have shrugged.

"Don't do that, Tor," she said, not turning.

"My sweet lark—" he began.

"I am not anyone's lark," she said. Her voice was so firm she barely recognized it.

"Okay," Tor said, "Clementine, is something going on that the kids and I need to know about?" He sat on the couch next to her.

"Nope," she said.

"You've got a bit of an edge to you, and these pajamas are pretty awful. You always get such adorable ones."

A few appointments tumbled out of Clem's chest onto the floor. She didn't even reach for them. Her phone buzzed with two reminders. One to pick up Evan's retainers at the orthodontist, the other reminding her that because of the snow, the truck picking up donation items would be running late. She ignored them.

"Torvald, if you and the kids want adorable pajamas for Valentine's Day, from now on, the four of you will need to do the ordering. This is the last set I will ever order."

Tor looked nervous. Had she ever seen him look nervous like this before?

Clem tugged Hagrid's tail through the hole in the end of his pajamas, then scratched his ear. "What do you think, big guy?" Hagrid's pj's had shrunk too. He looked like an overstuffed bratwurst.

"I can't believe you did this, Mom," Anna said, then stomped out of the room. Evan and Brewster followed. They left behind a cloud of disappointment.

Minutes later, the lights flashed and the power went out. The house was suddenly black as night, and a stillness snapped into place. What a relief.

"Anna!" Clem yelled. "Where did you put the lanterns?"

"The what?" Anna yelled back.

"The lanterns! You know, the ones you were to gather for the storm that is now here."

"Oh, crap!" Anna yelled from the second floor, then tumbled down the stairs in the dark. "I forgot!"

No surprise there.

"I'll get them from the basement," Anna said.

Clem heard her making her way down the steps.

"Ouch!" Anna yelled. "Mom, when are you going to get Georgia's furniture out of here? I killed my knee."

Once Anna returned with the lanterns, Clem sent them all to bed. "Off you go," Clem said, "before the house gets too cold to fall asleep."

She bundled up in layers, knowing that by morning the place would feel like an ice cube. Unlike their neighbors, Tor refused to install a generator that would run basic appliances and the heater in crises like this. He reveled in the challenge of a power outage. "We don't need a generator," he insisted every year. "We can keep warm enough. I'll cook over the camp stove and keep the fire going."

Each year it got worse, and the year before, Clem had suffered frostbite in her pinkie along with smoke inhalation and a few other power outage maladies—all while listening to the dulcet hum of the neighbors' generators. Midway through that storm, Clem and the kids had moved next door to Georgia's warm, well-lit house.

Tor cleared his throat, which she knew would lead to a speech about the importance of weathering storms without the assistance of modern technology.

"Don't," she said.

He didn't say anything else until he was climbing into bed, at which time he rolled away from her and grumbled, "I wish I had my green sweater."

"Me too," Clem whispered, thinking that if he did, she could wrap the sleeves around his neck and pull tight.

By morning, the snow had stopped completely and the power was back on. Despite the pajama drama the night before, Tor and the kids woke sure Valentine's Day was going to go as it always had. Even after all the *I prefer not to*s and the flubbed pajamas, not one of them went to bed thinking, *Mom is so done. There's no way she's going to have a Valentine's Day celebration tomorrow.* Despite all warning signs, they never saw it coming.

No matter. It became obvious that morning when she didn't wake them with hot chocolate and heart-shaped marshmallows.

Instead of the usual 6:30 AM wake-up call, she let them wake on their own. And when they finally did at 9:00, she was stretched on the couch in front of a roaring fire. She heard Anna first. "Mom? Mom!"

"Right here, Anna." Clem held a mug of steaming tea.

Anna thundered down the stairs. "Mom," she said, "it's Valentine's Day."

"Happy Valentine's Day, sweetie," Clem said. She turned, saw her daughter and the boys at the bottom of the stairs. This was going to be hard. If only Georgia were here.

"Well?" Anna said.

"Well, what?"

"Well, where's our Valentine's Day stuff?"

Clem was direct. "Anna, our Valentine's Day celebration is not happening this year, unless you and your brothers and your dad want to make it so."

The mouths of all three kids dropped.

"If *we* want to make it so?" Anna said. "*You* always make it so."

Clem shook her head. She almost preceded her next statement with *I'm sorry,* but she caught herself. "That is true, honey, but this year, I prefer not to."

Anna's face nearly exploded. Clem could see she'd had it with *I prefer not to.* Even so, Clem held strong, something that was getting easier and easier.

Clem saw Tor over Anna's shoulder. He was staring at her, shaking his head. In many ways he looked exactly like he had when they'd first met; in other ways, she didn't recognize him at all.

An hour later, Clem's phone buzzed. It was a reporter from the *Boston Globe* asking for an interview about the I PREFER NOT TO movement.

"I can talk now," she said. She looked at the snow piled up on the window, the wind still whipping through the yard, and the balls of ice weighing down the sycamore. Tor had headed outside to begin snow cleanup, and the kids were zoned out on their devices.

The reporter, Jillian, was warm and positive, and she had a long list of questions. Clem put her on speaker and sat down at the table.

How long have you worked at the library?

When did you first read "Bartleby, the Scrivener"?

What are some of the things in your own life that caused you to start the I PREFER NOT TO movement?

When Clem began talking to Jillian about her hot flashes, she realized that the HRT patch must be working. Her hot flashes were still coming regularly, but the intensity had eased. She made a note to put this on TikTok. There was hope with the right gynecologist. About thirty minutes into the interview, Anna came to the doorway and stood. She was listening. And the smirk was gone.

"And my last question," the reporter asked, "are you writing a book?"

"A book?"

"Yes, the story of how you came to represent women around the globe. The story of how your voice came to matter."

"I represent women around the globe?" Clem said.

The reporter paused. "Well, yes."

Anna moved into the room and sat next to Clem.

"And my voice matters?"

The reporter seemed surprised that Clem had to ask that question. "Yes, Clementine, your voice matters."

The thought of writing a book had never crossed Clem's mind, but now that the seed had been planted, it seemed as if the idea had been there all along.

Anna reached out and took her hand.

By midafternoon, the interview went viral and word of the I PREFER NOT TO movement was traveling even faster—woman to woman, person with uterus to person with uterus, state to state, country to country. The sound bite was blasting everywhere: "I prefer not to."

And at 5:00 PM, Clem received a third call from the funeral home. This time she answered. The woman on the other end had a warm and empathetic voice. Did Clementine know that Georgia's ashes were ready for pick up? Would she prefer they hold them a little while longer?

"Yes, please," Clem said. "I'm almost, but not quite ready for this next step."

The woman assured her that because there was no timeline for grief, she'd take good care of the urn until Clem felt strong enough.

Thank God.

Crunch, crunch, crunch.

CHAPTER TWENTY-EIGHT

A Room of One's Own

One thirty-eight AM, Clem's head:

My voice matters.
I am a leader.
I PREFER NOT TO is a movement.
Make a plan.
I am furious.
Turn anger into energy.
I want more.
Make more for yourself.
I want less.
Let go of stuff.
I have no space to myself.
Make one room yours.

The next morning, Clem pulled half of her clothes from the walk-in closet, dumped them into plastic bags, put them by the front door, and marked them for donation. She grabbed the toolbox from the basement, then dismantled the shelves and hanging rods. From her perch, which thankfully was spared, Frankie stared as if to say, *What's happening here?* Clem put the metal and wood in buckets and dragged them out the back door onto the snowy porch. Then she sanded the walls of the closet and painted them the same happy green they'd painted Anna's room the year before.

After lunch, she took a breath and went down to the basement. Georgia's bedroom set was there, waiting to be emptied and moved upstairs. Clem dusted it, but she wasn't ready. She enlisted Evan's help, and the two of them dragged Tor's old desk up the stairs to the bedroom. She dismissed them, then moved it herself into the closet and set up her computer and printer. She put her ring light on a shelf, then hung a few pieces of art. She printed a colorful sign, *I PREFER NOT TO*, then taped it to the wall.

She briefly considered removing one of the two chairs in front of the window. It was tight. But Georgia's spirit lived on in that rocker. It had to stay. She'd make it work.

When she was done, she nodded. She'd successfully transformed her closet into an office.

Make one room yours.

From I PREFER NOT TO headquarters, Clem began making TikToks multiple times a day. She ordered T-shirts and coffee mugs with the new I PREFER NOT TO logo on them. Her following was up to 1.7 million. Women were empowered. All around the world, they were watching her videos, then looking around at their lives, and responding, *I prefer not to.*

Can you make dinner?

I prefer not to.

Can you take the dog out?

I prefer not to.

Can you make me a dental appointment?

I prefer not to.

Can you drop off the car for an oil change?

I prefer not to.
Why didn't you do the laundry this week?
I prefer not to.
Can you plan Gigi's birthday party?
I prefer not to.
The flowers need to be watered.
I prefer not to.
Let's go on vacation together.
I prefer not to.

The second I PREFER NOT TO gathering in Byrock's town center drew well over a hundred people. With all the snow, Clem hadn't expected much, but as she sat on the steps of the gazebo, she watched carloads of women pull in. Jessica from the grocery store arrived with her book club buddies. The owner of the town bookshop showed up, along with Brenda from the bakery, Samantha and Meghan, and so many more. Five snowshoed over a hill. Nova, Rose, and Charlene appeared with a gaggle of friends. Astrid, as usual, wore yellow.

When Clem stood, the women cheered. "Hello, hot-flashers," she said. "Hello, overwhelmed moms, mental-load managers, and pissed-off people with periods. Welcome to the new world order." She knew people, men especially, would think the term *new world order* sounded a bit audacious. What the hell was wrong with that?

CHAPTER TWENTY-NINE
Poor Kara

The next day Clem infiltrated Dr. Sheffield's waiting room, tracking in dirty slush on her boots. She chuckled at the pregnant woman near the door who looked like she might be giving birth to a camel but had no idea that a fire-breathing dragon was nipping at her swollen heels. Looking deeper into the crowd, Clem spotted three hot-flashers near the window and began making her way in their direction.

The receptionist called to her. "Hello! Good morning! Can I help you?" Now that Clem had experienced the authentic welcome at Dr. Parker's office, the fake cheeriness of Dr. Sheffield's minion annoyed Clem more than ever.

"I sure hope so."

"Do you have an appointment?"

"I don't."

The receptionist looked confused.

Clem looked at her name tag. "Kara, I'm a patient of Dr. Sheffield's. He birthed all three of my kids. I'm now at the beginning of perimenopause. I'm having hot flashes. And recently I had my first night sweat. I nearly drowned in my own bodily fluids." Clem was speaking quite loudly, and the women in the waiting room were beginning to stare.

"Oh, my," Kara said. Her eyes were as big as Frankie's.

"Honestly," Clem continued, "when I woke in the middle of a night sweat, I thought I'd been bludgeoned and was covered in blood. I scared the hell out of my kids. Well, I scared one kid. The other two weren't very interested in my impending death."

Kara nodded. "And?"

"And?" Clem waved her hands wildly at the women in the waiting room. "And this!"

"What?" Kara said. Clem could tell she had no idea what she was going on about. "Would you like to make an appointment? Dr. Sheffield is booking fairly far out—March, I believe—but he had a cancellation next week. I can get you in."

Clementine shook her head. "No, no, I don't want an appointment, Kara. I've had enough appointments with Dr. Sheffield. I'm here to gather followers."

"Followers?"

"Yes, followers. Every single woman in here, pregnant or not, needs to know what perimenopause is. They need to be ready for it." Clementine pointed to the women around her. "No one prepares us. No one prepared me."

Kara picked up the phone and pressed a button. Clem figured she was summoning Dr. Sheffield, but she didn't care.

"I'm also here to protest," Clem said.

"Protest what?" Kara said, covering the mouth of the phone with her hand.

"The fact that we"—she pointed at herself—"the hot-flashing humans of the world, are not represented in this office. Where is the artwork that depicts our challenges? Where are the posters of sweating women? Where are the posters of women wandering the world in a brain fog with itchy ears? Where, where, where?" Clementine ran from wall to wall, waving dramatically at the pictures of expectant mothers.

Kara glanced at the door to the back offices. "I don't know. I just started working here last week. I'm only twenty-two. I don't know much of anything."

Right then, the door to the exam rooms opened and Dr. Sheffield stepped through. Relief flooded Kara's face. "Clementine?" he said.

"Hello, Dr. Sheffield." Clementine glared at him.

"You're back."

"I am."

"Can we help you? I'm sure Kara offered to make you an appointment."

"I don't want an appointment," Clem said.

"No?"

"No."

At this point, every woman in the waiting room was watching the exchange, and Clem saw that the lady carrying the camel had had it. "What in the world," she said, pointing at Clem, "are you rabbiting on about?"

Clem didn't blame her for the attitude. Carrying a camel was exhausting. She took a breath. "Are you sure you want to know?"

"I am. I've listened to you long enough." She pointed at her belly. "This is my fourth kid. It might pop out at any second, so please hurry."

Clem nodded. "Here goes. I just entered perimenopause, and no one warned me."

Dr. Sheffield cleared his throat.

"Warned you of what?" the woman said.

"The horror."

"There's horror?"

"Oh, yes. You think you're in hell now with your acid reflux and backaches, just wait. With perimenopause come hot flashes, this weird breathy thing that makes you think you're going to suffocate within seconds, discomfort in parts of your body you didn't know existed, itchiness in other parts of your body, brain zaps, and so much more. It's horrible."

All the women in the room looked from Dr. Sheffield to Clem and back.

"Is all this true, Dr. Sheffield?" the camel lady said.

Dr. Sheffield looked uncomfortable. "Listen, perimenopause is different for every woman. Clementine seems to be having extreme symptoms."

"Oh, no, Dr. Sheffield. My symptoms are not extreme. They are quite common. This degree of hot-flashing and brain fogging is experienced by women all over the world. I'm on TikTok. I know."

Three women picked up their phones.

"Clementine Crane," Clem said to them. "You'll find me under I PREFER NOT TO."

"Clementine, please don't upset my patients. These women are in other phases of life right now. They don't need to anticipate what's to come."

Steam shot from Clem's ears. "What? They are not children. Of course they need to anticipate what's to come. Or at least be given the option to consider it."

"Why stress them out about something that isn't going to happen for years?"

"You so clearly do not have a uterus," Clem said. "People without uteri should not be making decisions like this."

Dr. Sheffield corrected her. "Uteruses."

"Actually, either is correct." Clementine shook her head, then looked at each woman one by one. "Educate yourselves, ladies," she said. "Don't wait. Prepare yourself for the horror that will inevitably arrive. Those years Dr. Sheffield references? They go by fast. Damn fast." Clem turned to the lady carrying the camel. "You especially. Pay attention."

CHAPTER THIRTY
You Can't Unsee It

Samantha pinged her. Clem?

Clem?

Here.

Need to talk to you. Call me.

That was odd. Samantha avoided phone calls as much as everyone else.

On the phone?

Yes.

Why?

I watched your TikTok.

Which one?

Sweater Giveaway.

Clem laughed. "The Great Perimenopause Sweater Giveaway" was one of her favorites. One in which she donated favorite sweaters that, with hot flashes, were too thick and heavy to wear and then encouraged all perimenopausal women to do the same. After it went live, two national organizations that empowered and invested in women contacted her to team up. Perimenopause sweater giveaways were now happening on two continents.

I love that one.

Me too, but I still need to talk to you.

Clem didn't feel like talking. She was deep in content creation for the week. *Right now?*

Yes, please.

Clem called her. "What's up?"

Samantha was quiet for a moment.

"Sam, is everything all right? Did something happen at the library?"

"Clem, I need you to watch your sweater TikTok."

"What? Why?"

"Watch it. Then call me back." Samantha hung up.

Clem sat down in Georgia's rocking chair with her phone, clicked through to the sweater video, and hit play. She watched herself nattering on about the thick red sweater that made her feel like she was being smothered by a furry manatee, and the purple one that had nearly suffocated her during a hot flash. Death by purple sweater. "I'm not able to donate this one," she said in the video, "because I got so hot I cut it off my body with kitchen shears." She held up the mutilated sweater for all to see. This video had gotten nearly a million likes.

At the thirty-second mark, Clem froze. "Oh, shit." She saw what had made Samantha reach out. "Damn, damn, damn." Right behind her, in just a few seconds of footage, was Frankie. There was no mistaking her. The lighting perfectly highlighted Frankie's golden hues as she swam in a circle in her punch bowl. "Oh, no," Clem said, burying her head in her hands.

Her phone buzzed. Samantha, of course. Clem didn't pick up.

Samantha texted. It's okay, Clem. Don't panic.

Clem panicked. She ignored the text, watched, and almost deleted the video. But then she remembered that it had been stitched and dueted thousands of times by perimenopausal TikTokers who were telling stories about their own near-death experiences while wearing certain sweaters. She didn't have stats, but she knew those women were showing their sweaters to the world, then donating them to organizations in their respective towns and countries. They were brilliant videos that were making people across the platform laugh and cry.

"Shit."

Samantha texted. Seriously, Clem. It's okay. I already suspected. I haven't told anyone. Can we talk?

Clem did not want to talk. She searched *how to delete a TikTok and all duets/stitched videos.* The responses led her to Reddit. She hated Reddit. She clicked through anyway.

Clem's phone rang. She muted it. Reddit pointed her to the "Remove All" feature on TikTok. This, according to passionate Reddit-ers, was the key. If she used it to delete the original and all affiliated versions, she would be clean. No evidence.

With her heart thumping so hard, it was impossible to make her thumbs do what they needed to do. What if someone else had already spotted Frankie? Watched the video on repeat while doomscrolling until they noticed Frankie swimming laps behind Clem? Bathsheba? Local-Fish-Guy? Good god, how had Clem missed this when filming? She tried to be so careful.

When she finally located "Remove All," she hit the button and waited. Seconds later the video was gone. The stitched videos were gone. The dueted videos were gone. As promised by the all-too-wise Reddit-ers, all evidence was gone. Poof!

For a moment, Clem felt free, but then another thought pushed into her brain. What if someone had downloaded the video and was right now uploading it to the platform? Could people do that? Was it possible?

Of course it was possible. It was even likely. She held her phone to her chest and rocked, fear pumping a hole right through her middle.

The phone rang. Clem picked up. "Hi, Sam."

"Hi, Clem."

"I'm so sorry. I didn't intend to take Frankie. It's a long, hot story." She swallowed hard.

"Can I come over?"

The last thing Clem needed was a visitor. "God, no, Sam."

"We can talk it through."

Clem pressed her cheek to the frozen window and looked over at Georgia's empty house. When Evan was about four years old, they'd become obsessed with where people went when they died. For weeks, they'd talked endlessly about souls, spirits, graveyards, burial, cremation, and ghosts. Reincarnation turned out to be their favorite possibility, and they decided that everyone who died came back as their favorite animal. Maybe Georgia would be back as a bunny.

"I can't, Sam. I've got something to do this afternoon."

"Okay, but please find a way to return Frankie to the library. I won't tell a soul. Promise."

After hanging up, Clem turned to the punch bowl and said, "The gig's up." Frankie swam into her castle and disappeared. If only Clem could follow her.

An hour later, Clem drove to the funeral home, hid her tear-puffy eyes with giant sunglasses even though the sun hadn't been out in days, and picked up Georgia's ashes. They were in a round teak box that resembled the yurt she and Georgia had rented a few summers before in Maine. Georgia would approve.

Before setting off in yet another snow squall, Clem belted the vessel into the passenger seat. She didn't want Georgia rolling onto the floor the first time she hit a patch of ice. Once she was secure, Clem pulled into traffic. "Georgia," she said, "Samantha knows I have Frankie." She looked over, still shocked that all that was left of Georgia could fit into this small container. "I have to find a way to return her to the library. It's time, I know. I'm ready."

Right then, Clem pulled up to the four-way intersection outside Pet-O-Rama. Directly opposite her, in a pale-blue truck, was Douglass. She tried to slink down into her seat so he didn't see her, but it was too late. As she drove past him, he pointed a finger at her and mouthed the words "Give back the fish." Clem's heart thumped. He knew too.

CHAPTER THIRTY-ONE
Finally

The first sign that Tor was having a revelation of his own arrived via text.

March 24 is Stop Snoring Day.

Who says?

The American Sleep Association.

You looked up the American Sleep Association?

I did.

And?

It pointed me to a sleep disorder clinic in Boston.

And?

I've having a sleep test on March 24.

I don't believe it.

It's true.

It was March 5. A few months before, this news would have delighted Clem and set her nerves at ease. Now? She wasn't sure she cared.

Crunch, crunch, crunch.

Best novel about a cool brave woman by a cool brave woman! Go!

If Clem was actually going to return Frankie to the library, she needed a boost of confidence. Snowstorm Lit would help. It helped everything.

Meghan jumped in first: Malala's Magic Pencil by Malala Yousafzai.

Keisha followed: The Handmaid's Tale by Margaret Atwood.

Walter was next: Little Women by Louisa May Alcott.

Clem wondered what Jade was up to, because when Snowstorm Lit was about women, she was usually the first to post.

Jing: The Hunger Games by Suzanne Collins! Katniss, Katniss!

Meghan followed: Fry Bread: A Native American Family Story.

What? No author? Clem knew Meghan must be thinking about Frankie. She'd never made that mistake before.

Gong!

Clem filled in the name: *Kevin Noble Maillard.*

Bathsheba countered with Amy Tan's *The Joy Luck Club.*

Jade finally landed one: The Color Purple by Alice Walker.

Clem smiled. The game was starting to fill her with courage, just like she needed it to. Taking Frankie back to the library was going to be one of the hardest things she'd ever done. It would symbolize the point of no return.

Walter made a play: Isabel Allende's In the Midst of Winter.

Clem loved that one too.

Victor: How the García Girls Lost Their Accents by Julia Alverez.

Of course *García Girls* was an excellent choice, but that didn't matter if you spelled the author's name wrong.

Gong!

Autocorrect! Autocorrect! he sent, but out was out.

The thread zipped and zinged for four or five minutes.

A Wrinkle in Time by Madeleine L'Engle.

Mrs. Dalloway by Virginia Woolf.

Their Eyes Were Watching God by Zora Neale Hurston.

Wild Swans by Jung Chang.

Bath got gonged for that one. The subtitle was missing. The complete name was *Wild Swans: Three Daughters of China.*

As the game slowed, Clem knew everyone was resisting the urge to search for appropriate titles. Then Walter and Samantha sent the same title in the same second: *The Hate U Give* by Angie Thomas.

Gong! Gong!

Clem could be a tough moderator.

Then Keisha, too, fell victim to autocorrect.

Gong!

It was down to Jing and Jade.

Jing posted: L.M. Montgomery's Anne of Green Gables.

A good one, but Jade trumped her.

The Bluest Eye by Toni Morrison.

No one lost to Toni Morrison.

Jade won the gold trophy.

Game over.

An hour later, confidence bolstered, Clem called Amanda Chen. Hungry to talk to the local celebrity who was changing things for women all around the world, Amanda agreed to meet Clem at the library at four that afternoon.

Once everyone was out of the house, Clem tucked Frankie's punch bowl into a cardboard box, covered it with a small blanket, tiptoed out the door, and belted the box into the passenger seat of her car, right next to the vessel of Georgia's ashes. She was well aware of the irony of the situation.

Undeterred, she pulled into the parking lot of the library, ignoring the handful of parents banging tambourines and wearing those ridiculous orange-sequined Frankie hats. What a relief that after today, she wouldn't have to see or hear them anymore.

As soon as Clem walked into the children's room, Little Miss Blue Hat raced up to her. "What's under the blanket, Ms. Clementine?" she said.

Clem waved her off, then set the covered box on Meghan's desk. She texted Bathsheba, Samantha, and the rest of her colleagues, then waited for Amanda Chen's cameraperson to get set up.

"What's this all about, Ms. Clementine?" Bathsheba said. "There's a leak in the men's bathroom, and the members of the Not Only Bingo group are complaining because the members of the Only Bingo group want their time slot. I don't have a lot of bandwidth for whatever this"—she waved her hands at the box—"is."

"Bear with me, Ms. Bath," Clem said. "This won't take long." Her palms were dripping with sweat, but this time it wasn't because of a hot flash.

Minutes later, when the library team was finally gathered and the camera was ready, Clem stood next to Meghan's desk holding the corner of the blanket. Her hand was shaking. "Think about Georgia," she whispered to herself. "Georgia, Georgia, Georgia."

"I have good news," she finally said out loud.

Meghan looked at her quizzically.

"Georgia would be so happy I'm doing this," Clem whispered. She wiped her hands on her pants.

"Ms. Clementine, who are you talking to?" Little Miss Blue Hat said.

Clem laughed. "An old friend."

The girl rolled her eyes. She was too young to know how important old friends were. "Okay," she said, "but what's in the box?"

Clem started to lift the corner of the blanket but stopped. "Wait a minute," she said, then took her phone from pocket, clicked on TikTok, propped it up on a bookshelf so that it was focusing on her and the box, and went live. She needed to be honest with everyone—the library folks and her I PREFER NOT TO followers.

This time when she tugged the corner of the blanket, she let it slide off the box. Then she reached in and lifted Frankie's punch bowl high into the air as if it were some kind of sacred chalice. Her heart was pounding, and her legs wobbled like noodles. Thankfully, Frankie was swimming happy laps around her castle—as undeterred as ever by the sudden change of venue.

It took a moment for everyone to realize what they were seeing, but once they did, the library went from hushed to raucous in mere seconds. Little Miss Blue Hat screamed. Meghan squeaked. Bathsheba yelped. Victor and Walter said, "What the hell?" simultaneously, then covered their mouths with their hands. Amanda Chen jumped in front of her camera and began narrating the event, filling viewers in on the backstory. Only Samantha looked unsurprised. She smiled at Clem and clapped.

After the initial shock, all the kids in the room yelled, "Frankie!" and rushed the punch bowl.

Keisha leapt between them. "Children, please back up!" she said. "You'll scare her. Let's give her a moment, then we'll welcome her properly back to the library."

Questions were flying at Clem. From Amanda Chen. From Bath. From Little Miss Blue Hat. Where did she find Frankie? Was she healthy? Where did the fancy bowl come from? Did someone turn her in for the reward?

Clem waited until the room was still and quiet, then she cleared her throat. "I have a confession to make," she said. She imagined

Georgia standing next to her, holding her hand while nudging her with her elbow. The only path now was the truth. "Although this is hard to admit," Clem continued, "you need to know that Frankie has been with me this entire time." Clem took a deep breath. "I took her. I took Frankie."

The collective gasp rolled over her like a tsunami, and the look on Meghan's face broke Clem.

"I'm so sorry," Clem said. "I didn't mean to hurt or scare anyone." She folded the blanket into a square and squeezed it to her heart, then stepped aside to let Meghan and the kids converge on the beloved fish.

Upstairs, as she was packing her personal things into the box she'd used to carry Frankie back into the library, Bathsheba approached. "Clem, the board will be holding an emergency meeting tomorrow," she said. "Enough damage has been done, so I doubt we'll press charges. But it's possible they'll vote to fire you."

Clem cut her off with a wave. "No need, Bath. I quit." She pulled the *Connector of People to Magical Things* nameplate from its Velcro bed, then placed it into the box next to Craft Clem shooting from a bevy of flames.

"What?" Bath said. "Clementine, you may not love me, but I know you love this library. Don't you want to fight to keep your position?"

Clem looked around. Handfuls of the protesters had heard the news about Frankie and had gathered in front of the library. They were chanting "Frankie's home! Frankie's home!" and jingling their tambourines joyously.

"I do love this library," she said, "but I realize there's something else I need to be doing."

"What if the board votes in favor of your employment with a suspension?"

Clem shook her head. "I prefer not to," she said. Then she turned, picked up the box, and headed to the exit. More than anything, she wanted to text Georgia, but instead she looked up at the small patch of blue in the otherwise cloudy sky and whispered, "I did it."

An hour later, she saw the library's Instagram post: "Frankie is home!"

Clem got a DM. Local-Fish-Guy.

Well done. Your fish karma gained a level.

CHAPTER THIRTY-TWO

Magical Things

The following week Clem spoke to 250 women in a banquet room in a Boston hotel. The planned speaker had canceled, and Clem had been hired at the last minute to fill in. Despite the late addition, the Women in Business group had done a hell of a job decorating with banners and balloons festooned with Clem's tagline: I PREFER NOT TO. They'd even hung posters with a QR code for Clem's TikTok account.

When she stepped in front of the women, she said, "Hello, hot-flashers, overwhelmed moms, mental-load managers, and pissed-off people with periods. Welcome to the new world order."

Afterward, nearly every woman in the audience lined up to talk with Clem and get her autograph. Lynn Foster, head of the group, put her at a table with a vase of lilies on it as well as a sprinkling of red confetti. As expected, most of the women were from New England—Massachusetts, Maine, New Hampshire, and Connecticut. Each and every one told Clem how much she'd inspired them. They couldn't wait to get home and try out their new response on their husbands, wives, kids, and bosses: *I prefer not to.* One particular woman from Vermont mentioned that she was in a wreck of a marriage but had always been too afraid to leave. "You've given me courage," she told Clem. "Hearing you say *I prefer not to* was the most magical thing. I'll be out of my house tomorrow."

This *was* a magical thing, and she *was* the Connector of People to Magical Things. She didn't need anyone to bestow this title upon her. Not Bathsheba Wheaton. Not Torvald Crane. And she lived it more and more every day.

As the last few women approached the table, Lynn Foster said, "You're something, you know."

"It's not me," Clem said. "It's the movement. Women are ready for this. They need it."

Minutes later, the very last attendee approached the table. "Hi," she said. "I'm Aria Lewis. I'm so happy to meet you."

Clem shook Aria's hand.

"I hadn't planned on coming to this event," Aria said. She leaned close and whispered, "Actually, I wasn't even a member until yesterday. When a friend called to tell me that you were replacing the original speaker, I joined and registered immediately. I need to show you something." She rolled up her sleeve. Clem assumed that a hot flash was starting to build, but instead the woman held out her arm and said, "Look." Clem saw the words *I PREFER NOT TO* tattooed on her wrist.

"Is that real?" Clem said.

"It is," Aria said. "These words have made me whole. Like you, I'd been swallowed by the expectations and assumptions of the world. My husband, parents, children, boss, the universe, my own body. I'd juggled it beautifully for years, but when the hot flashes started, I began to flail. I realized I could no longer do everything, and I shouldn't have been expected to all along."

Clem leaned closer to Aria's arm. The letters were clean and neat, written in a powerful sans serif font.

"A few weeks ago," Aria said, "while scrolling TikTok, I saw you having a hot flash and talking about things you no longer preferred to do. It's like I'd been struck by lightning. I woke the next day, said 'I prefer not to' when my husband asked for pancakes, my kids asked for a ride to school, and my father called to have me solve his tech issue for the millionth time. I said 'I prefer not to' all that day—to the mailperson, a clerk at the store, a demanding colleague—and by dinnertime, I felt lighter and freer and more in command of my own existence than I had in years, maybe decades. I came here today to thank you and show you this."

"May I touch it?"

Aria nodded.

While Clem ran her thumb over the words, she thought about Melville's "Bartleby, the Scrivener" and the phrase that helped her understand the story: "the decremental extinction of a woman's spirit." Bartleby died at the end of that tale, alone and lonely, but Clem knew that she, and all women, had something he hadn't. Each other. With that, Clem knew their destiny could be different.

By the end of the week, Clem had signed a merchandise deal with a company that was going to emblazon I PREFER NOT TO onto T-shirts, jackets, coffee mugs, water bottle stickers, and anything else Clem wanted. "But no tote bags," Clem told her contact there. "Why the world thinks women need four thousand tote bags is beyond me. As if we need to carry any more crap than we already do."

When her TikTok following ballooned to 1.9 million followers, Anna volunteered to manage the I PREFER NOT TO merchandise. Clem almost asked why she'd suddenly jumped on board, but she realized she didn't have to know every reason for everything from her teen. All she had to do was accept the goodness.

The woman in China who'd left her husband and family to travel the country on her own was TikToking from Qingdao. She was making friends, eating new foods, and talking with other women in similar situations. Since the last time Clem had checked her account, the woman had painted *I PREFER NOT TO* on the side of her van in Mandarin. There was even an airbrushed likeness of Clem.

As the movement grew bigger, Tor was shocked into silence. The boys were weirded out. Women and people with uteruses were stopping her daily in the grocery, the kids' school, the pharmacy, Brenda's Bakery, the street. "Say it," they'd holler from a block away. "Say it!" She was always happy to oblige.

"I prefer not to," she'd say. "Now it's your turn. Say it with me. Three, two, one—"

"I prefer not to!"

CHAPTER THIRTY-THREE

Unsolved Mysteries

Crunch. Crunch. Crunch.

At 1:38 AM on March 24, the night of Tor's sleep test, Clem heard the giant beast. Excited, she leapt out of bed, pulled on her robe, and raced outside with Hagrid by her side. By the time she reached the backyard, the crunch was faint. She could tell the temperature was rising. The snow was sloshy and the balls on the sycamore were bare. She suspected that with the change in weather, this might be the last time the creature happened by. Was it possible she may never know if it was a woolly mammoth, a moose, or even a curious alien from a faraway planet?

Clem looked up at Georgia's house. For the first time in months, a soft light was on in the upstairs bedroom. As Astrid had promised, the new family had moved in, and through the window, Clem saw one of the moms rocking the baby. Sadness flooded her heart, but only for a moment. Georgia would have been so happy to have a baby in her house. Clem needed to make room for that kind of joy.

Crunch, crunch, crunch.

"Oh, Georgia," she whispered. "We may never know."

On March 27, Tor received an official sleep apnea diagnosis. He was surprised, and when the CPAP rep arrived to teach him how to use the machine he'd be sleeping with from that day forward, he balked.

"Do you really think I need this?" he asked.

"I'm the technician," the guy said. "I don't administer the tests or read the reports. They tell me where to go, and I arrive to teach the diagnosed how to use this machine." He patted it affectionately.

Tor nodded and cleared space on his bedside table. "It's bigger than I expected."

"Smaller than it used to be," the man said. He laid a mask, a long hose, and a few other bits and pieces on the bed, then showed Tor how each fit together. He explained the nightly routine and the weekly cleaning process. Clem tiptoed past the door a few times to eavesdrop and chuckled at the flabbergasted look on her husband's face.

The following day, the sun began melting the ice pack on the top of the fence in the backyard. This was one of Clementine's favorite days of the year, when she could feel that winter was truly coming to an end and spring would soon burst forth. The new family was settling in next door, and Evan was already babysitting for them.

That weekend, Clem, Tor, and the kids climbed in the car and drove across Massachusetts to the sugar maple farm in the Berkshires. Clem held Georgia's ashes in her lap the whole way, and once there, they trudged through the tall trees, following the directions handed to them by the man at the welcome cabin.

"Ms. Mark's name is already on the plaque with her husband's," he said. "And the plaque has been placed in the ground between their trees."

He gave them a bucket with soil and instructions to mix Georgia's cremains with the dirt before burying them. The nutrients would feed the tree and all the living things around it. Clem filmed a TikTok and tagged the Keeper of Living Collections. He would appreciate this place.

Georgia's tree wasn't the tallest in the grove, but it was, not unexpectedly, the most interesting. Its trunk was crooked, and it had a few lumpy bits here and there. It was, Clem thought, perfect.

As instructed, Clem mixed Georgia's cremains with the dirt in the bucket. The earth at the bottom of the tree had been loosened and cleared of snow, and the kids were happy enough to take turns with the shovel, digging a foot-deep hole.

Clem poured in the mixture, then Tor refilled the hole and patted it flat. Before departing, Clem knelt to touch the dirt one last time.

"Night, G," she whispered.

A few weeks after the visit to the Berkshires, Clem spotted an envelope leaning on the empty cookie jar in the kitchen. Her name was scrawled on it in Georgia's handwriting.

"What's this?" she asked Tor. Her breath caught in her chest.

"Astrid dropped it off. Said she found it in Georgia's papers."

"Tor, it's been months since her death."

Tor shrugged. "Leave it to Georgia to have one more thing to say."

Clem smiled.

"Are you going to open it now?" Tor said.

When Clem nodded, he turned to leave the room.

"Wait," Clem said. "Will you sit with me while I read it?"

Tor smiled. "I would like that very much."

Clem sat down at the table and traced the letters of her name with her finger. Even though Georgia's death was expected and appropriate, Clem had been left with so many big feelings. Sadness. Loneliness. Resentment. Nostalgia. It was hard to know what to do with them all. But holding this envelope in her hand, Clem recognized that with a little more time, only one of those big feelings would remain. Love.

"Here goes," she said. She opened the envelope and pulled a small slip of paper from it. There was a single sentence written on it in her friend's neat, round letters.

Dearest Clementine, she read silently. *Tor's green sweater is in the bottom drawer of my dresser. Love, Georgia.*

Clem blinked. This had to be a joke. How many times had Georgia asked Clem where the sweater was? How many times had she raised an eyebrow when Clem insisted she didn't know? And how many times had Clem crashed into that dresser in the basement on her way to the laundry area?

She chuckled, bit her lip, then laughed uproariously.

"What is it?" Tor said. "What does it say?"

Clem jumped up and grabbed his hand. "Come on! Come with me!" She threw open the basement door, switched on the lights, and ran down the steps. Tor followed.

"What is going on, Clem?" he said.

"You'll see!" she said. "Come on!"

When they'd both made it down the stairs, she knelt in front of Georgia's dresser and opened the bottom drawer. There, right on top, was Tor's hideous green sweater. The one he'd been searching for all these months.

"Hey!" Tor yelled. "My sweater!" He grabbed it and pulled it on over his T-shirt. "Why would Georgia have kept my sweater?"

Clem buried her face in her hands, first laughing, then crying, and then laughing once more. Georgia had had that sweater all along.

Clem and Georgia. Besties forever.

CHAPTER THIRTY-FOUR
The New World Order

In January 2024, Clem stuck her nose through the narrow opening in the curtain to peek at the nearly twenty thousand people, mostly women, who had battled a fierce snowstorm to see her. Women who had paid impressive amounts of money to listen to *her* speak at Madison Square Garden in New York City. It was astonishing, and it seemed impossible that in only ten months, she'd been shot like a human cannonball from misery to joy, from a mundane existence to worldwide fame. Yet here she was.

She pulled her nose back, and when the director gave her a wave, Clem took a deep breath, crossed her hands over her heart, and closed her eyes—the signal to her tech team that she was ready. The arena went dark, then silent. Clem counted down:

Five . . .
Four . . .
Three . . .
Two . . .

On *One*, in a perfectly timed move, the curtain rose, the lights went up, and Madison Square Garden erupted in deafening applause.

Clem walked to her mark at center stage. As she waited for the cheers and clapping to die down, she scanned the room. Once again, she was in awe of the many types of humans who were gathered together—nonbinary, Indigenous, Black, white, trans, Asian, Latino, tall, short, LGBTQ+, Middle Eastern. There were fancy women and plain women. Long haired, short haired. Wide, narrow. Corporate, artsy. Yes, her husband and sons were there, as well as a handful of other men, but for the most part, this was a uterus-only event.

From the registration forms, she knew there were Jews, Christians, Muslims, Buddhists, Hindus, and atheists sprinkled throughout the audience. Women in wheelchairs lined the first row, and a sign language interpreter was standing ready near the edge of the stage. Clem's manager had told her that a handful of attendees had flown in from Dubai, while others had taken the subway to 34 St–Penn Station. The youngest guest that evening was five. The oldest, eighty-seven. The same age Georgia had been when she'd died.

Twelve months before, Clem's shy, people-pleasing self would never have considered stepping onto that stage. She would have been too scared, too self-conscious, too awkward. Her brain would have been riddled with insecurities. What if she offended people? What if they misunderstood her intentions? Thought she was trying to be a savior to women everywhere—some sort of messiah? What if they booed her? Threw rotten apples? Wrote nasty things about her on Instagram? Left unkind comments on TikTok?

But up there on that stage, she didn't feel even a glimmer of fear.

Butterflies?

Yes.

Fear?

None.

She still cared deeply about what women thought, but she also accepted that pissing off a few people was part of the gig. How could anyone change the world without offending at least a handful of humans? Saying no to the patriarchy had united Clem in a common purpose with women all around the globe—and that was proving to be more powerful than all else.

As the crowd began to settle, Clem spotted Anna wedged between her brothers in the front row. Clem reached up and tugged on one of her curls. Anna smiled and did the same. Their secret sign.

Finally, the room quieted, and the lights dimmed.

Clem clasped her hands together. "I prefer not to," she said sotto voce. It was an intentionally dramatic beginning, and she felt a wave of energy roll toward her from the crowd.

"I prefer not to," she repeated, this time a bit louder, and as the hum built, she watched the women start to shift in their seats. She loved this call-and-response. It was like playing Marco Polo in a pool but with the opposite effect. When she called *Marco*, people swam toward her, not away.

She waited a beat, then repeated her now-famous anthem a third time, full blast. "I prefer not to."

The crowd thundered, and Clem soaked in their collective energy and determination.

A minute later, when the room was quiet, Clem spread her arms wide. "Your turn," she said. "On my count. Three, two, one."

The entire crowd chanted, "I prefer not to."

Clem cupped her hands around her mouth and called, "Three, two, one!"

"I prefer not to." The women jumped up, stomped, clapped, and wrapped their arms around each other's shoulders.

"One more time!" Clem hollered.

The crowd roared. "I prefer not to!"

When Clem felt the stage vibrating under her feet, she raised her hands high in the air and, like a seasoned orchestra director, ended the frenzy with one dramatic chop.

"Hello, hot-flashers," she said. "Hello, overwhelmed moms, mental-load managers, and pissed-off people with periods. Welcome to the new world order!"

Right then, the beat of a timpani drum rolled through the Garden, and Clem would later claim that the crowd had actually levitated when the words *I PREFER NOT TO* flashed on the giant screens. She smiled. She loved everything about this. Every damn thing. And as she reflected on the journey it had taken to get here, she spotted Torvald a few seats down from Anna. Like the women around him, he was standing and applauding, sporting his signature orange *I PREFER NOT TO* T-shirt. When their eyes met, her husband smiled and shook his fist in the air. He was trying hard, she knew, but at some point in the not-so-faraway future, she also knew she'd have to decide whether or not to stay married to him—a question she didn't yet have an answer to. Until then, she was simply going to bask in the wonderment of just how much things had changed.

When the crowd in Madison Square Garden quieted, a question flashed on the big screens all around the arena: *What do YOU prefer not to do?*

"Enough about me," Clem said. "I want to hear about you. What do you prefer not to do? Tap the green button on your app if you'd like to talk. Someone with a mic will come to you. If you prefer not to speak in front of the crowd, you may type your response in the app and hit send. I read every response at the end of the day." She did, too.

Clem's tech team had created a fancy system for handling the crowds of people who wanted to tell their stories. It included accessibility options for those with disabilities and those who preferred anonymity. Through the dozens of talks she'd given in recent months, they'd been able to iron out the bumps. The process was seamless.

"I prefer not to cook for my family."

"I prefer not to listen to my doctor drone on and on about crap that has nothing to do with me."

Huge applause.

"I prefer not to listen to misogynistic music."

"I prefer not to put up with my husband's drinking."

"I prefer not to join the PTO at my kid's elementary school."

"I prefer not to cut vegetables."

"I prefer not to eat vegetables."

The crowd roared with laughter.

"I prefer not to be listed as the primary parent with my children's doctors."

"I prefer not to sacrifice time with my girlfriends."

"I prefer not to take public transportation."

"I prefer not to make every damn decision for a family vacation."

"I prefer not to go on a family vacation."

"I prefer not to date."

"I prefer not to put up with, well, anything."

"I prefer not to back down about accessibility issues."

"I prefer not to let men talk over me in meetings."

"I prefer not to go to church."

"I prefer not to wear dresses."

"I prefer not to wear hearing aids."

"I prefer not to have Thanksgiving with my parents."

"I prefer not to drive everyone everywhere."

Hundreds of people shared that afternoon. Some responses were funny, some serious, others heartbreaking. When everyone who wanted to speak had done so, the lights dimmed and a spotlight beamed down on Clem. "Thank you for coming. Thank you for trusting me. Thank you for the opportunity to connect all of you to magical things."

Outside the wind roared. The air was bitter and cold. Many people in the arena would struggle to get home that night. Roads were icy. Airports had shut down. Subways and buses were experiencing long delays. Hotels were filling up. But even so, the energy in the Garden was bright and fiery.

As the crowd filed out of the arena, Clem smiled at her team. Charlene was there. Nova and Rose. Samantha. Astrid. The energy was kinetic, and Clem realized this was what she'd been working toward her whole life. And it was a magical thing.

ACKNOWLEDGMENTS

Clementine Crane Prefers Not To was fueled by hot flashes, night sweats, brain fog, rage, sleepless nights, and an overwhelming urge to crawl into the freezer. I bow to all the brave perimenopausal warriors out there. We deserve better—deeper medical research, more compassionate support, and a world that sees us.

Thank you to Barbara Poelle, agent extraordinaire, whose humor, spot-on instincts, and well-timed kicks in the arse always propel me forward.

Thanks to my editor, Melissa Rechter, whose patience and insightful questions helped shape this story into its most powerful and compelling form.

Huge gratitude to the stellar editorial team at Alcove Press. Your dedication and belief in this story strengthened it in ways even Clementine would have to admit she prefers.

I'm wildly grateful to the brilliant and buoyant Becky Stelmack—my cheerleader, sounding board, and, often, direct line to sanity. Our texts and breakfasts (but especially our retirement plan) keep me going.

Acknowledgments

Chris Bernard, thank you for your writerly camaraderie and generous spirit. You are a steady source of inspiration and encouragement.

Jotham Burrello—long road, friend. I am grateful.

Thank you, Katrin Schneck. Your unwavering presence and perfectly timed cups of rooibos tea make life infinitely better.

Thank you, Mom and Dad. Your influence, in big and small ways, has guided my journey.

Hugs and hearts to my three sisters—Traci, Nancy, and Amy. Honestly, who would I be without you?

Love-drippy gratitude to my kiddos. Orion, you are human starshine. Your fierce ingenuity and expansive heart will impact the world in significant ways. And, Yao, your comedic timing and sense of drama leave an indelible mark (whether we're ready for it or not).

To my husband, Andrew—chief mischief-maker and chaos-endurer. Forever thankful to you for keeping life interesting and full of laughs.

A high five to playwright Henrik Ibsen, whose *A Doll's House* planted seeds way back in high school—seeds that took root and blossomed decades later in these pages.

A double high five to Herman Melville for "Bartleby, the Scrivener: A Story of Wall-Street." I read it in grad school and carried its *ka-boom* until it found its home in *Clementine Crane Prefers Not To.*

To the intrepid scientists on a mission to de-extinct the woolly mammoth, I stand and applaud. Your audacity and genius boggle my mind in the best way.

To the booksellers, reviewers, book bloggers, librarians, and all other passionate champions of stories, THANK YOU!

And, finally, to each and every reader. Thank you for trusting me to tell you a story.